THE AMERICAN GIRL WHO BROKE LONDON

ALICE BRICKSTONE, BOOK FOUR

TYLER PIKE

BEFORE YOU BEGIN

Please consider signing up for Tyler's mailing list for updates on future releases.
tylerpikebooks.com

Enjoy *The American Girl Who Broke London*.

CHAPTER 1

Another lawyer flashed that British "I am not impressed" look. Alice Brickstone had received ten others just like it in the past five minutes. She didn't understand their disdain for her. Yes, she was six feet two inches tall, but when was height criminalized in the UK? Why should a teenager in a t-shirt inspire British scorn? And she wasn't playing the part of an obnoxious American tourist. Alice was never loud. As a person with selective mutism, she struggled to speak to anyone in public.

Maybe it was her shirt? It bore the lettering "oxygen is over-rated," the tagline of one of the American college swimming programs she had turned down to come to London. Alice wore it today, not as a reminder of what she had given up, but instead as a statement: elite swimmers are tougher than everyone else, in and out of the pool. But toughness was not the same as confidence. Now, at the threshold of this new phase in her life, she was so full of doubt she felt sick.

Everything felt wrong. It didn't feel like those tearful but exciting college send-off moments in movies. Perhaps that was partly because Chancery Lane was a weird place for an ancient and prestigious university. It was, instead, lined with London's oldest legal firms. This was their turf, and she a trespasser. Everyone here probably thought she had committed some violent crime and was on her way to consult with a legal firm. No one would guess she was here to attend university.

And that was because none of these lawyers even knew the university existed.

She was only a few minutes away from the secret gate now.

"But how can a parent say goodbye without even seeing the campus?" Dad pleaded. "To us, you're still our little girl." That did it. His tears were flowing properly now.

Alice felt her tears rising, so she looked away. Her baby sister Connie waddled beside Mom, trying to explain what the big red box was for ("It's a phone booth"). The cute little girl was blissfully oblivious to the gravity of the moment. Alice would miss her badly, and she knew Connie would miss her big sister even more. This thought also made her want to cry, so she looked over her shoulder and checked that her best friends Karan and Madison were still behind her. The fact that the three of them had all made this stupid decision to come to Chancery Gate was only slightly reassuring. Had Alice coerced them into coming? Would this place destroy their friendship?

Alice caught their eyes, each in turn. They smiled back, eyes twinkling with excitement and anxiety. Her long legs propelling her purposefully in front of the others, Mad looked like she had already left everything behind. Karan was nothing like Madison. Her eyes darting everywhere, Karan exuded anxiety from every pore in her skin. Madison's parents (Karan's foster parents) were trying to reassure her.

"Oh, for God's sake," Alice's dad exclaimed, wiping his tears on the sleeves of his flannel shirt. "I forgot my credit card at the pub."

As Dad ran back down Chancery Lane, Karan caught up with Alice.

"Hey," Karan said. She was almost as tall as Alice and nearly as muscular, but that was where the similarities ended. Karan was blonde and fair-skinned with movie star good looks. Only up close did one notice the network of scars all over her face. They had faded slightly over time, or perhaps Karan was getting better at disguising them with makeup.

"I keep seeing this guy in a hoodie," Karan said. "The same guy. I think he's following us."

"What? Where?" Alice scanned the street but saw only stone buildings and lawyers in suits.

"I just get glimpses, and he's gone. Like a ninja or something."

"A ninja. Like from feudal Japan? Here, on Chancery Lane?"

"Yeah. One second he's there; the next, he jumps out of sight. Like in a kung fu movie."

"Um, I think you're mixing your martial arts there," Alice said.

"I'm not joking. I've seen glimpses of this guy the whole time we've been in London."

"Seriously? Why didn't you say something?"

"I wanted to be sure."

Alice thought it was unlikely Karan's anxiety was causing her to get paranoid. Despite her mental health challenges, she was usually reliably observant.

"What's up, you guys?" Madison asked. Her jet-black hair was in a perfect topknot, her bangs cut like a knife across her high forehead, and her nose was long and sharp like the beak of a bird of prey. She wore a lacy black blouse and black trousers with black boots.

"Karan saw a ninja."

"Cool," Madison said, obviously thinking it was a joke. "Can you guys believe it's finally time? Are you nervous?"

"Hey," Karan objected. "I'm being serious here about...."

"Very nervous," Alice interrupted, deciding she didn't want to think about the possibility they were being stalked right now.

"But honestly, I'm just hoping the Vice Chancellor was right about this place. She guaranteed I'll fit in." She hastily added: "And I'm sure you two will also."

"Yeah, but it's her job to sell this place. How convinced are you?" Karan asked. "On a scale from one to ten?"

"Five or six," Alice said honestly.

Suddenly, Alice thought she saw a shadow disappearing down one of the many tiny laneways that lead from Chancery Lane. Then it reappeared, and a man started jogging toward them. But he looked nothing like a ninja. He had flaming red hair and was dressed in a smart casual outfit that restricted his running. For a second, she thought he might be an employee of the pub coming to return Dad's card, but he stopped well ahead of them and touched the shoulder of a woman dressed in a black T-shirt over black trousers, like a barista or something. She had been pushing into the door of a small café Alice hadn't noticed before.

They were too far away to be overheard, but they didn't seem to be having a happy conversation, and it quickly grew louder until finally, the barista shouted: "You used a siddhi against me? To get into my pants?"

The guy looked around wildly and saw Alice and her friends. He would have been mortified, and not only because of her accusations. Alice knew it was ill-advised to talk about their unique abilities, or "siddhis," in public. Even Alice and Madison's parents had no idea about them yet. The university had ways to introduce parents very slowly to the world of "siddhas," which they call people who had "siddhis." But when it came to sexual assault, who cared about some secret code of conduct? Alice wouldn't have blamed that woman even if she had screamed her accusations from the rooftops.

He turned back to the barista and said something that looked like it was meant to calm her down.

"No," she roared. "Imagine how I felt. I thought we were

meant for each other. But all that synergy and chemistry... it turned out to have been all your stupid mind-reading!"

The guy was flustered but couldn't stop the woman's tirade.

"That's sexual abuse. No better than drugging me. And believe me; you're going to regret it."

She entered the café and left him standing there, running his hand through his red hair. He gave Alice a rueful and nervous look and hustled away.

Alice looked back at Karan, who started to laugh.

"When we got our letters," she said, "and they said most normals like Mad and me acquire siddhis before we graduate, I was hoping for some variety of Jedi fighting skills. Now I'm not so sure—maybe mind reading has its perks."

Madison looked thoroughly disgusted with Karan. "I can't believe you would even say that. You, of all people. There are no perks when it comes to sexual abuse."

"I, of all people, want to get laid, and I, of all people, seem to have a face like a baboon's ass and need all the help I can get."

Mad and Alice had to reassure Karan about once per day (with complete sincerity) that she was gorgeous, scars or no scars. But before Alice or Madison could even open their mouths to do so again, Karan pulled two little drawstring bags out of her pocket and handed one to each of them.

"Anyway, I got something for you guys," she said.

Both girls pulled out bracelets. Mad's was made from black metal, and Alice's was rainbow-colored and light, like aluminum. They both had a matching pendant resembling a series of interlocked circles and swirls.

Karan held hers up, which matched theirs. "They're called Celtic knots. They appear in lots of early Bibles and such. Cool, eh?"

"Oh my God, Karan, it's so beautiful!" Madison gushed, always more polite than Alice.

"Yeah," Alice agreed, trying to look pleased. It looked expensive, and she was not a jewelry type of person.

"I got them at that Jubilee Market in Covent Garden the other day. Celtic knots symbolize unity and stuff, and I thought we could use a bit of that this year. Just in case."

Just then, they heard someone call their names from further up Chancery Lane. "Ms. Brickstone? Ms. Percival? Ms. Fremantle?" It was a British accent—formal, commanding, confident. It belonged to Professor Pippa Bird, Vice Chancellor of their new university. It meant the time was upon them.

They all proceeded to the steps where Professor Bird stood. She looked the same as she had a few days ago when Alice and her parents had met her. But somehow, up close, she was much more impressive. Tall and thin, though probably a few inches shorter than Alice, she had short, straight jet-black hair. She wore a women's business suit not unlike those worn by the local lawyers on Chancery Lane, but it looked completely natural on her. She wore super cool, oversized, retro horn-rimmed sunglasses. Her expression was relaxed but businesslike. She looked like she owned the building. Maybe the whole of Chancery Lane. Like even the law firm executives would curtsy and bow to her.

What were *her* abilities? They must be amazing for her to be in charge of the whole university.

She spoke slowly and steadily in a deliberate, posh British accent. "Did Mr. Brickstone have a prior engagement? I must say I was hoping to address you all together today."

They were spared the need to answer as Alice's dad came running up, holding his credit card in the air like a trophy.

"Ah, excellent." Professor Bird clasped her hands and smiled slightly.

Dad took his place next to Mom, Connie quieted down, and Mom set her onto her little feet. Mr. and Mrs. Percival stood at attention. Alice, Madison, and Karan stood off to the side, aware Professor Bird needed to address the parents.

"I wish to thank you in person for supporting your young women in their decision to attend Chancery Gate. I do not have children, so I can only guess how hard it must be to face the prospect of being separated from them by an ocean. This is a momentous and challenging step for parents to take. But I assure you that your young women will have the time of their lives here, and I personally guarantee they would not have received a better education anywhere else in the world."

Alice turned to look at her and Madison's parents. The Percivals seemed convinced, while Alice's mom and dad did not.

"The other consolation I can give is a reminder that our scholarship terms cover unlimited international flights between semesters. Provided that a student's marks are kept above credit level, they are encouraged to travel home for holidays. I am confident you will all be reunited for a white Christmas in lovely Colorado."

Dad looked like he wanted to ask again why he wasn't allowed to see the campus, but before he could open his mouth, Professor Bird wound up her speech.

"Well, the moment has come. As you might expect, many groups are coming through today, so I must ask you to make your goodbyes." Turning to Alice, Madison, and Karan, she said, "I'll wait for you at the mouth of Broken Passage. Don't be long."

The goodbye was, in fact, terrible. The worst was the last hug with Connie, who had finally realized something big was happening and had gotten scared and started to cry. Alice had been Connie's primary caregiver for much of the last two years, so this separation would be traumatic for her.

After finally peeling herself out of the last embraces, Alice wiped her tears and walked away with Madison and Karan.

CHAPTER 2

P rofessor Bird smiled at them as they reached Broken Passage, a tiny, winding pedestrian laneway leading off Chancery Lane.

"Come with me," the Vice Chancellor commanded.

All their luggage had been taken in advance, so they only had small backpacks. The girls were elite athletes, yet Professor Bird was still hard to keep up with. She strode past the side door to an old pub and deeper down the tiny lane. The walls were brick back here, the ground paved over, and there were the occasional bits of garbage you'd expect to find down a dark alley near an urban pub.

There were no other people down this far into the passageway, so it was odd when they encountered an older man in tweed waddling in the other direction, perhaps out to the pub for a drink. "Afternoon, Vice Chancellor."

"Good afternoon, Professor Shirk."

Then something even odder happened: the short professor looked sideways and scowled at Alice, looking her up and down as though she was wearing something that was glaringly inappropriate, which brought him and his entire world into disrepute. He even lifted a finger and almost looked like he would scold Alice. Then he mastered himself, shook his head, and walked on.

Alice turned to Madison for sympathy, but her friend seemed oblivious and glassy-eyed, overwhelmed by being so close to entering the fabled university.

Professor Bird stopped to face them. Alice hoped she would explain why Professor Shirk had been so rude, but no.

"As you know," Professor Bird said in her businesslike tone, "the university is cloaked. This small passageway leads to the main entrance.

It did not look much like a hallowed university, nor the approach to one. It was more like a back alley where you might get mugged.

The passage wound left, then right, and appeared to dead-end at the high stone wall of another nondescript building. To the left and right were the sides of two other buildings—all old stone. The gray, English sky loomed above that.

A man in sunglasses emerged from a door from the building on the left. It was like a scene from a movie in which the good guy would reveal himself to be the bad guy and gun them all down.

As Alice's wary eyes flicked from the guy in sunglasses to the walls that surrounded them on three sides, she suddenly sensed something peculiar about a spot on the wall in front of them. She tried squinting at it, but it revealed none of its secrets. Closing her eyes, she instinctively took a deep breath and dropped into the meditative state that helped her read someone's mind. When she opened her eyes again, she jumped back as though from a fire.

That nondescript rectangular section of stone wall was seething with something brighter and more awesome than fire —prana; whorls and swirls of it, in all shades of crystalline blue, some currents moving fast and others almost stationary. It was the most intense concentration of prana she had ever seen.

"Mad," she whispered, "can you see that?!"

Madison looked at her curiously, her hawk-like brows raised, obviously having not seen anything unusual. Of course, she couldn't have seen prana—even massive concentrations of it like that magical doorway. Alice had been told that only rare siddhas could see it, and Madison wasn't even a siddha. Yet.

Giving Alice a knowing look, Professor Bird continued calmly. "Now, I must apologize in advance." She gestured toward the guy with sunglasses. "David here is our duty sentry today, and he will ask to read your mind before you enter. This procedure is required for every person entering Chancery Gate. Thankfully, entering the gate is the only time you will be forced to submit to mind reading during your time here."

"Um," Karan stammered. "Why? What's he looking for?"

"He is under strict instruction to read only your identity and confirm you have a valid reason to enter. He will read nothing else. It's our version of an ID check."

"What would stop him from poking around wherever he wants? Why should I trust my most private thoughts to a random stranger? A man, even?" Karan protested.

Professor Bird placed a hand gently on Karan's shoulder. "It is a matter of trust. And I guarantee that each sentry you encounter has earned the university's trust."

Karan still looked worried.

"I understand your concern, Karan. Unfortunately, it is a necessary security measure in place for three centuries. Even I am not exempt. Our sentries are very well-trained, and I guarantee no sentry will 'poke around' our students' minds. In time, you'll regard it as no worse than scanning an identity card."

"Yeah, but what if I think something really embarrassing, and he sees it by mistake?" Karan insisted.

"It simply doesn't work like that. You'll see."

Professor Bird removed her spectacular horn-rimmed

sunglasses, stood face-to-face with the sentry, nodded, and stood aside.

Madison stepped forward for her turn. She was three inches taller than David and used every inch to look imposing and stare him down. But he apparently got what he wanted, and then it was Karan's turn, then Alice's.

Alice had been read before, but this was a more intense experience. The sentry was powerful. She had no way to resist him. He knew exactly where to go to find her name and confirmation that she was an incoming student, and then his presence disappeared.

Alice took this as a personal challenge. One day she would find a way to block the sentry from reading her. Just for the hell of it.

"Are you ready to see your new home?"

They all nodded.

"Come. Always enter to the left."

Professor Bird strode straight through the rectangular cascade of blue prana.

Wide-eyed, Madison reached out and touched what she must have seen as cold stone. Alice expected her to withdraw her hand, raw and burned, but she seemed fine.

"Well, what the hell," Karan explained. "What's the worst thing that could happen? A bloody nose?" And she walked through the prana. Madison quickly followed.

Alice hesitated. This felt like a big moment. She looked back and got a reassuring nod from the sentry. Then she turned back to the pranic doorway and strode through.

She felt a rush of intelligent warmth course through her body, as when she used prana to fly. It was nourishing in a way that nothing else was. The closest thing to the experience of being bathed in prana was a hug from a kind friend in a moment of need. It was a gift of pure, unconditional love that reached every cell and neuron of her body.

The first thing she saw on the other side of the pranic doorway was Professor Bird squatting down, patting a yellow Labrador that looked overjoyed to see her. It was wagging its whole body.

Alice spun around and saw the wall as solid and stony as ever. The prana seemed to have disappeared, or perhaps her ability to perceive it had.

Then she let herself slowly turn back to look at Chancery Gate University, her new home.

Rather than large, stately, stone buildings, they were surrounded by two long rows of cute little terraced houses with bay windows and flower-covered balconies. Hundreds of young people were milling around, scoping each other out. She couldn't help comparing it with the scenes of Diagon Alley in the Harry Potter movies; here were the same kinds of narrow, old buildings crowding in over each other with leaded windows leaning out over a cobblestone footpath. But this was no shopping street for wizards. Nothing was for sale; there were no shops with colorful signs. Instead, this was a solemn and functional space designed for students. Through some nearby windows, she could see some students studying and others chatting intently.

"Welcome to Chancery Gate University," Professor Bird said, giving the dog one last pat before standing up. "Most of it is underground, of course. These buildings serve primarily as classrooms and a few offices. That is our Great Hall over there."

Alice saw a larger building to the right where Professor Bird was pointing. It boasted a wide, stone staircase up to some imposing oak doors. Above the doors was the colorful sign: "Welcome First-Years!"

A bored-looking girl in a hoodie and jeans shuffled up behind Professor Bird, who seemed to feel her presence and spun around.

"Ah, Ms. Bridish. You're just in time." To Alice, Madison,

and Karan, she said, "I leave you now in Nick Bridish's capable hands. She is a fourth-year student and will take you on a little campus tour and answer any questions that may occur to you."

To the Labrador, the professor said, "Sit!" and "Stay." It did, but its wary eyes followed the professor's every move as she left through the stone wall, leaving the dog, Alice, and her friends with Nick.

"You guys Amazons or something?" Nick asked in a New York accent. Dressed in all black but with none of Madison's style, Nick looked thin and angry, like a caricature of a disaffected young woman. She was only around five feet tall and had to look up at Alice and her friends.

Alice was instantly on alert. She hated being made fun of for her height or weight. At the same time, she felt her mutism coming to claim her, preventing any quick retort.

"Nice to meet you," Madison said calmly. "I'm Madison, and this is Karan and Alice."

"Hey," Nick said. "So, what do you want to see?"

"Um, like everything?" Karan suggested, gesturing around her. "We're kind of, like, excited?"

Nick rolled her eyes and mimicked Karan's exaggerated hand gestures. "So these are all super-old buildings. Professors sit around in them devising new ways to torture students."

"Excuse me?" Karan was alarmed.

"Just a figure of speech. They make you work hard here."

"You don't like working hard?" Madison asked.

"Duh. Any more questions?"

"So, I guess the big question anyone would have is how is this entire place hidden in the middle of London?" Madison asked.

Nick shrugged her shoulders. "No idea."

"Seriously?" Karan asked.

"It's cloaked, obviously, by a bunch of siddhas from the

seventeenth century. Nobody these days knows exactly how they did it."

Madison scrunched up her formidable black eyebrows. "There's no book that describes the school's history or anything?"

"Books suck," Nick spat.

Karan finally burst out laughing, which didn't go over well with Nick.

Suppressing a smile, Madison asked, "Hey, can you just show us around a bit?"

"Where?" Nick's face had assumed an aggressive expression like she was about to lose her temper.

Madison turned to Karan and Alice, and they shared an intimate look of astonishment at their new tour guide's behavior.

"Just have her start with the cafeteria," Alice said quietly to Madison, as her mutism prevented her from speaking to Nick directly. "Then the cafe. Then the gym. Then the library. Those are my priorities, at least. Or whatever you guys think. I can't speak to her. Mutism."

Nick appeared to soften. Evidently, she'd overheard and realized Alice had an anxiety condition.

This made Alice even madder. Now, not only did Nick think she was an overgrown Amazon, but she also felt sorry for Alice because of her condition. This was not the magical first impression of the university Alice had expected.

But her anger melted away as they started walking. They began to the left, away from the building Professor Bird had called the Great Hall. The place was amazing.

"Was all this stuff seriously built in the seventeenth century?" Karan asked as they passed another flower-bedecked, narrow building leaning precariously toward the lane.

"I guess so," Nick responded, adding, "They built it after the great fire of London, blah blah blah."

"What's the 'blah blah blah' part?" Madison asked. "Pretend like we're new here."

Nick took a deep breath, exasperated. "So everything in the old city got torched in 1666, right?"

"Right."

"And these early English siddha superfreaks took advantage of the chaos and built this place. That's all I know. I'm not a professional tour guide. They just stuck me with you guys because we're all American. Yay, team."

"But even if it's cloaked, surely the city planners and civil engineers and surveyors would have figured out there was a big, empty space in the middle of the most expensive real estate in the world?"

"Apparently not," Nick shrugged. "Maybe they're all idiots. Most people are."

"What about GPS?"

"The cloaking fools GPS too. I don't know how. Anyway, all that stuff you asked about is downstairs." She sauntered toward one of the medieval wooden doors, which was open. As Alice stepped on the stone threshold, she noted how the stone was worn down in the middle with use, like a saddle on a horse. Seriously old.

She walked through the doorway and traced her hand along the smooth wood of the door, feeling the weathered grain of ancient, heavy planks held together with decorative iron bands.

As they proceeded into the building, she noticed how the carpeted floors were all slanted, and the fancy wallpapered walls were made of wood as aged as the door, as were the white ceilings with their exposed support beams.

Then they came upon an anomaly—one of many they would encounter at the school. It was a modern glass elevator.

"Most of the campus is underground," Nick reiterated as she

called the elevator. "There are only so many of these elevators, and sometimes they get crowded."

They got in, and Alice was again surprised to see so many buttons. They had fifteen floors to choose from. The first five floors were dorms; the deeper levels were mostly classrooms, one was labeled *fitness center*, another *dining hall*, and the bottom one read *loading dock and warehouse*.

"Where first?" Nick asked, bored, looking at her watch.

"How can a loading dock be at the bottom?" Karan asked. "What's down there?"

"I don't know. We're not allowed in. You need a special key card to even press the button."

"Let's see the dining hall first, please," Madison said, pushing the button for B14.

The glass elevator gave them amazing three-hundred-and-sixty-degree views of each floor they passed.

First were the multiple dormitory floors. Alice had expected something like the basic dorm rooms she had seen at Hardrock College back home, but these "dormitories" were more like giant mansions in the English countryside. They saw huge, high-ceilinged rooms with fireplaces and floor-to-ceiling book-shelves. Students lounged around on leather couches, reading or staring at their phones. A few were cuddling, and one couple made out with wild abandon. Alice noticed and shot a look at Karan. She had a kind of longing in her eyes.

Then the elevator passed through the levels labeled *lecture theatres*. Beyond the glass doors, Alice saw cavernous spaces like hotel lobbies with modern sculptures everywhere and furniture that looked like artworks, on which students lounged in pairs and threes. Alice assumed the classrooms were behind doors branching off from these spaces. Then they descended past the fitness center, and Alice's jaw dropped. For an athlete, it was a dream come true. It was an enormous, open space about the size of two football fields. There was a fifty-meter pool in which a few people were lazily swimming laps, an expansive weight room full of people working out, lots of cardio equipment, a large stretching area, tennis courts, basketball courts, and a giant track around the outside edge that looked like it was about a half kilometer long.

Then they arrived at the dining hall.

The space was wide open, like a church but with hundreds of wooden tables and thousands of chairs. Large oil paintings covered the walls, and a high ceiling decorated with fancy wood brackets and giant candelabras. Some stained-glass windows were up at the far end, glowing brightly. Alice guessed electric lights backlighted them; this place was far underground.

They must have been a half-mile deep. A vague sense of claustrophobia gripped her.

"It's open twenty-four hours, like a buffet. You just go up to the front and see what they have. It's great if you like boiled vegetables and leathery meat."

The dining hall was largely empty, probably due to the time (it was 3:00 p.m.). But some students were having coffee and sandwiches. One skinny-looking young man was hunched over a giant bowl of ice cream.

"Is there good coffee?" Madison asked.

"Just normal brewed coffee. Better than instant, I guess. There's a decent coffee cart up on Top Lane. But you have to bring a keep-cup. There are serious limits on trash around here."

"And on enthusiasm," Alice commented as she walked away from Nick toward the giant buffet. It looked a lot better than Nick had intimated. There was a massive salad bar with plenty of healthy options and some less healthy. She wasn't going to starve. Just for fun, she poured herself a big mug of coffee and then topped it with soft-serve ice cream—her two favorite food groups.

Karan and Madison came over and did the same thing while Nick slumped in a chair. It finally occurred to Alice to wonder what, if any, siddhis Nick had. Maybe behind all that heavy pessimism lay some super-being. But maybe not. She didn't even look that healthy.

They finished their coffee-ice-cream floats and got back in the elevator.

"We all must be at the Great Hall up on Top Lane at five o'clock for Professor Bird's welcome address. So, I guess I'll help you find your dorm rooms so you can do ... whatever."

They traveled back up and stopped at one of the dormitory levels. Nick must have known their dorm room number.

As the doors opened, the scent of a wood fire immediately struck them. It smelled like home.

CHAPTER 3

The fireplace was ginormous, and the fire within was crackling and glowing. Alice expected the air to be stale and smoky, but instead, it was fresh and smoky, like the air in a forest near a campfire.

Madison was obviously wondering about it too. "How do they get air in here?"

"Yeah," Karan said. "I would have thought an underground dorm would smell like farts and dirty socks."

Nick shrugged. "I think it's piped in from some forest somewhere."

"Wow. Where's the nearest forest?" Karan asked, elbowing Alice in the ribs. She knew Alice needed nature almost as much as coffee.

"Who knows? Trees suck," Nick shuffled off, and Alice and friends followed, laughing at Nick's apparent hatred of ... basically everything.

They wove their way around the leather couches on one of which sat the snogging couple they had seen from the elevator. The two students were red-faced and trying to act cool until Alice's group passed out of sight and earshot.

After they passed, Alice saw Karan turn to watch as the

couple resumed their passionate kissing. The hungry look was back in her eyes.

They passed through an arch into a hallway with modern doors on either side.

"Toilets and showers," Nick said.

Then they went through another arch into a smaller shared room that wasn't palatial or fancy like the main room. Alice liked it better. It was more like the living room in Madison's house in Hardrock. Normal couches, lamps, a TV, and a thick carpet with a few Labradors lounging.

"What's the deal with all the dogs?" Karan asked.

"They're nicer than people, that's for damn sure," Nick said.

"But other breeds of dogs are nice too. Why Labradors?" Madison asked. Alice knew Madison had grown up with them.

"Some crap about how they're easier to read than other dogs. I can't read minds, so I have no idea."

"But where do they all poo?" Madison asked.

"The mind-reading thing makes them easier to train compared with other breeds. They all know to take themselves to the dog bathroom. It's near our bathrooms." Nick took a deep breath and said, "You guys are in that room. Mine is number four over there. Let me know if you're on fire or something. I'm done here." And she left.

"Wow," Karan said, her eyes wide.

"Yep," Alice agreed. "Let's check out our new room."

They did and found a large, pleasantly furnished space with three double beds and large closets. They jostled for the beds they wanted, showered, and changed clothes. The bathrooms were adequate, and Alice wondered where all the water came from and where the sewage went.

The three of them had wondered for months what their dorm room would look like, and here they were. They were highly thankful their applications had been accepted and that they were to share a room rather than be split up to meet new people.

Mad and Karan then persuaded Alice to chill in the big common room before returning to Top Lane for the welcome address.

They settled on a couch next to the fire, Karan sighing with satisfaction, then looking around to perv on any kissing couples. There were none left, unfortunately for her. The room was pleasantly silent. Pleasant, at least, for Alice, who was close to imploding from social anxiety and needed this moment of quiet. She scanned the vast room and decided she'd prefer a corner away from the traffic next time.

Then two people walked toward them, dispelling Alice's temporary illusion of peace. One of them was a small, thin, Indian woman their age who was fashion-model gorgeous. The other was none other than the red-haired guy they had seen getting chewed out by the wronged woman earlier on Chancery Lane.

It became apparent that the former was practically dragging the latter.

"Mind if we join you?" the Indian woman asked in a formal British accent.

Alice shook her head, but Karan nodded so furiously that they sat on the couch across from them.

"I'm Supriya. I'm a second-year student, and I had trouble making friends last year, so I promised myself I would go out of my way this year to help new students connect with each other. I met Jon just a half-hour ago and noticed he seemed unhappy. I felt like he could be experiencing some of the same feelings of alienation I did last year.

Supriya had spoken so quickly and confidently that Alice felt swept up by her, despite the absurdity of her trying to make a sex abuser "happy."

Karan looked over at Alice and widened her eyes comically. Supriya didn't see her gesture.

"That was when Jon saw you three lovely people sitting here," Supriya continued breathlessly, proceeding like it was simply inevitable she would. "He disclosed to me what happened to him outside the front gate and that you all were there as observers of his mishap. I told him it was fate that we were all in the same dorm. I don't believe in coincidences, and I insisted we come over and say hello to you to make things right."

"Um, hello?" Karan said awkwardly.

"Pleased to meet you. I just wanted to ensure you didn't get the wrong impression. Jon is a really nice person who made a mistake."

Jon, the red-haired guy, looked like he was trying to sink into the leather couch and disappear forever.

Madison noticed that Karan seemed about to burst into laughter and decided to take over as spokesman. "I'm Madison, this is Karan, and that's Alice."

"Did you grow up in siddha families?"

"None of us did," Madison answered.

"Well, then you might be able to understand Jon's situation. If you don't have your family to support you when your abilities show themselves, it is bloody hard to know what is right and wrong. Growing up, I'm sure you used your abilities to your advantage. It just seems natural to do so. Like using our eyes or our ears. We don't understand it creates an unfair advantage. So you completely understand how Jon feels about what happened. Certainly, he understands now it was an error. You must reach out and support him, not condemn him. Most of us are in the same boat, and attending Chancery Gate is our chance to reset and start fresh."

As Supriya took a massive breath after saying so many

words in a row, Karan again directed comical expressions at Alice and Madison.

Supriya noticed this time and frowned.

Undeterred, Karan spoke. "Actually, Supriya, I'm not a big fan of sexual assault."

Only Karan could pull off a comment like that. Alice could see Madison squirming in her seat.

"I think Jon's victim is the one who needs understanding and support," Madison said.

Jon looked like he wanted to sink deeper into the couch or even be swallowed by the Earth.

"But as a person with no siddhis," Karan continued, "I reckon mind reading would be a fun way to spice up a relationship. Imagine the possibilities!"

Supriya gave Karan a kind of patient smile. "I'm not sure about that. The thing we must be clear about, though, is that consent is the operative term. Consent is the key. Jon understands that now. Completely. You will acquire siddhis over time. There's no doubt. Everyone does. And you'll learn that using siddhis against another siddha without consent is against all the rules of siddha society. It's vital now because of the security situation."

"What security situation?" Madison asked, clearly alarmed.

Supriya leaned in conspiratorially and widened her eyes. "My parents tell me there is a rumor they have found a supersiddha. Someone with powers so rare it has reopened the Great Rift."

"What is that? The Great Rift?" Madison asked.

"I have no idea what the Great Rift is. My parents told me not to worry about it, but I got the sense they were quite concerned."

Alice saw that Supriya, though clearly proud she was the only one from a siddha family, seemed like she was being honest with them and really didn't know. But she knew enough to communicate a deep-seated fear of whatever the Great Rift was supposed to be.

"And what's a super-siddha?" Karan asked.

"No idea. Someone with mythical abilities. Like in the Ramayana and the Mahabharata (those are Indian scriptures). The new person they found is supposed to have abilities nobody has seen for thousands of years. And the cool thing is that I heard it might be an incoming first-year student."

"Wow," Karan said nervously, glancing at Alice and then back at Supriya. "And would that person, hypothetically, be, like, fully accepted here? I mean, would everyone treat them like any other student?"

Supriya appeared not to have noticed Karan's furtive glance at Alice. "I can't speak for anyone else, but I do know this: my parents and most siddhas in India would think of them as a divine incarnation and treat them accordingly. But here, among so many different cultures," she added ominously, "he might well be persecuted. People can be fearful and sensitive in some cultures when someone very different comes along."

"Understatement of the millennium," Karan said.

"But I'm worried about this security situation. We weren't told about any of this when we enrolled. Have you heard anything specific?" Madison asked.

Supriya shrugged. "Oh, don't worry about it too much. I'm sure we will notice a few restrictions, but if they are tightening security, they'll focus on the deep basement Loading Docks. I hear that's where all the most sensitive stuff is."

"What sensitive stuff?" Karan asked.

"Chancery Gate is not the only entrance to the university. Except for students, everything else—food, supplies, rubbish, staff, Company agents—travels through underground tunnels. And all those tunnels lead to the deep basement loading dock. That's probably where the real restrictions would be."

She looked at her phone and then at Jon, who was now

almost an unrecognizable part of the couch. "We had all better get up to Top Lane for the VC's address!"

As she bustled Jon away, Alice almost felt bad for the guy. But then she remembered the bitterness written on over the face of that barista woman on Chancery Lane, and she knew Jon deserved more than a bit of humiliation.

When they were alone again, Karan burst out, "You don't think they mean *you*, do they?! Alice Brickstone, super-siddha? Divine incarnation?"

"Lay off, Karan," Madison warned. "I'm more concerned about the security thing. What if there is some threat to the university they're not telling us about? What if the British army storms campus one day, and we all get sent to Guantanamo Bay?"

That was a serious buzzkill; even Karan didn't have a quick quip.

In truth, none of them knew what to expect. One thing was sure: Alice needed to keep her abilities secret, at least the flying.

But what was all that stuff about a rift? Alice needed to find out if it was for real, then she needed to make sure she was never, ever, mixed up with it. And she also wanted to see the loading docks herself.

They sat there for a second longer before the crackling fire before following Supriya and Jon to the elevators.

CHAPTER 4

When they emerged from the elevator to natural light, Alice breathed a sigh of relief. Having been underground since coming through the secret gate a few hours prior, the dull, fading London daylight felt like a Colorado summer day in comparison.

Top Lane was crowded with the jolly little terraced classrooms and excited, chatting students making their way toward the larger student union building. Only hours ago, Alice would have felt a kind of hopeful kinship with all these strangers and their unknown abilities, but their chat with Supriya weighed on her. She felt wary of everyone and was not looking forward to the VC's address.

Just then, their cynical guide from earlier approached. "Dorm room okay?" she asked while staring at the ground.

Alice nodded curtly, but Nick probably didn't see or care what Alice thought of the dorms.

"Well, let me know if I can help." As Nick turned to walk away, she added, "Just kidding. I hate helping people."

"Seriously?" Madison asked disapprovingly, her prominent eyebrows lifted.

"I think I like her," Karan smiled.

Alice just wanted to get this over with. She strode up the stone steps of the Great Hall with Mad and Karan right behind.

They entered the atrium, where alphabetically sorted tables were staffed by jolly-looking student volunteers. The newcomers were meant to line up according to surname to pick up a welcome pack, and they did so.

The three of them regrouped, each holding a small but relatively heavy drawstring bag with the school's name and logo on the outside.,

"Let's open them on three, k?" Karan said, looking more excited than she had earlier. The prospect of cool little gifts was appealing to her. Alice had to admit it was kind of exciting to her as well.

"One, two..." Before getting to three, Karan jerked her bag open and dug around inside.

"I thought it would be a nice pen or something, but this is amazing!" Karan said, holding up a brand-new smartphone.

Alice's bag had one too, and she pulled out a smaller but potentially even more valuable item. "Did you guys get one of these?" she asked, holding up a Visa credit card with her name embossed.

"Whoa, yes, I did," Madison replied. "Are they seriously giving us free money? Or is it, like, just something set up for us, but we have to pay it off ourselves if we use it?"

"Who knows?" Karan said. "Let's go online and buy something ridiculously expensive, like an airplane, and see what happens!"

"Let's not," Madison said, switching on her new phone. "But seriously, this phone is an expensive welcome present."

"Hey, mine knows it's me!" Karan held her phone up and showed them it was preloaded with her name, a new email address, and a phone number. Her contacts list was already populated with Alice, Madison, and many professors' phone numbers. Alice noted the Vice Chancellor's number was not listed.

"And it has apps with our class timetable, book lists, links to the bookstore, and even lists of local swimming clubs!" Madison gushed. "They have done their homework on us."

"What classes have you got?!" Karan asked. "My schedule has nothing magical about it. Aren't we supposed to be learning siddhis here or something?"

Alice tapped into her schedule and saw a very standard-looking list of subjects:

History 101

Ethics 101

Physics 101

Literature 101

Business 101

Each class seemed to have one or two lectures per week and a bunch of tutorials. Below this was a note probably aimed at the high achievers like Madison: "Note: These are required subjects for all first-year students. The subject matter will differ from any units you have taken in high school."

"How could physics be different?" Madison fumed. "Have the laws of physics changed when I wasn't looking?"

"Maybe they have, Mad," Karan said. "Did your advanced placement physics class account for how siddhas can do what they do?"

As Madison harrumphed, Alice noticed her schedule was very, very full. She compared it with Madison's and Karan's and confirmed they all were in the same classes.

"Um," she said, "weren't we supposed to have more study time in college than in high school?"

"Yeah," Karan agreed. "Our schedule looks busier than high school. Maybe siddhas don't have to sleep."

"All the tutorials are in Top Lane. We even have some at night," Alice commented.

A bell rang like in a theatre announcing the show was about to start. So, they all filed into the lecture theatre, which looked more like an opera house. They found seats together in the back of the grand circle on the main level at Alice's insistence so she could quickly exit.

It was a vast, intricately designed, gorgeous space that rivaled any theater she had ever seen, including the Theatre Royal in London's West End.

There were five levels of galleries up the walls on all three sides. They couldn't see the galleries above them, but they could see the ones that lined the sides to their left and right. They were elaborately decorated with floral arches and were full of older-looking students. Perhaps the first-years were relegated to the primary seats in the grand circle. Maybe the first- *and* second-years; she couldn't tell. Alice suspected the third- and fourth-year students didn't need to attend the VC's address. Graduate students were also attending Chancery Gate, but surely none were here.

The ceiling was a series of domes inlaid with gold writing, which she couldn't decipher.

Dominating the whole space was an enormous stage lit with spotlights and populated with what appeared to be all their teachers sitting in straight-backed chairs. They were wearing robes and weird hats—*maybe formal academic dress*, Alice thought. Her dad wore something like that in his graduation pictures. But the hats were not just the square-topped ones she was used to. They were elaborate and extreme—some teachers looked like they were wearing giant couch cushions on their heads. Or like the oversized cushions were wearing teachers below them.

"Welcome, all," a warm voice rang through the sound

system. Alice saw Professor Bird had stood up in the center of the line of professors.

"It's a great honor to address you all. I'll try to keep to the facts. My first duty is to explain the contents of your welcome packs. You'll be pleased to learn your new credit card has no limit, and the school will fully reimburse your purchases. Being a siddha has perks."

Alice looked at Madison to her left and Karan to her right. They both returned her look with their eyes wide and mouths hanging open. They had suddenly just been gifted...infinite money? Was that a joke?

"The catch is that you cannot make any purchases that draw attention to yourselves or our university. The consequences of doing so are serious, and you will likely be forced to pause your studies to help The Company manage the coverup. Even small coverups may require you to take months away from your classes and studies.

"Your new phone is set up to make calls and use as much data as you need, and you will never see a bill. It is set up on a secure telecom network operated by The Company exclusively for siddhas. With that said, we have an earnest request to make of you. Or rather, it is a demand, I'm afraid. You must avoid using your old phones while you are studying here."

There were discomfited murmurs among the new students and knowing smiles in the galleries.

"This place is, as you know, cloaked from outside view. Even GPS satellites cannot see us. Our cloaking has evaded the most sophisticated surveying techniques. It stymies mobile phone tracking as well, to an extent, but our scientists and engineers have developed additional layers of protection in our IT network, of which your new phone is a part. When you use your phone, you are given your own data cloaking. This cloaking is effective even when you are wandering around outside of our campus. Another advantage of your new phone is that our IT department can locate it whether you are on campus or off. This feature helps us find lost devices and may help locate you and provide assistance should you ever require it.

"Where do we get all this money and IT wizardry, you ask?"

Alice did not ask and was feeling too tired to listen anymore. For a girl from a rural town in Colorado, there were too many details and rules for her to take in. And her anxiety levels were still high from her encounter with Supriya and Jon.

She reached into her gift and pulled out a pamphlet she hadn't seen before. Unsurprisingly, it contained another bunch of rules and warnings. "Don't go out in London at night alone," was one of them. Alice recalled the ninjas Karan said she saw and wondered if London was teeming with them. They would attack stragglers like a lion picking off the weaker gazelles.

The pamphlet had a million other "natural laws of siddhis" and "Corollaries," and it went on and on and on.

She sighed and put it all away.

Looking around her, she wondered what her year would be like. She searched for Jon and Supriya but didn't see either of them.

Supriya's talk about a "super-siddha" and a "Great Rift" had sounded like gossip rather than fact, but it still stressed her out. At least the VC had not yet mentioned any heightened security.

"And finally," Professor Bird said, "there is heightened security on campus this year as a preventative measure. I will leave it to Professor Shirk to discuss the ramifications for the annual Game."

Great, Alice thought. *Everything Supriya said was probably correct, then.* Which meant Alice needed to find out what this Great Rift thing was.

A bearded older man with a substantial academic cap stood up laboriously from a chair beside the podium. Even though academic robes covered his tweeds, she recognized him from the passageway earlier in the afternoon. A surge of anger ran through her as she remembered how he had seemed to want to criticize her for some grievous error she had committed without knowing it.

"Greetings," his deep, quiet voice purred into the microphone. I am pleased to reveal the protocols around this year's Game."

Alice noticed all the returning students in the galleries were leaning forward in their seats.

"For those of you who are new, The Chancellor's Game is one of this school's most cherished competitive traditions. It pits six teams against each other in their efforts to solve a little mystery contrived by your teachers."

At the words "little mystery," Alice saw most returning students burst into laughter. Clearly, there was nothing little about it.

Professor Shirk's quiet voice continued, and the laughter immediately subsided. "This year, we return to a rather more traditional format. I am happy to announce that this year's game will again take place in pubs in central London."

He held up his hands to quiet the returning students, who seemed pleased.

"Full details and rules are available on your phones. Here, I wish to emphasize one crucial difference this year. Unfortunately, our security situation demands that first-year and second-year students may participate in the Chancellor's Game only under the close supervision of their team captain. Captains must be physically present to supervise any mind-reading attempts in pubs and research activities. Company agents will be posted in all pubs to ensure compliance."

Alice noticed much grumbling and handwringing among the older students in the galleries.

"We have also removed essential research materials most relevant to the Game from the main stacks and placed them in the Vice Chancellor's collection. Entry is restricted to team captains and three team members at any given time. We acknowledge this will severely limit participation by first- and second-year students, as there are one hundred eighty of you and only six team captains. However, the alternative was either canceling the game or banning first- and second-years from participation.

"All first-year students have been automatically assigned to a team. All other students may freely choose which team to join. Information is on your phones. Any freelancing will result in disciplinary action for the individual and possible disqualification for their assigned team."

After a few seconds' pause, he leaned close to the microphone. "As usual, Camden Town is out of bounds. No clues have been left for you in any pub or venue in Camden. Furthermore, we highly recommend you avoid the area altogether. It is not considered friendly to anyone associated with Chancery Gate University."

He leaned back a little and picked up his cane. "That is all. I am available during office hours should you have any questions. Good luck."

Professor Shirk seemed satisfied with himself and stepped away from the podium. Everyone got up to leave, catching Alice by surprise, as she had planned to get out before the crowds. She dropped her new phone on the floor and had to bend down and dig around at Madison's feet. By the time she had it in hand, it was too late to avoid long lines to leave. She felt highly claustrophobic and desperately looked around for a sneaky alternate exit but saw none.

Sensing Alice's discomfort, Madison put a hand on her shoulder.

"Hey, I bet the VC's library has stuff about the Great Rift," she said in the voice she usually used to help Alice calm down during moments of anxiety. "I saw which team we're on. We should contact the captain tomorrow morning and develop rapport with him."

Alice couldn't respond; sucking up to some older student was the last thing on her mind. She was getting some info on the rift thing, but she was going to do it tonight, and she was going to do it her way.

CHAPTER 5

After finally getting out of the Great Hall, Madison and Karan wanted to mill around with other students in Top Lane and debrief. Alice made her apologies and struck out toward the dorms alone as quickly as she could walk.

Arriving back at the array of glass elevators before most other students, she was lucky to get in one with a skinny guy in a lab coat with an official-looking key card. He seemed nervous about her presence. Leaning as far away from her as he could, he reached over and swiped his card. But before he could press his button, Alice quickly pressed the button for the lowest floor: the loading dock.

He looked up at her with frightened eyes. "Are you authorized to go to the docks?" he asked her in a tinny, strained voice.

Alice nodded.

"Why didn't you use your pass?"

Alice just glared at him threateningly.

She could almost hear his remaining resolve collapse, and he nearly fell as he stepped away.

He pressed the button to the next floor and rushed out as soon as the doors opened wide enough to let him through.

Then she was alone.

The elevator traveled a long way down, past the fitness center, all the dorms, lecture halls, the dining hall, and finally slowed down at the bottom floor. When the doors opened, Alice found herself in a massive cavern lit by floodlights. It was the size of several football fields.

Immediately to her left was a line of fancy, fast-looking cars and a few bright-yellow motorcycles. To her right was a set of massive freight elevators, huge garbage dumpsters, and recycling containers.

Otherwise, it was just a vast, empty space.

The presence of stalagmites and stalactites implied this was a natural cavern, but it was reinforced with colossal columns of concrete and concrete walls.

In the distance, she could see the walls were broken by a series of arched tunnel entrances, like in a railway station. One was significantly larger than the rest. It looked like a small airplane could fit through.

She felt happy down here, probably because it was a huge space with no people. She would like to walk around for an hour or two and unwind.

"Excuse me," a polite British voice rang out and echoed behind her. "Do you have a pass to be down here?"

Alice turned and saw a tall man in a security guard uniform approaching her. He was stocky and broad-shouldered, yet his hair was completely gray and his eyes a bit tired. She saw he had been in a chair right by the elevator door, and in her awe of arriving in such a place, she had walked right by him without noticing.

She shook her head in response to his question. She felt her mutism was at an ebb, so she asked: "Where do all those tunnels go?"

He smiled like he thought Alice was making an inside joke. "I'm not at liberty to say, as you well know. May I ask if you are a new student?"

Alice nodded.

"I'd like to tell you all about the school's underground passages, but unfortunately, they are one of the most guarded secrets we have, and students are not permitted down here."

Alice nodded.

He looked kindly at Alice. "It's natural to be curious about everything—I was myself as a student. Back then, they allowed teachers to bring some of their senior classes down to explain the basics. Just showing them the entrances does no real harm, as you can't tell where the tunnels go."

He gestured toward the elevator door behind her. "I'm afraid in my capacity as a loading dock security guard, I must ask you to take the next lift back upstairs immediately. I'm sorry."

Alice acquiesced to being led back to the elevators and smiled sympathetically at the man as the doors closed. He smiled back and seemed genuinely sorry to have booted her out.

REJOINING MADISON and Karan back in their dorm room, Alice explained her experience in the loading dock.

"So," Madison said, "let me get this straight. Supriya gossiped about a super-siddha on campus who threatened to open a Giant Rift. Because of this, the university has tightened security, particularly in the loading dock area. You're worried this super-siddha is you and that the heightened security is because you are here. Is that all accurate so far?"

Alice nodded reluctantly, knowing where Madison was going.

"So, you sneak down to the loading dock and get caught. Which all but guarantees those rumors about you will get worse."

"Not my finest moment, I guess," Alice said. "But you know how I am. I was anxious, and it gets worse when I feel people are hiding things from me."

Karan laughed as she threw herself under the covers.

"And at least the security guard down there didn't take down my name," Alice reasoned.

"And surely a university with nearly infinite financial resources wouldn't have any CCTV cameras down there or in the elevators," Madison said in her most sarcastic tone.

"Oh," Alice said.

Karan yawned. "Look, Mad. It's been a stressful day. Not everyone behaves rationally all the time. Let's go to sleep."

Alice realized then how tired she was and could barely stand to be awake one more second. But she dragged herself to the shared bathroom and got ready for bed.

None of them even had time to comment about how great it was to spend their first night in their new room together before they were all asleep.

IT FELT like only seconds had passed when Madison was waking her up. "Rise and shine, you two!" Madison sang. Alice noticed Mad was fully dressed and looked fresh.

Karan and Alice both vented their rage at her and threatened to sleep all day, but Madison persisted. "It is our first morning here together! Classes start today, and we have tons to do before then!"

"Like what?" Karan grumped.

"Like looking for information about the Great Rift in the VC's library," Madison said. "I have already organized it with Nick Bridish, that depressing girl from yesterday."

Now fully awake, Alice rolled out of bed and dressed quickly. Karan wasn't far behind her.

She had a renewed sense; a new beginning was possible. Perhaps her fears about being labeled a super-siddha were utterly unfounded. Maybe they would find out this Great Rift was some outdated argument between people wanting to keep women out of the university or something that seemed important at the time but sounds silly now, like whether students had to wear formal clothes at dinner.

Alice knew, however, that she couldn't feel comfortable here until she could be sure she wouldn't have a target on her back. That meant she had to put the Great Rift thing behind her.

Moments later, they had walked the entire length of Top Lane, which was surprisingly long, and had reached a kind of turret that stood at the end. Nick was slumped against a stone wall waiting for them.

"Thanks for agreeing to meet us, Nick," Madison said, smiling.

Nick coughed a bit before she responded. "No problem. I hate helping, but I love helping people get into trouble."

Madison's expression changed. "Why should we get into trouble?"

"Kidding me? Breaking into the VC's library? On your second day here? That's monumental. I had to be here to see it."

"But...I thought you had access..." Madison stammered.

"I don't have access to the VC's library. You asked me to bring you there, I agreed, that's it. So do you want to do this or not?"

"But won't you get in trouble too?" Madison asked.

"Not if I show you the door and leave before you're caught, which you will be. But don't let me talk you out of it. I think it's a fantastic idea."

Alice and Karan looked at each other with wild glows in their eyes.

Karan turned to Nick. "Is there a chance we won't be caught? It's just a library, after all. Right?"

"Anything's possible."

"Can you help? I mean, help us not get in trouble? If it's not against your nature?"

"Sure," Nick said, though she clearly didn't believe it. "Come on."

"No way," Madison said. "As you said, we're not doing something that would get us in trouble on our second day here."

"I knew it. You guys suck."

Madison shook her head in disbelief. "Come on guys, let's go get some breakfast."

"Mad, let's just see what Nick has in mind," Karan said. "If it doesn't look promising, we'll take off."

"That's the spirit," Nick said.

"Come on, Mad," Karan insisted. "Let's just see the outside of it as long as we're here."

"Only the outside," Madison said. "Right?"

Karan nodded with the same naughty gleam lighting up Nick's face.

Alice smiled. She was just as hesitant to get in trouble as Madison. Still, unlike her conservative friend, Alice had the compulsion to get her questions answered, uncover hidden things, and ensure authority never asserted itself too strongly over her.

"Follow me." Nick turned and walked toward a worn wooden door. She looked left, looked right, pushed it open, and disappeared into the darkness. Alice was the first to follow, and she sensed Karan and Madison close behind her.

Nick was halfway up a narrow stone staircase hemmed in by unadorned stone walls. Alice hurried to follow. Their feet made only scraping sounds.

The top of the stairs inexplicably ended at a landing big enough only for a wooden bench, which Nick shifted out of the way. As soon as she did so, another door of roughly hewn wood slats appeared as though by magic.

Alice looked back at Karan and Madison, but they seemed not to have seen the absence of a door seconds before.

Looking back at the door, she realized it must have been cloaked, like the front gate. Was this place full of cloaked entrances to secret spaces? The idea sent a thrill through her.

Nick pushed through the door. Alice noticed she was breathing hard and wheezing. *No athlete, this one*, she thought.

The door added to the noise of Nick's heavy breathing, as the hinges were unoiled and old. Nevertheless, they all hurried through and closed the creaky door behind them.

Now they were in a brightly lit hallway, and they all took Nick's lead, pressing their bodies against the wall.

At the end of the hall was a glass door with an electric lock, next to which was a button. It looked like something you'd press to leave, meaning they were inside a secure space.

In the other direction, the hall held several doors.

"Which one?" Alice asked Nick in a whisper, pleased she could speak to her.

Nick seemed equally pleased Alice had managed to over-come her mutism and address her. "The last door leads to the VC's library. I don't think there would be anyone in there now. Teachers are all preparing for classes today, the VC is probably busy, and students don't yet have any reason to be in there. Maybe."

"That's reassuring," Karan whispered.

"When you're done, leave by that glass door. I'm going to block this one again."

"Got it," Alice said.

Madison looked betrayed. "You said only the outside!" she hissed.

"Too late. We're inside now," Karan smiled.

Nick turned and left, pulling the squeaky door closed.

"Now what?" Madison asked.

"Let's just have a quick look," Alice said.

They tiptoed down the hall expecting the VC to emerge from one of the doors along the way at any second, but she didn't.

Professor Bird was sitting in the library, though.

They opened the door and probably looked utterly ridiculous as they piled up on each other in the doorway.

Professor Bird was surrounded by books and a laptop. Her dog leaped to its feet and wagged its tail in passionate greeting.

"Ladies," Professor Bird said with a distinct tone of dismay, "may I assume from your demeanor that you are aware you're not allowed in here?"

"Yes, Professor," Madison replied in a panic. "We were led here just to see where it was. We didn't mean actually to come in."

"Led by whom?"

Snitching on a friend, even one who would be laughing at your doom, was worse than the doom itself, so they all remained quiet.

Professor Bird looked at them for a moment and then closed her laptop.

"Follow me, please." To her dog, she commanded, "Misty, come."

Their hearts beating like mad, the three of them followed the VC and Misty through another set of doors, silently down a hallway, and paused in front of a doorway. A cacophony of voices, laughter, and even what sounded like video game sounds echoed off the stones. Alice read "Vice Chancellor" on the doorplate.

Professor Bird held her arm out for them to enter before her. It was a promising gesture, Alice thought. Perhaps they wouldn't be reprimanded, at least, if the Vice Chancellor intended to be polite. But then again, maybe English people were just polite no matter what.

Alice and her friends found themselves in a large, circular, stone room with a high-vaulted ceiling. It must have been the top of the turret they had seen from below. Sloping lead windows lined the edges of half the room, all looking out over the nearby buildings toward Top Lane.

The room seemed to be organized roughly into four sections: a workspace with a giant desk overlooking the largest window, a little dining area, a personal library area with floor-to-ceiling mahogany bookshelves and three leather chairs, and a mad-scientist area full of high-tech gear. There were also monitors covering most of the walls. Most showed empty hallways or poorly lit basements, so Alice assumed they were security camera feeds. Others showed views of classrooms and lecture halls, many of which were already in session, with the voices of professors carrying over one another. A few screens showed sci-fi films playing at low volume, and several others were playing what appeared to be British sitcoms. The hum of conflicting voices and soundtracks sounded like a games arcade.

Professor Bird noticed their astonishment. "I have an obsessive-compulsive disorder. The films, TV shows, and games are a kind of reassuring background noise."

Alice couldn't imagine this woman having any disorder. She seemed perfect in every way. Alice wondered what her siddhis were.

They looked at the security feeds, and Alice saw dozen showed the landing bay. She saw a different security guard patrolling near the elevator. Had Professor Bird been watching last night? Could any one person monitor all these feeds efficiently? Surely the VC had a team of assistants to help her.

Alice turned to look at Madison, who seemed to be experiencing a mild variant of a heart attack. She and Karan ran to her, but she shook them off. "I'm fine. Just low blood sugar."

Professor Bird rushed them over to her little dining table, sat Madison down, and sighed. "You're probably hungry. Eat something while I attempt to impress upon you that rules are relevant even to first year-students from Colorado."

Karan didn't hesitate. She plopped down, greedily took two croissants onto a plate, and began stuffing herself.

Alice followed suit, attempting to eat in a slightly less horrific way, and Madison just sat stiffly, recovering, ready to be chastised.

Misty sat near them, clearly hoping for a handout.

"Before I learned there was a whole world of siddhis out there, I believed science could resolve all my unanswered questions. Why could I see the thoughts in other people's minds? Was it normal to have visions of events happening far away? I poured my heart and soul into science, but it had no meaningful answers."

"It turned out the answers were here at this university. But I'm still a scientist at heart. I'm hoping siddha science can genuinely answer the big questions in the universe. Like where life came from, if we are alone in the universe, and how we can cure stubborn illnesses like cancer.

She appeared to have a thought. "Excuse me for a moment," the VC said.

Alice watched her walk over to her desk and pick up her remarkable sunglasses. It occurred to Alice they made Professor Bird look a bit like Audrey Hepburn in an old movie.

"Please call Nick for me and ask her if she has time to come to my office," she said, then put the glasses down again.

It dawned on Alice the glasses must serve as her phone. It explained why she almost always wore them, even in the gloomy English weather. Like the VC herself, the glasses blended classic style with contemporary science and technology.

"But now I have no time for pure science," the VC continued. "I'm comfortable with that fact because my job as Vice

Chancellor requires me to devote my time elsewhere, and I love my job."

She walked over and placed her hands on their table to ensure she had their attention.

"Do you know what my job primarily entails?"

They all knew better than to venture an answer. Their mouths were also stuffed full of buttery croissants. Even Madison had given in and taken one.

"I spend nearly all of my time ensuring the survival of Chancery Gate University. Because it is always on the verge of discovery, as it always has been. To be discovered is to invite our destruction.

"I am often critical of how overprotective we are of our students. We should be more honest with you about the precariousness of our existence because there is not the faintest possibility any of you would take unnecessary chances or break rules if you knew the truth. Every rule here has a purpose; ultimately, they are all essential for the university's continued survival. Essential. But as the university always overrules my appeals for a more honest approach with our students, I must be content with finding allies to my cause wherever I can. I sincerely hope to count you among them?"

They all nodded.

"Excellent. I only request that you each make an appointment with the head therapist at Chancery Gate. She will help you with any issues you may be experiencing in your transition here. Now I know you have a busy day ahead of you, and so do I. Ms. Bridish will help you find your way out."

They suddenly noticed Nick slouching in the doorway, looking dismayed.

Once back downstairs, she turned to them and asked, "So, you guys get discovered in the VC's library, and she feeds you croissants?"

Madison explained what had happened, and Nick just shook her head.

"Sorry to disappoint you," Madison said, annoyed.

"What did you morons hope to find in her library anyway?" Nick asked.

Madison clammed up, which Alice thought was more than a little bit childish of her.

Karan explained the rumor about the super-siddhi and the Great Rift.

Nick looked down at the ground for a second and then began to walk away.

"What did I say?" Karan asked Alice.

"No idea," Alice responded.

"Come on." Karan ran to catch up with Nick, and Alice and Madison followed.

After they fell in with her, Karan asked, "What did I say?"

"Oh, you're still here," Nick said in mock surprise. She stopped and faced them again. Now, rather than annoyed, she just looked strangely exhausted. "Look, there are always rumors about super-siddhas. It's an annual thing here. Nothing but disappointment if you ask me. There hasn't been a real super-ish siddha here since your buddy Dean got booted out."

"Dean?" Alice asked. "Dean MacRae? The English cowboy who recruited us to come to Chancery Gate?"

"Yeah. Is he a cowboy now?" Nick scoffed.

"Top to bottom," Alice answered.

"Dean was *expelled* from this place?" Madison looked shocked.

"Sort of. I don't know the details."

"Why?" Karan asked.

"Why what?"

"Why was he expelled?" Alice asked.

"Dude could knock planes out of the sky with toy arrows," Nick answered. "It scared some people."

"So? Were they scared of him because he could shoot things with arrows, which was potentially aggressive, or just because he had a siddhi other people didn't?"

"Probably both. I don't know. People are jerks."

"But surely people have other siddhis here besides mind reading?"

Alice saw Nick flash her a quick look. It was the first time she had seen her looking nervous rather than bored, cynical, and tired. Did Nick know about Alice's siddhis? The VC knew about her healing abilities, for sure. Dean would have told her. But nobody here knew she could fly. Hopefully. Besides, why would Professor Bird share private stuff about one student with Nick, who was just another student?

Nick looked down and resumed her bored look again. Maybe it was a mask she chose to wear.

"Everyone here is different," she said, finally. "But unusual siddhis like Dean's attract attention."

"So surely Dean had to do something to get expelled, right?" Madison pressed.

"No idea. Way before my time. He probably got sick of people treating him like a freak and shot someone's balls off with a dull arrow. That's what I would have done."

"And that's against the Corollaries," Madison said, nodding. "So, if he hurt someone, they would have to expel him."

"Not anymore. After Dean, the VC fought for the right to manage deviants like you people in-house. If you break a Corollary, her sister owns you."

"Sister?"

"The head therapist is another Bird."

Karan looked confused. "What are the corollaries? Some heart attack thing?"

"Haven't you read that pamphlet?" Madison asked, incredulous.

"Nope."

Madison took it out of her pocket and showed Karan and Alice. It was the list of rules Alice had not wanted to read earlier and didn't much care to read now. Clearly, Karan had ignored it too.

"Look, guys, I'd love to chat with you all day, but I have somewhere to be." She looked genuinely exhausted, so Alice nudged Karan.

"What about the Great Rift?" she asked.

Nick sighed. "It is a kind of old political debate. A bunch of idiots are all worked up about it. That's why the VC had to beef up security."

Alice closed her eyes in embarrassment. After all that running around, all they had to do to learn about the Great Rift was to ask Nick. It was yet another reminder for Alice that she should resist that angry voice in her head that urged her to take risks.

"What kind of political debate could pose a risk to the university?" Madison asked, an intense look on her face.

"Everything is a risk to the university."

"But who are they?" Madison asked. "What's their problem?"

"Two basic factions in the siddha community. One likes the status quo, one doesn't."

"And?" Karan pressed.

"Conservatives think we should keep our abilities secret. Other people think we should use them more. To prevent wars, mostly."

Alice thought back to what Professor Bird said about finding cures for diseases. "Which side is the VC on?"

"Seriously? Everyone in the university and The Company are conservatives. Most siddhas in the world are. Can you imagine if someone like Dean went out and started wasting bad guys everywhere?"

"He'd be noticed," Alice said.

"Right. So no, the VC is not on their side."

"So, if everyone is conservative, why the security thing?" Karan asked.

"Probably just a bunch of overbearing mommies and daddies putting pressure on the VC because they're scared about their precious kiddies."

Alice looked at Madison and Karan, knowing they were thinking the same thing. They'd all imagined the siddha community was a nice safe space full of love and harmony. Or at least harmony.

Karan looked increasingly annoyed. "These 'mommies and daddies' are worried about centuries-old conflict?" she asked.

"I guess."

"Just because society is split between conservative and liberal?"

"Yep. Except they're not called that. The two sides are called Conservatives and Interventionalists."

"Great," Karan said. "So we just traded stupid American politics for stupid siddha politics. Fantastic. Do siddhas troll each other on social media? Is there even social media here? Are there nasty political tabloids, like one for the conservatives and one for the liberals? Do you people fight over which newspaper is fake news?" Without waiting for an answer, Karan started walking back toward the elevators. "I hate it already."

CHAPTER 6

Their first lecture was History. Between getting ready for class and eating a second breakfast, Madison and Karan scheduled their counseling appointments with Agnes Bird, PhD, SEP, but Alice put it off. She had never liked counseling and had no reason to expect a siddha therapist would be any better than the ones she had been subjected to throughout her childhood.

Keeping a low profile was hard for a six-foot-two female, but she had a lot of practice from her years being "that dumb tall girl" in high school with a lot to hide. The technique was to always sit in the back of the classroom, as quiet as a tree, ensuring she was last in and first out, not lingering in public spaces. There was no reason to think that strategy wouldn't work here.

The difference was that back in high school, she always had swimming and flying to look forward to. Now? She was excited about her new campus and its possibilities, but anxious everything would come crashing down on her head when people here learned what she could do.

At least she still had Madison and Karan sitting with her in the back of the hall.

The class was surprisingly non-magical. They weren't taught any siddhis. The lecturer—an extraordinarily meticulous and well-spoken woman named Professor Dunstan—ran through a history of the university, gesturing with an old-fashioned pointer stick toward images and maps projected onto a giant screen. She had gray hair and the plummy, brittle voice of an older, upper-class British woman. But there was something odd about her. Even watching from her distant spot at the back of the lecture hall, Alice felt sure this professor had the physique, energy, and general appearance of a twenty-year-old, not an older woman. Perhaps there was a siddhi that gave its possessor eternally youthful deportment?

Alice was intrigued by her story about the university but started wondering about the practical details, like where they got their electricity and how they had dug out all the underground parts of the campus. It would have involved a massive amount of excavation. Where did they put all the back dirt they dug out? Some farmer outside of London must have noticed a new mountain in his potato field.

But as class ended, her anxiety rose, and her curiosity was replaced by plans to get herself out of the lecture hall without chatting with anyone. She decided to leave early and headed straight for the practical tutorial up on Top Lane.

Thankfully, she found the designated room empty. It was on the second floor of one of the terraces leaning over Top Lane. It was furnished with six chairs, a table, a trolley with an electric kettle, a container of loose-leaf English tea, sugar, milk, and a tea set. It looked civilized and relaxing compared to the packed lecture theatre she had just escaped.

Alice sat back in her chair and gazed beyond the flowers in the window planters at the steady flow of students and dogs on Top Lane.

Ten minutes later, Madison and Karan joined her, followed

immediately by a graduate student who said she would lead the tutorial. She had dyed-blond hair and delicate features.

Soon afterward, three other students came in. These guys were all Asian in appearance, around five feet tall, stocky, and angular. They must be gymnasts, Alice thought. There couldn't have been three people on the planet who looked more different from Alice, Madison, and Karan.

She looked at Karan and willed her to avoid cracking any short-person jokes.

But she didn't, and after some smiles and nods, the session began.

The grad student wrote *Niamh* on a whiteboard. "None of you are locals, so I assume you need help with my name. It's pronounced Neeve." She spoke in a bubbly Irish accent like Saoirse Ronan, which flowed like a song. Alice liked her already.

"These practical sessions are the fun part of the university. This is where we discuss siddhis and practice them. Em, strictly speaking, siddhis can't be learned like magic tricks, but we can show you what to look for when your abilities manifest."

Alice saw Karan and Madison lean in. The gymnasts seemed to relax in their seats, so Alice assumed they already had siddhis and expected this class to be beneath them.

"Mind reading is a crucial skill, but it is not the same for everyone. Some experience it as a physical sensation; for others, it is sensory; for others, it is more like a download. By the time you leave Chancery Gate, it will feel natural, like a summer breeze, but you will also know that your experience of this siddhi is unique to you.

"You should know this: never will I or any other tutor or teacher ask you to compare yourself with anyone else. This is not a competition, and your experience is private. I ask that you remember the crucial step of asking for consent before attempting to read another siddha. Consent is assumed to be denied unless it is enthusiastically given. Any questions about that?"

The six students all looked at each other. Alice knew they were all wondering the same thing: will I allow that person to read me? Alice knew her answer already: definitely, emphatically, no.

"To illustrate how diverse the range of skills that is possible, there is a crude, four-level scale. I don't find it helpful to think of it too literally. Level four should not be automatically considered better than level one. You'll see what I mean in a moment.

"Level one describes a person who requires lots of space and quiet to be able to read another person. Most of us in the siddha community are level-one readers. In addition to consent, they will require their subject's full, undivided, and willing attention.

"A level-two reader can read another when the other is distracted or unwilling. Most gate sentries are level-two readers. They still require eye contact and some degree of peace.

"A level-three reader is rare; they can read another without eye contact. They only need to be close to their subject or at a moderate distance.

"The fourth level describes a defensive rather than an active-reading skill. Put simply, a level-four siddha can block someone else from reading them. Blocking abilities can range from partially or completely successful."

One of the gymnasts raised his hand but didn't wait to be called on. "Have you ever met anyone like that?" Alice couldn't place his accent at all.

"Sam, is it?"

He nodded.

"Yes, Sam, and so have you. Our VC is one. But I only mention her because she has permitted me to use her as an example. I must also remind you that these are not cut-and-dry categories. They say nothing about the quality of a reading experience. A level-three reader might, for example, be completely unable to choose what they read in another person. What they see is, therefore, completely random. On the other hand, a skillful level-one reader might only pick up a single word or image, but it is exactly what they were looking for."

Once again, Alice saw everyone looking around at each other, wondering what everyone else could do. If only they knew she could do everything Niamh described, except perhaps the level-four defensive stuff. She made a mental note to work on level four as hard as possible so that nobody would ever find out she was probably the only student who was as good as the VC at mind reading.

Sam's gaze lingered on Alice and turned to Niamh again. "So what about that video going around of the super-siddha first-year student? They seem to have all four levels of abilities. Lots of people are scared."

Sam's friends laughed as though he had said something funny; then they looked at Alice and her friends like they should be in on the joke too.

It was weird. If they were talking about her, what was so funny? What video could they be talking about? Why would she be expected to be in on the joke?

A video. Alice thought hard. A group of kids had filmed her flying last year, but Alice was 100 percent sure they would never pass that footage on to any other soul and would never let it out on the internet. When she met Karan a few years ago—or rather, when she had rescued Karan—someone had filmed her flying, too, and someone had taken that footage with absolutely nefarious motives. She had assumed she'd meet that person someday, find out what he wanted from her, and then make him regret he was alive. Somehow. She hadn't considered that he could have just been biding his time until he dropped the video on the internet to ruin her life. Could that be what this was?

Niamh seemed to pick up on Alice's discomfort and glared at the gymnasts. "I am not aware of any super-siddhas nor of any videos, and I would encourage you to focus on yourselves."

Chastised, the gymnasts sank back into their chairs.

"As I was saying, these skills are fluid. They may come and go depending on our energy levels and health. Meditation and good food improve our abilities, while alcohol and illness degrade them.

"And finally, they can spread like a virus. We don't know how or why, but it is one of the main benefits of attending Chancery Gate: our siddhis rub off on each other.

"So, let's practice. And no, we won't be reading each other today. Today, we'll sensitize ourselves to that mysterious substance that enables all our siddhis: prana. We must first get a feeling for the presence of prana. Prana concentrates around the edges of things. It seems to be attracted to borders and boundaries, and vertices. Therefore, we can feel it most intensely when someone makes a big decision, has a bad fall, or near-massive natural upheaval or change. It concentrates on births and deaths, for example. It is equally attracted by growth as decline."

Niamh got up and flicked the button on the electric kettle, and the water began to heat up.

"And," she said, pouring tea leaves into the pot, "the strangest characteristic of prana is this." She poured boiling water into the teapot and stirred it with a teaspoon. "Prana likes tea."

The other five students laughed, thinking Niamh was joking. Everyone but Alice, who had seen it before: wisps of curling blue prana flowing from a cup of spiced tea. She saw it now, though less prominent than before. The liquid crystalline substance flowed above the teapot like a feature in an impressionist painting, vibrant, blue, and alive.

Alice quickly looked away before Niamh noticed her staring.

"No one alive can actually see prana, of course. That skill has been lost for centuries. But we can all learn to feel it. And I was not kidding when I claimed that prana likes tea."

Alice once again squirmed in her seat, realizing she had yet another skill thought to have been lost for centuries. Not even Madison and Karan knew Alice could see prana.

Niamh poured them each a cup of English breakfast and asked them to relax and extend their feelings to their teacups.

LATER THAT DAY, as they walked to an ethics lecture with Professor Shirk, Madison told Alice she swore she had felt something over her tea, while Karan thought the whole exercise had been ridiculous.

"Why should prana like tea?" she asked no one in particular. "This whole thing sounds too hard. I can't imagine ever getting any magical powers and landing one of these siddhi jobs with infinite income."

"*Of course* you'll get a siddhi, Karan," Madison said. "They practically guarantee it."

"Um, how are you guys liking it here so far?" Alice looked at her friends and was suddenly overcome with a deep sense of shame. Since arriving yesterday, she had been totally caught up in her worries. She hadn't given one second of thought to how Madison and Karan were coping.

They looked at each other and sighed.

"We're both struggling a bit," Madison admitted.

Alice felt guilty. "I'm such an ass for not checking in with you guys before now."

"It's pretty much just like they said in history class," Karan said. "Imposter syndrome."

"What's that? I must have been spaced out."

"Professor Dunstan was just giving us a pep talk before the lecture," Madison said. "She said imposter syndrome is really common, and not just here. She said she used to teach at Princeton in the US and saw the same thing there. New students almost always feel like imposters. Like everyone else is smarter, better, better-looking, more athletic, more popular, or better adjusted. They get paranoid and think everyone, including the teachers and their roommates, is looking and laughing at them. They think they'll be found out. They worry they'll bomb out, and the news that they failed will get back to their friends and family back home. They worry it was all a mistake that they were admitted to the university."

"So you guys feel like imposters? But you're totally not, you know. I really think you guys do have siddhis. Just not the standard ones everyone else here seems to have."

"Oh, come on, Alice," Karan said. "I'm just good at finding stuff online. It's not a supernatural ability."

"And I'm just well-organized," Madison added.

"You both put up with me," Alice said firmly, "and that makes you both unnatural freaks, in my view."

Alice felt slightly better and more confident that Madison and Karan had her back no matter what. Together, they rushed to the glass elevators and down to class. Soon they were settled into the back row of Shirk's lecture.

The short, bearded Professor Shirk stood up from a chair in the front row and strode confidently to a little stool behind the podium.

Alice clearly remembered the look of deep recrimination on his face yesterday near the gate.

"Welcome to Ethics 101," his smooth voice intoned over the excellent sound system in the lecture hall. "Even though this unit is intended to be delivered in lecture format, I prefer to encourage as much discussion and debate as possible. As the Tibetans and Greeks understood, ethics is a subject grasped only through asserting arguments and counterarguments."

Alice looked around nervously. She hoped she wouldn't be forced to speak in front of others, especially in such a big class on their first day.

"We'll start with the siddhi laws and corollaries; then, I want you to introduce yourself to someone you've never met. I'll give you a hypothetical scenario to debate with each other."

Oh, brother, she thought. More about those corollaries. She saw everyone pulling out their little pamphlets from yesterday, and she did the same.

The professor put a slide up on a wide screen in the front of the lecture hall:

The Four Laws of Siddhis

1. The supernatural abilities we call "siddhis" grow through selflessness and are suppressed by greed. Selfishness begins with "Me" and extends to "my people, my preferences, my beliefs, " ending in mistakes, conflict, and war.

2. The fundamental substance that enables siddhis—"prana"—is drawn to relaxation and health and is repelled by stress and disease.

3. Siddhis beget siddhis.

4. Prana protects prana.

"These aren't 'laws' in the civil, social sense of the word," he intoned. "Rather, they are more like statements of scientific facts. Like the laws of thermodynamics."

Alice saw a lot of students nodding their heads, but she wasn't convinced. She could think of counterexamples from her personal experience for each law.

"Recently, however, questions have been raised about the

universality of these four laws. Please introduce yourself to someone sitting nearby and discuss any complications with the Four Laws.

Not gonna happen, Professor, Alice thought. Thankfully, there were too many students in this lecture theatre for one professor to monitor. Surely he wouldn't notice if Alice didn't participate.

"Hey," a male voice said from behind her. She spun around and saw Sam, the gymnast, had come to partner with her to discuss the laws. He must have stealthily risen and snuck around behind her. He wore a tight T-shirt that could hardly contain his striated arm muscles.

Naturally, Alice couldn't reply to him.

"She has selective mutism," Madison announced. "But I'm happy to chat with you."

When they had debated for a while, Professor Shirk tapped the mic.

"Excellent," he announced, quieting most of the conversations among students. "I'm glad to see you all engaged in meaningful debate. I hope you've noticed that even these so-called laws can be problematic. It is the nature of the problem we deal with here. Whenever we think we understand the world we live in, we are humbled by gaps in our knowledge."

He flashed another slide onto the screen, reading:

THE THREE COROLLARIES to the Four Laws:

1. Siddhas must support other siddhas and never harm or expose them outside the siddha community.

2. Likewise, a siddha never exposes his/her/their siddhis outside of the siddha community.

3. The best use of siddhis is preventing conflict and mishaps. Siddhas never engage in conflict but rather intervene at the highest levels to facilitate peace, minimize harm, speed reconciliation, and prevent future conflict.

. . .

"Here, we have three seemingly reliable guiding principles. It won't take you long, however, to discover their inherent contradictions."

He seemed to glare straight at Alice then. Her seat in the back row was so distant from his podium that he could not even make out her features. But perhaps her height was distinctive? Hair color? Was that even possible?

She instinctively slumped deeper into her seat. Like most very tall girls, Alice was well-practiced in this tactic. And yet next to her, Madison and Karan sat straight in their seats. *Lucky them*, she thought.

Professor Shirk continued, "Please discuss any contradictions that occur to you with your new debate partner."

Alice thought about it. *We should support siddhas.* Sure, no big deal. So long as she didn't have to be nice to jerks and idiots. Oh, wait a minute, she sounded cynical like Nick.

Never expose your siddhas outside of the siddha community. She was totally on board with that.

Siddhas never engage in conflict. Um, that was a problem. Alice had fought that guy Tyler last year. But she had to, didn't she? Otherwise, Tyler would have just let Asher die in that cave. But then, when she had pursued Tyler off the cliff, Tyler died from his injuries. Could she have saved Asher while still "minimizing harm?" Maybe, maybe not.

And what about Jon and his female victim? After she shouted at him in public, it seemed like they would have broken Corollaries, even though only Jon was to blame.

When the class finally ended, Alice wanted nothing but solitude. She intended to skip her remaining classes and go straight to the pool, and she told Madison and Karan as much.

"Wait, Alice," Karan said. "Just one second. I found something you'll find interesting."

"When?"

"My debate partner in there knew about that video thing Sam mentioned. It's not you."

Alice felt relief wash over her like cool water.

Karan held out her phone. "He shared it with me."

Alice saw the tear-stricken face of Jon's victim, the barista from Chancery Lane. She accused him of breaking Corollaries to take advantage of her and described how hard it had been for her ever since. It was sad, and Alice felt terrible for her— much worse than before. Alice couldn't imagine what being sexually abused felt like. Supriya hadn't understood the extent of Jon's lousy behavior.

Just then, Alice looked up and found herself hemmed in by Sam and his two friends on one side and Professor Shirk on the other. Where had they all come from? Shirk glared up at Alice and her friends. He was only about half Alice's height. Once again, Alice got a vibe of deep disapproval from him. He looked like he wanted to say something but instead turned to Sam and his gymnast friends (who were short, like him) and did something astonishing. Professor Shirk and Sam appeared to read each other without warning or polite permission. It seemed like they were just used to communicating that way.

When they were done, Shirk just walked away.

Alice had no idea why Shirk hated her, but she was sick of it. She was sick of people like Jon and people like Sam laughing at Jon. In fact, she was sick of all of this. The crowds, the politics, the judgment. Then, she recognized the extent of her anxiety and that it had engulfed her and was coloring all her feelings. She couldn't let it continue to build any longer; she had to address her anxiety. Right now.

Once Alice and her friends had walked far enough away from the ethics lecture hall that she felt confident they were in no danger of people trying to talk to them, she thanked Mad and Karan for their support, muttered something about anxiety and needing a workout, and headed for the pool.

The gym always reminded her of her mentor back in Colorado. Deputy Nancy Oakland was a beleaguered member of their local sheriff's department and had alternately helped and arrested Alice several times over the past few years. As part of Alice's unofficial parole, she had been forced to lift weights with Nancy a couple of times a week. And Nancy, despite her short stature, was the strongest woman in the gym and on some days, the strongest person, period. She and Alice had developed a weird but healthy bond, which was unique in Alice's life. It was inspiring how Nancy always seemed to do the right thing, fought for herself in the man's world, and held her ground with strength. Alice often considered following in Nancy's footsteps and pursuing a career in law enforcement. Now, she wished more than ever to go home and start over.

On the way to the pool, Alice passed through the weight room and decided to text Nancy to say hi. She took a photo of the gym too. She didn't know if messages like that would have been considered a breach of any Corollaries, but she sent them anyway.

Instantly, Alice's phone rang.

"Are you kidding me?" Nancy said.

"What?" Alice said, breathing hard. "No 'Hello, Alice, I miss you'?"

"Thanks for the pics. That gym of yours is where I imagine I'll go after I die."

"What time is it in Hardrock? Isn't it like five in the morning?"

"I'm in the gym too. Anyway, hello, Alice, I miss you. Like you care."

"That's it?"

"You got more?"

"Don't you want to hear about how my first day of classes went?"

"What am I, your mother? Get back to your workout. You have, like, a hundred machines in that gym to try and report back to me."

"Nice to talk to you too," Alice said, but Nancy had already hung up.

She smiled and walked through to the pool, which was empty. Alice had been a competitive swimmer in high school and hadn't been in the water for weeks, so it was bliss to do some laps. But the happy feelings and endorphin rush from exercise were short-lived. After showering off, her thoughts returned to her, worrying that the students objected to her presence on campus and would circulate some hate video of her, or worse.

It was only day two on campus, but she already felt claustrophobic and stifled. She needed something resembling fresh air. She wanted to see the sky, at least, and not just the sliver of gray above Top Lane.

Then it occurred to her: she was in one of the greatest cities in the world. Why not take her unlimited credit card for a spin? She knew she had been advised not to wander London alone, but maybe that advice didn't apply to someone as big and powerful looking as her.

With a sense of rebellious excitement, she changed into a blouse and slightly darker jeans—her only "dress" outfit—and took the elevator up to Top Lane. She emerged into an early afternoon, twilit, oppressive dullness, but it felt like freedom was near.

Alice made her way toward Chancery Gate. She had no idea if she would be allowed off the campus and had even less idea how getting out would work.

She passed a few familiar people but kept her eyes averted. She thought she saw Professor Bird's Labrador, but the dog didn't come up and lick her leg or anything. What was it like to read a dog's mind? Could those dogs report back to their masters somehow?

Then she was at the weird stone wall that looked very solid.

She was alone and had no way of asking anyone for help. There were no sentries on this side.

So, she just walked through it.

CHAPTER 7

A lice emerged right next to the sentry at the gate, who
today was a friendly-looking lady who could have been
someone's grandma. Alice had never known either of her
grandmothers, but she expected this lady to say something like:
"You turn your tail right around, young lady."

But instead, she just nodded politely at Alice, who nodded
back. Alice took a few tentative steps down the passageway
away from the wall, but the grandmother sentry didn't call out
to her. Alice kept walking left, right, left again, and a final right.
She kept walking and began to hear the unmistakable clamor
of cheerful voices in a restaurant or pub.

She knew it must be The Pickled Chicken. Her family had
had several fun dinners there in the week they had been in
London together. She felt the urge to go in and reclaim those
warm times with her family. She yearned for her mom, her dad,
and especially her baby sister. She wished they were still here,
waiting for her in the pub, everyone smiling in the warm glow
of the publican's friendly service and the heavy English pub
food.

But she knew they were gone, thousands of miles away. The
pub would feel empty to her. Also, English pubs were more the

domain of older men. She had no desire to run into someone like Shirk tonight. So as soon as she reached Chancery Lane, she turned away from the Pickled Chicken and strode north, away from the River Thames.

When her family was there, they saw all the major sights like St. Paul's Cathedral, Big Ben, Westminster Palace, Trafalgar Square, Tower Bridge, and Shakespeare's Globe Theatre. They had walked miles and miles and taken several tours on double-decker buses.

Now, rather than sightseeing, all Alice wanted to do was wander. To attempt to claim a little bit of the city for herself. To express herself and find freedom from the anxiety that burned in her. She was just going to wander and see what happened.

She walked and walked and walked for what seemed like hours. She would turn away whenever she found herself near a familiar monument. She just wanted to find little surprises, like plaques on doors indicating which famous people lived in which terrace houses. It was well past dark when she found herself walking along a decidedly less genteel street lined with grungy, graffitied buildings. She caught a street sign and realized she was in Camden Town. Perhaps her legs had followed a subconscious urge to defy Shirk's warnings about this area.

Well, she thought, *why not enter the lion's den?* Ordinarily, she would want to avoid crowds, and she knew she should be cautious, as Shirk would have had his reasons for warning students away from here. But tonight, she felt rebellious, and her rebellion was helping clear her anxiety. She searched for the kind of bar that would most offend someone like Professor Shirk.

Then she found just the place. A two-level cocktail bar advertising "drag and bingo." Did she have the courage to go somewhere like that? Alone? A group of kids back home liked dressing up in drag, and they were probably the most excellent and most tolerant people at her high school.

She looked hard at the people milling around the entrance and spilling out onto the upstairs balcony overlooking the street. They were primarily young people in couples or small groups. A few were even alone. Maybe it wouldn't be bizarre for a single woman to walk in alone? She might get hit on by someone, but perhaps her size and height would put them off. And she knew about drink spiking, but she didn't intend to buy anything—just pay her cover charge and walk through— mainly because Shirk told her not to come anywhere near here.

And that's what she did.

The place was surreal. Everything was lit with blue lights, including a very long blue bar. The walls were covered with graffiti lit in blue. She couldn't see any drag shows or bingo and guessed it was upstairs, so she headed up.

The show was not on at the moment, so everyone was mingling. It felt crowded and claustrophobic, so Alice immediately headed through the doors onto the balcony. Ten tables were set up for quiet conversation, but there was still enough room for people to stand around in twos and threes. And that's when she saw him.

Shirk. There was no chance he had seen her. His back was to the door, and he argued intensely with a woman. While earlier Alice had seen his disapproving look—because he had leveled it at her—his expression now was one of pure loathing. Like he wanted to hurt the person with whom he was speaking.

His anger didn't suit him, dressed as he was because Professor Shirk was dressed in full drag. Not glam, not sexy, but matronly, like a ninety-year-old woman with an impeccable fashion sense. Like the Queen of England, maybe. Shirk had a gorgeous yellow skirt suit with a pearl broach and a matching yellow hat at a rakish tilt. On his feet were black high-heeled shoes that probably cost more than Alice's whole wardrobe. It was his short stature that gave him away. Although she couldn't hear exactly what he was saying, she could make out his voice's unmistakable droning, pompous tone.

The woman he was sitting across from had shoulder-length black hair and plain features. What was unique about her was that she looked like she relished Shirk's fury, as if she was feeding on it like a vulture feeding on a corpse.

Alice didn't mind someone treating Shirk like carrion, but this woman was alarming.

There was no way Alice could get close enough to eavesdrop, so she relied upon observing body language. They looked like people who had some serious dirt on each other. Like they knew there was mutually assured destruction. It was obvious that Shirk was here because he assumed no Chancery Gate students would be. He looked like a regular. But that was just a guess based on how comfortable he was in drag.

But what Alice wanted to know was what dirt did that woman have on him?

That was when she noticed a young person standing near Shirk's table. They looked as gender-neutral as humanly possible. Like the kids back home who identified as non-binary. They looked like they were an expert at blending in and looking invisible. Alice had to look twice to make sure the person was really there.

That was when Alice noticed this person appeared to be eavesdropping on Shirk's conversation.

Alice watched Shirk seethe and lecture his adversary, who continued to soak it up like fuel. She responded to his lectures with short answers and occasional shoulder shrugs. Finally, she showed him something on her phone, which contained something that outraged Shirk. Then she just stood up and left.

Alice watched Shirk compose himself, rise from his seat, and rejoin some friends inside. They looked much younger than him, but all were as impeccably dressed as he was. It was like a subculture of people dressed in upper-class mid-century women's clothing.

Alice walked over to the nearly invisible person, stood beside them, and tried to breathe deeply and think relaxing thoughts. Her experience with Jon and his abusive behavior had convinced her mind reading was to be used as a last resort. She wanted to try this the old-fashioned way: through words rather than mind reading.

But for a person with selective mutism, even someone like her, who had come to accept her condition and make some strides, speaking to strangers was still a massive challenge.

Fortunately, they seemed to understand. Some people just had a basic grasp of human nature and didn't need siddhis to read people.

"Hey," they said, smiling wryly as though completely understanding what Alice wanted.

"Hey," Alice replied, smiling back.

"So I'm guessing you know the queen but not the nasty woman, right?"

Alice nodded sheepishly.

"And you're wondering what they talked about."

Alice nodded again.

"The queen called the nasty woman Needley."

Needley, Alice thought to herself. Had she ever heard that name before? The woman had not looked familiar, but she could be a teacher or admin person at the university she hadn't seen yet. But if Shirk was meeting her here, Alice guessed she wasn't from the university. The question remained: was she a siddha? If not, why was Shirk having a clandestine meeting with her?

"The two of them seem to be working together on a project," Alice's confidant continued. "But there's a problem. The nasty woman wants a name, and the old queen won't give it to her. The queen has a brother who died. It was some kind of a big deal. Like a scandal. And Needley knows something about it that isn't public information. She's threatening the queen that she'll post it on social media unless she is provided a name. But I got the impression it was the name of a different person altogether, unrelated to the brother thing. Someone important."

Alice waited, wondering what kind of name the woman wanted from Shirk. The name of a student a Chancery Gate? Of a teacher? Why was it of interest to her?

"That's all I heard," they finished. "Hope it helps."

"It does," Alice said. "Thank you."

"No problem." They smiled again—one loner to another—and walked back inside, leaving Alice alone on the balcony.

Alice pulled out her phone, looked up "Needley," and found about a million accounts on Twitter. Hopeless.

Alice gave it up and left the bar, relishing being out of the noisy, crowded space and happy to be leaving the urban grunge of Camden Town. She reoriented and decided to head back toward the Thames and follow it back toward Chancery Lane. Soon, she was passing expensive apartment buildings and well-lit corner grocery stores.

By the time she reached some reassuring landmarks like the stately University College London and the classic columns of the British Museum, she found herself relaxing back into her wandering spirit. She was hungry and thought it might be fun to get something to eat before heading back to campus.

She reached the river and followed it past the massive facade of Scotland Yard. She thought of Sherlock Holmes and wondered what Nancy would have made of that guy. She probably would have trusted him only as far as she could throw him, although that might have been quite far.

Then she was gazing up at Big Ben, which her dad had insisted was called Queen Elizabeth Tower. It was pretty cool: a sixteen-story Gothic clocktower and, to her at least, the national symbol of Britain. It occurred to her how fun it would be to climb up to the top and jump off, amazing all the terrified tourists below with a graceful low roll before she flew into the sky.

Then she heard the happy murmur of voices indicating a pub was nearby and saw a side-lane entrance to a lively little place. She was thirsty and hungry and wanted to try out her new credit card, but she was hoping for somewhere quiet with fewer older men, so she backed away again.

Then she saw an interesting sign on the floor above the pub that read "The Library" in a whimsical font. Judging by a table of young people she could see through a window, it was clearly not an actual library. She observed them for a moment longer and saw them drinking lurid cocktails. One of them was eating something that could have been a pie, burger, or something similar, and her stomach grumbled with hunger.

Well, she thought, *any place called The Library couldn't be too bad.* Alice loved libraries. It appeared you got to the cocktail bar through the downstairs pub, so she stepped through the doors. The pub was packed, but mostly with older men, as expected. She was immediately impressed with the pub's primary feature: a prominent grandfather clock and a bell. In fancy writing beneath it was a sign that read: Westminster Division Bells to call MPs back to vote in parliament. Once this bell rings, MPs have only eight minutes to return to the chamber, so consider shouting them their beer! She again thought of Shirk and recoiled.

Alice remembered in the United Kingdom, MP was a Member of Parliament, like a congressman or senator back home. She looked around the pub and located several men who could have been MPs judging by their age and dress and the busy coteries trying to get close enough to speak to them. If Alice closed an eye and squinted, she could almost see these few individuals as centers of gravity in the large room.

One man seemed to exert the strongest pull. He was older, rounder, and red-faced. She looked carefully at him and thought she could detect a cold, shrewd mind underneath the falsely jolly exterior. He was surrounded by what seemed to be bodyguards—strong men in ill-fitting suits who were always looking away, scanning the room. One of them saw her and gave a sleazy wink.

Disgusted, Alice pushed past a crowd of suited men and women who looked like they worked for the politicians and walked purposefully toward the stairway. But just then, a group of young people lined up on the stairs waiting to be taken to a table or something.

Alice felt a bit overwhelmed again by then, and her anxieties confused her. Almost by magic, a path opened to the bar, and she just walked forward to get a drink while she waited for the stairs to clear. She had never bought herself a drink before. She had the occasional glass of something with her family, and Karan had managed to buy beers from liquor stores for them a few times, but openly and legally buying a drink was a milestone. She had chatted with Mad and Karan about the drinking age here being eighteen, not twenty-one like in Colorado, and they had made excited plans to go out together to buy their first drink at the earliest opportunity. But Alice knew that, for her, the time was now. It was appropriate she took this step on her own. She needed it.

"I'll have a beer, thanks," she said, surprised and proud that she could speak to a stranger.

"What kind?" the young bartender asked. "Just a lager?"

Alice looked around and saw the red-faced MP-looking guy drinking a big, amber beer with a creamy top. It looked like a latte, so she turned to the bartender and said, "Whatever he's having over there. The creamy beer."

The bartender raised an eyebrow and silently placed a large glass under a tap labeled *Doom Bar*, manually pulling the enormous wooden lever back and forth to make the beer come out. This manual pulling motion seemed unique to English ale. He let it sit there, and the foam settled a bit, then he pulled the rest of the beer in. It seemed that more foam than beer ended up in her glass, which suited her fine, as she was hoping it tasted as much like a latte as it looked.

Alice tapped her shiny new credit card, wondering if it would work, and it did. Then Alice walked off with her own beer in a pub in London, alone, an adult.

She took a sip, and it tasted...gross. Flat, room temperature, and bitter. Not much like the beers she had had before. But in its favor, it was creamier than beer back home, and texture was at least something, so she did not set it down and walk away in disgust. She also didn't want to draw attention to herself.

Alice looked up and saw she was directly under a huge chandelier and suddenly felt like she was under a spotlight. She was also near the division bell and began to wonder if it was ear-piercingly loud. Would everyone stare at her if it rang?

Come on, Alice, she urged herself. *You're a grown-up woman now. Just chill. Enjoy this. At least nobody here will call you out for being a supernatural freak.*

She tried another sip of her room-temperature beer, and somehow it tasted slightly better this time. She focused on the creaminess and chugged half of it down. And then, it happened. She started to feel like she did fit in. She *was* an adult and belonged in this pub as much as anyone else did. It was probably the alcohol, but she didn't care. She felt her inhibitions draining away. She swallowed down the rest of her beer and went to order another one.

"I'll shout you one, young lady," a deep, posh, British voice said beside her. She looked around and saw that the red-faced MP guy had sidled up to the bar beside her. He gave her a toothy grin, which was horrific because his teeth were crooked and stained.

She shook her head and tried to stay calm.

The MP nodded at the barman, who obeyed and poured two ales.

Alice knew all she had to do was turn around and walk away. But she paused because she also felt scared of breaking some cultural norm. Would someone chase her down and demand she accept that guy's beer? Would everyone stop talking and stare at the weird American giant who turned down a polite offer? By then, she realized she had paused too long, and a beer was set before her.

"Care to join me at my table?"

She shook her head quickly.

"Oh, come now."

She turned around and walked briskly away, pushing through a group of besuited junior-politician wannabes, all staring at her and the MP.

She saw the stairway upstairs was finally clear, so she climbed away from the hideous man and his pub.

A smartly dressed young man ushered her through a door, and she found herself back in the twenty-first century. The space was sleek, modern, dark, and humming with a different kind of youthful enthusiasm. The music was cool, though it wasn't anything she recognized. The library theme was stylistic only. Books lined the space everywhere, but no one was reading. The bar was even made from old leather hardbacks. While it was a relief to be out of the pub, Alice hoped The Library would be quieter. Then she caught a glimpse of a back room and walked through. It was much less noisy back there and had fewer people. She found a table and sat down with a sigh, pleased to have some space to breathe.

A prim waitress took her order.

Alice sank deeper into the chair, taking long, slow breaths.

A few couples were eating up here, but nobody looked at her. And she noticed a tall, skinny boy in a black *Star Wars* T-shirt. He was utterly nerdy but surprisingly cute as well. He was about her age, sitting in front of a chessboard with a beer on a coaster. He was reading a dog-eared novel with the help of the light on his phone. So, at least one person was reading something here. Of all the people in this cocktail bar, he was the only one who seemed to take the name seriously.

"Excuse me," a voice said from behind her, surprising her. "May I join you?"

With complete dismay, she turned and saw it was the guy who had looked like a security guard for the old MP downstairs. The one who had winked at her. He looked like a total jerk: slick black hair, a sneering, sad smile, lots of muscles, and a little belly sticking out through his suit jacket.

She shook her head firmly, but he sat across from her anyway. She looked around and prepared to leave, but she saw another big guy in a suit standing in the doorway. She was trapped.

"I work for Michael Longblood," he said conversationally, in a weird English accent very different from Professor Bird's. He leaned back in his chair and stared at her, expecting her to be impressed.

She had no idea who Michael Longblood was, so she shrugged her shoulders at him.

"Part of my job is to clean up messes he makes. I need to know if he made a mess with you."

So that red-faced MP was called Longblood, she realized. Alice lifted her palms to indicate she had no idea what mess he was talking about.

"Are you...let's see...do you, um, work for a living?" he asked.

Alice squinted at him but remained silent. What the hell kind of question was that? She pointed at her mouth and shook her head, trying to get the message to this guy that she couldn't talk to him even if she wanted to, which she didn't.

"Not very talkative. You're not making this easy, so I'll be direct. Are you a prostitute?"

That did it. Alice was furious, her space and privacy had been invaded, and she wanted this guy gone. She didn't look anything like a prostitute, did she? She was about to stand up and throw something heavy at him when a thin, high voice interrupted.

"Hey, leave her alone, mate." The *Star Wars* kid from the corner had come to Alice's rescue, which made a bizarre situation even stranger.

She wanted to tell him she needed no one's help, but she couldn't speak.

"Can't you see she can't speak? How could she possibly have caused Michael any problems?"

The security guard scrutinized her, seemed conflicted, and nodded at the *Star Wars* kid. He rose to his feet, nodded again, and went back downstairs without another word.

Then her savior went back to his corner table and his book.

Alice found herself staring at the guy. The authority he had over that security guard was so weird. He seemed to even be on a first-name basis with that MP too. After finishing her food, she found herself so intrigued that she ordered a random cocktail she had never heard of and went to his table. It was uncharacteristic of her to be so socially courageous, but it was a night of firsts, and the alcohol helped.

He looked up and indicated the chair across from him, setting his book down.

"My cousin has selective mutism," he said to her in that same high, thin voice. "Is that anything like what you have? Sorry to be so direct. You don't have to answer that."

Wow, of all the speech impairments she could have had, this guy nailed it in one. Not knowing how to feel, she just nodded and smiled weakly.

"I kind of recognized the signs when Eric accosted you."

She raised an eyebrow.

"My mother knows Longblood, and his security guys know me a little. She has some influence, so they give me the benefit of the doubt."

Alice looked down at the chessboard.

"You play?"

She nodded, having played a few games of chess on her phone.

He told her his name was David. After he ordered himself a fresh beer, they played a game in complete silence. Being in a completely foreign country, in a cool cocktail bar, with a guy was thrilling. Her. Alice Brickstone, the tall, dumb, country kid who couldn't speak.

She wondered why he hadn't even asked her name. Was that British politeness?

A few times, Alice was tempted to read him and figure out why he and his mother had such influence over an MP and his security, but she felt it would be rude, especially as he wasn't even asking her questions. She also remembered how hurt Jon's victim had been when she discovered he had been reading her. Not that David would ever know.

After losing to him in chess in a spectacular fashion, she smiled, got up, nodded at him one last time, and left the pub. Thankfully, she didn't see the MP or his security guards on her way out.

Then she recognized the familiar weight of her anxiety and realized she was exhausted from a bizarre night out. She tried to recover that fleeting thrill of sitting with the *Star Wars* guy, but waves of stress and exhaustion were rising.

She felt conspicuous. Tourists were mingling below Big Ben, strolling on the Thames, taking pictures of Parliament House and St. Beatrice's church, and she felt like they were eying her, wondering what such a tall young woman was doing out on her own.

She thought she saw a hooded figure dash behind the statue of Winston Churchill, but it must have been her imagination. Two drinks' worth of imagination.

Despite her effort to persuade herself that she had seen nothing out of the ordinary tonight, she remained unconvinced.

Turning on her heel, she walked the half-hour back to campus, her anxiety rising with every block.

Finally, she passed the Pickled Chicken, still emanating a hum of cheerful voices, negotiated the winding passageway, and approached the sentry, a large, bearded man this time.

"Good day, young lady," he said in jolly tones.

She tried to smile at him and stood still to allow herself to be read. It was over in a second, just like yesterday. And as she did before, she swore she would find a way to block their reading of her someday.

Then she was through the strange stone wall and into Top Lane. The old, twinkling streetlamps and candlelit windows were storybook-cozy in the evening. Conflicting emotions struck her. Already, she felt attached to this mysterious place and was drawn to the idea of being part of a community of people like her. But she couldn't bear the thought of becoming a pariah here. It was her worst nightmare.

Mad and Karan were already in bed when she arrived in her dorm room.

"Did you seriously go out without us?" Karan cried as she saw Alice. "Did you go to the Pickled Chicken? Did you get laid?"

Alice smiled despite herself. "No, I just walked around the city. I ended up in a cocktail bar near Big Ben."

"Did the credit card thing work?"

"Yep."

"I'm so jealous. Please take us with you next time."

"I may have seen your ninja," Alice said, surprising herself.

Even then, she hadn't been sure she had seen anything, but now she felt confident.

"Where?!" Karan asked, startled.

"Near the bar. They were spying on me. And in another bar in Camden Town, I saw Professor Shirk dressed up like the late Queen of England."

"What?!" Karan gasped. "Our Professor Shirk? The old English gentleman?"

"Sure," Madison said, yawning. "Why not?"

"What was he wearing?" Karan asked.

Alice described his yellow outfit and explained what her loner friend had overheard: some unnamed scandal involving Shirk's brother and the nasty woman's attempt to use it to blackmail him into coughing up someone's name.

"Was this Needley a siddha?" Madison asked.

"How would I know? She wasn't wearing a name tag."

Karan sighed. "I'm going to see Shirk in a different light from now on, that's for sure."

"What else happened out there?" Madison asked.

Alice explained being hit on by the red-faced MP and then being accused by his security guard of being a prostitute.

Predictably, Madison was horrified and insisted Alice never go out by herself again.

Which, just as predictably, made Alice angry. Madison was not her mother. She had planned to tell them about David, but there was no way she would do so now. Besides, it felt good to keep David to herself for now, partly because Karan would grill her about it mercilessly, partly because she wasn't sure how she felt about him in the first place.

After Madison and Karan had exhausted their questions and the room and the entire dormitory grew quieter than a tomb, Alice lay in bed thinking about David. She fell asleep thinking of everything he had said and done and everything she wished she had said and done in response.

CHAPTER 8

O ver the following days, Alice tried to reclaim some of her initial enthusiasm for the university. She mostly failed. Every time someone raised their hand in class, she thought she was about to be named a super-siddha Corollary-breaker and a freak to be feared. Just as she had in high school, she turned into a solitary, quiet shadow in the back row, last one in, first out.

And yet, at the same time, it wasn't like high school. Outside class, she was free to do whatever she wanted, including wandering around one of the world's greatest cities. She had unlimited funds and could spend them on almost anything she wanted. Whenever she got anxious and paranoid, Alice invariably reminded herself, "This place does not revolve around you. Don't be so self-obsessed. Remember, Alice, everyone feels self-conscious their first year of university. Imposter syndrome is the most common cause of first-year dropouts," and the like. But all this self-talk just raised the clamor in her already noisy head, and rather than keeping herself grounded, she was freaking herself out.

To make matters worse, her mutism was reasserting itself. She even found herself growing increasingly quiet around

Madison and Karan. Alice had initially wanted to support *them* as they adjusted to this place, a university for people like her; they were only here as close contacts of a siddha. Sure, who wouldn't want to go to a secret, magical university? But it must be hard to be competing with people with fully developed siddhis, and Alice felt personally responsible for making sure they were adjusting okay. So far, she was failing them. Alice was turning into a maladjusted nutcase who needed *their* support.

Regardless of how quiet or stressed Alice grew, Karan and Mad remained steadfast in their support of her.

"Alice," Madison said to her one morning, "get out of bed. I found something amazing. You and Karan have to come with me *right now.*"

Karan was instantly up and reaching for clothes, but Alice was exhausted from another night of poor sleep.

"Alice, I'm serious. I have just found the most magical, mysterious room anyone has ever dreamed of."

"Oh yeah?" Karan said, pulling on a bra and T-shirt. "More magical than the wardrobe in the Narnia books?"

"Well, that was more like a portal."

"Semantics," Karan added, kicking Alice's mattress to get her moving. "Is it more magical than Doctor Who's Tardis?"

"That was a spaceship, not a room," Madison said, grabbing some of Alice's clothes out of her closet and chucking them unceremoniously onto her bed for her.

"Oh, fine." Karan faked a sigh. "Alice, get the hell up. We have to go see this stupid room that won't even take us to a magical land or time travel."

"It's way better than both of those, Karan," Madison said.

Alice finally rolled over, hoping Madison had discovered a room that would magically cure her anxiety and lift her mood. Still, she didn't know how anything or anyone could fix the confusing mess that her head felt like today.

She didn't want to deflate Madison and Karan's excitement,

so she dressed and even tried to participate in the banter. "Is it like that room in the Harry Potter books that turned into whatever you want?"

"Better," Madison said, leading them through the common room toward the elevator.

"Hey," Karan asked as they walked by the couch that had hosted the kissing couple the first time they had seen this room, "do you guys know how this room always looks so clean every morning? How is that even possible?"

"No idea." Madison shrugged as they waited for the elevator. "Maybe they have cleaning staff?"

"If you had an unlimited credit card, would you take a janitor job here?" Karan asked.

"Maybe they hire people from the outside."

"And wipe their memories daily, and hire new ones the next day?"

"I guess not. Weird."

Madison took them down to a level Alice had never been to, and the doors opened onto a vast, bright, warm, open space.

"Puppies!" screamed Karan, diving forward out of the elevator.

A group of twenty little football-sized bundles of yellow fluff dashed toward her, and she practically dove to the ground to meet them at their level. Karan's blonde hair mixed with the puppies' yellow fuzz, making it look strangely like the reunion of a mother with her children. It was hard to tell who was happier, Karan or the puppies. They competed madly to lick her scarred face until she finally just rolled onto her back and let them attack her with their joy.

Madison looked at Alice, and both smiled. Alice experienced a wave of happiness for the first time in days, though she suspected the feeling would be brief.

She sat down on the polished concrete, which seemed to be

heated from underneath and was soon mobbed by her own little flurry of puppies.

And in another pleasing surprise, Niamh appeared. "So, you managed to bring your friends down," she said to Madison. "Nice work."

Alice was too busy playing with her puppies to be annoyed to learn Madison and Niamh seemed to have planned this together.

"Alice, Karan, Niamh is this term's volunteer puppy school manager."

Karan surfaced from her smother of puppies, wiped her face, and said, "This place is totally better than Narnia."

"I'm glad you think so," the Irish woman enthused. "Not only do our puppy school graduate dogs go on to be wonderful siddha companions, but we also find that the school is itself a balm to troubled students."

"Troubled," Alice mused. Understatement of the year.

Niamh stooped down to cuddle an older puppy. "Labs need quite some training to sit still long enough to be read. But the university discovered years ago that even having the little guys around had a healing effect on some of us when nothing else worked."

Alice looked around. Within the football field–sized area, there must have been hundreds of puppies playing and engaging in training activities.

"Sometimes, one of these beautiful creatures takes to the training better than the others. Like Professor Bird's dog, Misty. She is so smart she can communicate simple thoughts and questions to her master, who can, in return, answer her. Their relationship is more like that between two people than between a dog and her master. I have even seen Professor Bird ask Misty to deliver a package to someone on campus and return via the staff kitchen to get herself a reward. Misty will do anything for the VC."

There were bunches of students among the golden little bundles. Some looked like they knew what they were doing, others not so much. Were they all troubled? Was Professor Bird troubled?

LATER, as they filed into the back row of a lecture hall for their second literature class of the week, Alice's warm, fuzzy puppy cuddles had worn off, and she was bracing herself for another class. Karan whispered encouragingly to Alice, "This is my favorite class so far! Wasserstein is *the best*."

Alice did remember Professor Wasserstein from last time. She was a small middle-aged woman with a tight bun and a naughty smile. She wielded her smile with intention, too. Nearly every controversial comment was followed by that slight quirk of the lips on one side and a raised eyebrow; then, she smiled outright as she watched the penny drop around the room. Alice also remembered laughing when she finished her class with the line, "Comments? Compliments?" followed by her trademark smile.

But even Wasserstein's flamboyance wasn't enough to thaw her anxiety today.

Professor Wasserstein put her first slide up and read it aloud: "Hierarchy of Siddhis in Hindu Epics."

Flying was second from the top, right below immortality. Alice's healing abilities were not listed, but Dean's magic archery was in the middle, next to the *ability to cloak physical spaces and objects.*

"Your teachers here aim to serve," the quirky professor began. "We try to look dashing up here in front of the podium and customize our lectures to be relevant to current events.

"We have each heard a disturbing amount of useless gossip

in the hallways concerning new students here with unusual siddhis."

Alice saw nearly everyone looking around the room, trying to see who besides themselves had been gossiping.

"How have we heard these rumors, you wonder? We never read your minds without your permission, but we are not deaf. In my experience, gossip is a sign that you are yearning for the guidance that an historian, such as myself, may provide. Over the last few days, the hallway chatter has sounded more like TV melodrama than discourse befitting students at a prestigious university. I am here to reassure you that the sky is not falling."

Professor Wasserstein's naughty smile did not convince Alice she was about to be reassured.

"The legends claim these flying immortal siddhas lived tens of thousands of years ago. For those of you who are new, remember: 'siddha' is a person with 'siddhis.' I, for example, am a siddha with the siddhi of impeccable taste."

Everyone laughed but Alice. She realized Wasserstein was kidding, but it unnerved her how so many people here seemed to care deeply about "taste." Alice felt like she had none, at least not any that these people would consider "impeccable." Not by a long shot.

"In my opinion," the professor continued, serious again, "the top three or four siddhis on this list are either fictitious or so exceedingly rare we will see only one every ten thousand years, give or take a millennium. In any case, they have never been seen by anyone associated with the siddha university system."

Alice sighed and tried to turn invisible, which was, unfortunately, not an ability she possessed.

Professor Wasserstein pointed to the bottom set of siddhis and said, "On the other hand, mind reading (telepathy), precognition (seeing future events), and clairvoyance (seeing persons and events distant in time or space) are abilities we hope some of you will obtain and master before graduation.

"Finally," she said, pointing at the middle of her list, "I must tell you this list of rare siddhis is incomplete. There seems to be no limit to the typology of strange and extraordinary abilities that are possible in humans. We used to have a teacher here who had the uncanny ability to locate lost keys, for example.

"And now, we come to the main point."

Alice noticed the room grow quiet as everyone leaned forward in their seats.

"This year, we are blessed with a student or two with unusual abilities not even listed on the slide before you. I will not name these siddhis or the lucky students who possess them, as they are highly private. If they choose to do so, it is up to those individuals to make their siddhis public. But I must emphasize these abilities are natural and to be celebrated, not feared. As you know, siddhis are often infectious, so to speak. I wouldn't be surprised if a cluster of students with new, wonderful siddhis were to blossom.

"You people, and perhaps your parents, too, seem concerned that a student with unusual siddhis threatens siddha society. You are worried they will inflame the debate between factions in our society concerning the role of a siddha in the world. Despite my youthful appearance, I have been around for quite some time, and I wish to assure you: that never happened and never will. Never before has a rare siddhi upset our society to the extent predicted by the gossipers in the hallways. Forget it."

Professor Wasserstein opened her arms wide as though embracing the whole room. "I urge you to put aside your prejudices about what is expected and what is not. Accept each other for who you are. You need each other. Ninety percent of you have suffered the same traumatic mistreatment growing up. You have been excluded because of your differences.

Don't turn around and exclude each other. Embrace each other.

Alice closed her eyes and pressed her fingers into her temples as Professor Wasserstein cooed, "Comments? Compliments?"

After the lecture, Alice couldn't utter a single word to Madison or Karan about her feelings. She knew her silence was frustrating for them, but she could do nothing about it. She just wanted to swipe her magic credit card for a flight back home to Colorado.

After the other two had gone to study somewhere, Alice started changing to go to the gym in a futile attempt to lift her spirits. That was when she hit rock bottom, or so she thought. She just sank on her bed with her head in her hands. And in the darkness behind her hands, she felt like the only way forward was to get out. If not to Colorado, at least off campus.

She dropped her hands, put on her "going out" clothes—jeans, the same blouse she wore the other night, and the rainbow-colored Celtic knot bracelet Karan had given her—and set off toward Chancery Gate.

This time she walked confidently through the stone wall, silently past the sentry, and then embarked on a direct route toward Big Ben. It was raining, so she bought an umbrella and pressed to Westminster. She strode straight through the pub doors and toward the stairs leading up to The Library.

It was just as she remembered from the other night. The Division Bell on the wall and the giant chandelier hanging over huddles of suited politicians and younger staffers. The two men behind the bar pulling on big beer taps. The warm lighting and the smell of wet wool. Thankfully, that jerk MP, Michael Longblood, and Eric, his security guy, seemed absent.

She climbed the stairs to The Library and asked to be seated in the quieter room in the back. She was disappointed to find her savior nerd wasn't there.

She sat down heavily at the same table as before, ordered the same brand of ale to go with some food, and took a deep breath. She had to admit that even though her foolish hope of finding Nerd Guy had been dashed, getting off campus had been a good move. She already felt quite a bit better. And she was getting that same feeling she had the other night when she felt so grown-up ordering her beer.

Just when she was feeling relaxed, Longblood's security guard Eric appeared at the doorway. He saw her and walked straight over.

"I'm so glad you're here," he said, walking up to her, blocking her way out. "I've been hoping to finish our chat."

Her first impulse was to push him out of the way and leave. He was big and tall, but she was the same height he was and probably outweighed him. Especially after the rich diet she had been living on for the past few weeks.

She sat back down at her table, pretending to acquiesce to his request to "finish their chat." but then she got mad. What the hell was it about these guys? Why pick on her? She had to know why. And she knew exactly how to figure it out.

"I think we got off to a poor start the other night," Eric said as he plopped himself down in the seat across from Alice, pulling off his ill-fitting suit jacket and tossing it over a third chair.

Alice realized she had underestimated his bulk the other night. He did have a gut, but he was also jacked. Muscles made his white, collared shirt look like it wanted to burst open. She also noticed that the calluses on his hands were more like those of a rancher back home. His were not the hands of a regular gym junkie.

"You see, I had no idea you were a friend of David's," he continued, slumping back in his seat. "I looked up selective mutism, and I think I understand your condition," he said, winking at her conspiratorially.

Alice said nothing.

He pulled out a pen and paper and pushed it across to her.

"So, where are you from?"

Alice made no move to take his stupid paper.

"I like your bracelet," he said, indicating the bracelet Karan had given her. "I have lots of respect for LGBTQ." Alice hadn't thought of it as having anything to do with gender or sexual preference; it was just colorful and interesting. She just sat there and waited. She didn't look forward to what she had to do, however. Reading people subjected her to their inner worlds, and in most cases, it was not pretty.

"You look like an athlete," he continued. "I can tell. I was a rower myself. I still go out for a paddle sometimes. We athletes should stick together. What's your sport?"

As she continued to wait, Alice enjoyed watching him start to get twitchy. He was nervous about this situation. He was under pressure to get some results. He needed something from her, she guessed. *All will be clear in a moment*, she thought.

"I have your pal David's best interests at heart, too," he continued, leaning forward. He was almost pleading now. "I just have to make sure all is above board."

Alice said nothing but was pleased he was finally getting to the point. It would make it easier for her to sort through his stupid head. *"All above board" regarding what?* she wondered.

But then something changed in Eric. He tensed his hands and narrowed his eyes, glaring at her. He seemed like he would explode or reach out and strangle her.

She had to do it now.

Alice locked onto his angry eyes and mentally reached for him.

With a rush, she was in. His mind was a disgusting, messy shouting match, as expected. As he sat there, outwardly dazed, Alice guided him through the noise toward substantial facts.

Little by little, as the seconds ticked by, the whole story became clear.

His name was Eric Johnson, and he was a momma's boy through and through, except for one thing: against his mother's wishes, Eric worked for Michael Longblood, the independent MP downstairs. Longblood was considered to be the champion of the British alt-right. He had ambitions to become prime minister, but he needed something big to happen to launch him to power. Something that would alter the whole political landscape. Something...

Eric began to fight. He wasn't aware of Alice's presence in his mind, but he had been trained to keep his master's secrets, and this information had been disclosed to him and him alone. Among Longblood's confidants, he was the only one trusted with this secret. So, Alice had to expend much mental energy and force Eric to where he didn't want to go.

And then she had it: Longblood was planning to stage a major act of terrorism in London that could be blamed on foreigners.

Alice forced Eric to reveal one more piece of information: "Break London with two Hermans under ten."

Deeply shaken, Alice withdrew from Eric's mind. The ominous phrase, "Break London with two Hermans under ten," rang in her head like a forbidden spell.

As Eric shook his head to clear the fog she had created, Alice thought quickly about what she could do next to get him to leave her alone.

"So?" he started up again, slightly calmer than before. "What is your interest in Michael Longblood?"

She couldn't and didn't respond. Instead, she looked around, hoping for an opportunity to stand up and walk out. She was preparing to do just that, to fight with Eric and anyone else who tried to stop her—or maybe start screaming—when

David appeared at the top of the stairs and immediately saw the look of panic on Alice's face.

He rushed over and stared down at Eric. "Mate, why are you bothering my friend again?"

"You've got it all wrong. She invited me to join her."

Alice shook her head vigorously.

"My friend doesn't seem to agree." David took out his phone, tapped it, and held it to his ear. "Mum, I'm here at the pub, and Longblood's man Eric is harassing a friend of mine." He paused as though listening. "Yes, I agree."

"Okay, you win," Eric said, standing up abruptly, holding his hand up. "But David, you don't know who this woman is. You need to be very, very careful." With a final look over his shoulder, the goon walked downstairs to rejoin his boss.

David sat down in the seat Eric had vacated and smiled at Alice. "I didn't call my mum." He held his phone up to show her an open chess app instead of the dialing screen. "We're not really that close."

Alice smiled back at him, temporarily relieved to be rid of Eric. Then she remembered Longblood's plot, and her stomach lurched.

Alice was about to leave when David flagged a waiter and ordered an ale. "Can I get you one?" he asked Alice.

She looked at the stairs, then back at David, and nodded. She felt like returning to campus and telling someone about the terrorist plot, but here she was with this cute guy who had saved her for the second time. He was nerdy, yes, but that was part of the attraction. He was also quite confident, at least in the way he dealt with that security guard.

As she sipped her creamy, warm, flat beer and scanned the room constantly for signs of any siddha agents or a re-emboldened Eric the goon, a thought occurred to her—a wonderfully relieving thought.

What if Eric and Longblood were somehow part of The Chancellor's Game? Could the siddha university plant people like that here? The game was, after all, supposed to be set in pubs. Of course! After the VC's opening address, Professor Shirk said, "We have planted fragments of information in various pubs across London and the rest of England. Your goal is to discover enough of these clues to prevent a fictitious terrorist attack in London."

Alice felt stupid. Perhaps she had been frightened and shocked for no reason. "Two Hermans under ten" was probably a coded phrase that would earn her team points.

This train of thought relieved Alice so much that she discovered she could speak to David. She knew it would sound weird, as they had been silent for quite a while. *But what the hell*, she thought.

"I'm Alice," she said. "Nice to meet you, David."

He looked up at her from his phone, where he had been playing chess, and smiled in surprise. He didn't seem shocked; instead, he seemed like he expected her to overcome her mutism and was happy that it had been sooner rather than later.

"Another beer?" Alice asked.

They ordered another round and then another one. Halfway through her third beer, Alice felt herself getting quite drunk. She had never been so drunk before but thought she liked it at first. She couldn't do much but utter one-word responses to David's questions like "What's your favorite book" and "Have you ever been to the Cotswolds? They're really cool," and such.

After quite a while, perhaps a measured silence, David spoke up. "So that's an American accent, isn't it?"

Alice nodded but seemed to have temporarily used up her speech quota.

Instead of persisting with questions about her, he seemed to decide he owed her some information about himself in return. "I grew up in Stroud. It's in the Cotswolds, west of London. About an hour and a half by train."

She nodded politely. Her mom had wanted their family to visit the Cotswolds on their next trip because of its cute little market towns with medieval cottages and winding laneways with canals and old-growth forests. Dad had agreed enthusiastically because he had heard there were fantastic old pubs there.

David let that much settle in for a while, and then he looked at Alice and gave an awkward smile. She interpreted it as a question: should he keep talking or not? So she nodded.

"I moved to London for university," he said tentatively.

Alice took a big gulp of beer, then a deep breath, and said: "Why was that idiot so afraid of your mum?"

He smiled and then frowned. "Well, I'm not very proud of this, but my mum is... a kind of online political influencer. Eric knows my mum could seriously hurt Longblood's political standing with a single post. I just wish..."

Alice knew what he wished. He wished the world wasn't such a crappy place and his mother wasn't involved in making it so. She completely understood that feeling. David's mother was probably Mary Poppins compared to Alice's mom. But she couldn't say all this to him even if she wanted to. All she could manage was, "You guys write 'mum' over here instead of 'mom,' right?"

He smiled, and then his expression darkened. "Right. But mine doesn't deserve either title."

"Why?" Alice asked, thinking of the failures of her mother.

"She is a narcissist who cares more about her image as a mother than the actual job of mothering. And she operates on drama, not love. Growing up, especially after Dad died, I can only remember one drama after another. Each drama revolved around her. She was the diva; I was only part of her audience or sometimes a supporting actor."

Alice had never known anyone like that. David's mom sounded horrible, and Alice sympathized with his traumatic childhood.

After a moment of reflective silence, he said, "I hope Eric didn't say anything too vile to you."

Alice shook her head, though, of course, he had. The jerk's accusation she was a prostitute still hurt.

He paused for a second as though trying to find the right words. "Um, please don't take this wrong. But I'm only here today because I hoped to see you."

She stared at him, dumbfounded.

"I'm not like a stalker or anything," he insisted.

Embarrassed, she looked down at her beer. She wanted to believe that he actually liked her, but something inside her wouldn't or couldn't. It seemed likely he was acting, just like Eric and Longblood. Maybe his act was coordinated with theirs. Perhaps everyone was acting, in some way or another. But what if...what if David was just being truthful? Could there be a guy out there who genuinely liked someone like her, despite her mutism?

She looked up again and saw he appeared to be mortified.

So she picked up her beer and held it out. "Here's to crappy mothers."

He smiled awkwardly, and they settled back into silence. And then they ordered one more beer, though Alice knew it was a mistake. She was already too drunk and didn't like the feeling anymore.

But when the beer came, she found herself drinking it anyway. She discovered her vision and thoughts had begun to fog to the extent she could only focus on David. She couldn't and didn't want to think about anything else.

It occurred to her she was at risk of making a total fool of herself in front of this guy, and she needed to stop drinking. Now.

She pushed her half-drunk beer away and stood up to go. She wobbled, then steadied herself. He stood up, too, nervously.

They exchanged numbers, and David followed her downstairs and out the front door. He said goodbye, and she nodded back, and there was an awkward moment when nothing happened when something should have. A kiss? A handshake? What? But Alice turned and walked away. She imagined he was standing there, watching her go, a perplexed look on his face. She wondered if he was staring at her butt. But she didn't look back.

The night air refreshed her a bit, yet she knew she was drunk. She didn't much look forward to returning to the confinement of the campus and potentially having to explain to someone why she was so off her face, but she set off toward Chancery Gate anyway.

She tried walking purposefully and confidently but knew she was probably weaving ridiculously. She still had a kind of tunnel vision where she could only see and think about the space right in front of her. She craved a return to clarity, but there was no chance of that right now.

She kept swiveling her head left and right in a fruitless effort to recover her peripheral vision and take in her surroundings. She probably looked like an escapee from a mental hospital. But during one of her sideways glances, she thought she saw something behind her. She stopped and turned fully around, coming face to face with two of those hooded ninja people. They were only about ten steps back. They didn't even try to dash into the shadows this time.

Her breath stopped. Who were these people? They were head to toe in black, their heads covered with black hoods, and their mouths and noses covered with black masks—like ninjas, just as Karan had claimed. Oddly, they even wore little logos on the center of their chests. It looked like a line drawing of a ninja in a crouched stance. There was something weird about the design of the logos, too, but Alice couldn't see well enough to figure out what.

She squinted at them and tried to see beneath their hoods. They were grim, androgynous, and gaunt. They had the eyes of hunters. They reminded her of a pair of mountain lions back home that had killed several hikers before being captured and euthanized. Alice wondered if she was going to be their prey. She tried to read them but was too drunk to concentrate. She was unlikely to be able to escape an apex predator in the state she was in, wobbling on her feet.

Just then, a crowd of revelers emerged from a side street and walked between Alice and the ninja mountain lions. The hooded pair shot Alice one more look and accelerated into the darkness down the side street like a mountain lion would.

She knew she should turn the other way and run but immediately did the opposite. As she sprinted clumsily after the ninjas, weaving a little, memories flashed through her head of the other times she had seen one of these weird people. She had glimpsed them the last time she came to the library bar. Maybe they had been following her wherever she went. Alice was surprised at how quickly her anger rose as she thought of it.

The two were loping down the dark street, and Alice followed. She saw one of them turn their head, then a glint of a smartphone screen. It looked like they had just taken a photo of Alice. And then they just kept...jogging. Not sprinting, not running. Just jogging. Before, she had seen them move quicker than she thought possible, and now they were just jogging. Why?

But rather than abandoning her chase, she sped up, guided by curiosity, frustration, and alcohol rather than heeding the warning bells sounding in the back of her murky mind.

The hooded pair easily stayed ahead of Alice, teasing her

and taking her on a merry chase through central London. To other people, they probably looked like a little jogging club. At one point, Alice saw the stone lions of Trafalgar Square and realized they were about halfway back to campus. Then she lost the hooded figures around a corner. She felt pretty sick by then, and her anger had dissipated somewhat. She was about to pull out her phone to ask for her map to guide her to Chancery Lane when one of the hooded figures popped out of the darkness just ahead of her. She lurched forward and cut down one of those tiny passageways between buildings.

Alice squeezed into the sliver of darkness, and they were there, facing her again. Nobody spoke; Alice just stood there swaying, trying not to show that she was tired and drunk, quieting her heavy breathing and standing tall. The two hooded figures just stared at her with their predatory eyes. There wasn't enough room for them to stand side by side, but she could clearly see the one in front. Their weird logo appeared to be glaring at Alice, too.

Then the one behind did a sort of cartwheel onto the closer ninja's shoulders, pushed up one wall, crab-walked up to a higher point on the opposite wall, then dove in through an open window on the other side. Just like that, the person was gone. It was like something she had seen in a documentary about some French guys who taught themselves to free-run through urban environments. *They call it parkour*, she remembered.

The other hooded figure just stood there, staring at Alice.

Shocked, she tried to lock in to read their mind, but the effort again failed. Either alcohol messed with her abilities, or she was up against someone who knew how to block a mind reader.

Then suddenly, the hooded figure turned and bolted down the narrow alley, clearly at full speed this time. But before Alice could even process what she had just witnessed, her quarry opened a little blue door in the wall up ahead and disappeared inside.

Fighting against what was now a screaming instinct to turn and run, Alice walked tentatively over to the little door. It was still open. She turned and looked toward the window on the opposite wall but could see only darkness. It was beyond the door: just a few concrete steps leading down into the black.

Suddenly, a voice called from down the stairs, "Alice!"

CHAPTER 9

Should she run away? Or plunge down a dark stairway and probably fall into a trap?

She tried to think it through, but her brain wasn't working. All that came up were the questions: Why would this ninja know her name? What did these people want from her?

Alice tottered, both mentally and physically. She fought the voice in her head that was vigorously demanding that she withdraw and return to the safety of campus.

The safety of campus...with a rush, she realized she *was* coming to think of it as a sanctuary. Right now, she truly wanted to be in the warm glow of her dorm room, protected by a system of ancient cloaking and a bunch of sentries. It was safer than her family home in Colorado had ever been.

Or was it? She looked back up at that dark window, and a thought occurred to her. There was no question these hooded people had some serious abilities. But were those abilities siddhis? If so, they might have access to campus. With a shudder, Alice realized someone on campus could have sent them. If so, she had no sanctuary anywhere.

Which made her mad.

She wasn't going to learn anything by standing around, so she bent over double to fit through the tiny doorway and plunged down the dark stairs, stumbling at first, then descending steadily.

When it grew too dark to see, she turned her phone light on and continued descending. Far above and behind her, she heard a door close, confirming her suspicion that this was a trap. But she didn't care. She wanted information, even if it meant taking a huge risk.

After five minutes of descending, the stairs finally leveled into a large, concrete cavern. It smelled musty, like an underground train station. "Where are you?" she shouted but saw no one and heard no response. She walked deeper into the cavern and thought she saw a bright, hunched shape near a dark archway. Instantly on alert again, she crept forward until the figure revealed itself to be a motorcycle. Yellow. Exactly like the ones she had seen in the prohibited bottommost level on campus. She passed it and walked through the dark archway, which intersected with a long, straight pathway leading left and right into more darkness.

Surely this was one of the secret tunnels to campus. Why had those hooded people brought her here?

She walked past the bike and shone her phone left and right. There was no indication which way led to campus. Maybe neither did. Despite her drunken state, she somehow remembered the compass app on her phone, which she consulted. Then she oriented herself and set off briskly down the path that led east, where, hopefully, the campus lay waiting.

After a ten-minute stumbling walk, she thought the tunnel was getting brighter. She turned off her phone light, realizing she could see well enough without it. The light grew until the tunnel curved slightly, and suddenly she could see the opening into the brightly lit loading docks of campus. She stopped, forcing herself to be careful. She knew she was still massively affected by the alcohol and didn't want to make a dumb, drunk mistake now.

She had failed to find the hooded people. She didn't know who they were or what they wanted from her. She had, however, been shown a secret tunnel to the campus, which meant she now possessed a secret known only to the Vice Chancellor and a select few others. This meant she would now have to be very careful not to be discovered.

Then she got a weird feeling. It was hard to describe...something like being watched. She swiveled around and saw nothing. It was bright enough here that no one could conceal themselves. She saw only a concrete wall. And yet, the feeling remained. If it wasn't a person watching her, what was it? She scanned the wall for surveillance cameras but saw nothing. She reached out to touch the cold concrete, and her hand went straight through. Her skin tingled with the intelligent warmth of prana, just like she did when passing through Chancery Gate.

She withdrew her hand, stared at it stupidly, and put both hands through. Then she poked her head through and saw another set of stairs. These were helical. She stepped onto the landing and craned her neck to see how high the stairs led, but they seemed endless.

She ascended the steps cautiously, squinting up the whole time, wary of seeing someone or being seen. After a while, the effort of climbing numbed her worries a bit, and she trudged on and on for what felt like ages. She almost fell over when the stairs abruptly ended, and she stood on a tiny landing surrounded by stone walls. Once again, she got the weird feeling that she was being watched, which she now interpreted as indicating she was near a cloaked doorway. Groping with her hands, she quickly found it and poked her head through.

Now she was in a dark, broad hallway. It turned a corner to her right and disappeared, while to her left, there was a large door that appeared to lead outside, judging by the light. She looked down, fearful of making a noise, and was pleased to see a thick, dark-colored carpet. The lights were low as well. She stepped onto the carpet and crept to the door. Unsurprisingly, it was in Top Lane at the dark end, next to the Vice Chancellor's turret. Alice felt a rush of relief as she saw students walking casually around in twos and threes, not a care in the world. There were no weird ninjas in sight. A fat Labrador strolled over and looked up through the window quizzically, so she ducked back out of sight and back to where she had emerged from the secret stairway. It looked like brickwork, but she sensed the same feeling about it as before. She put her hand through just to be sure.

Then she returned to the door, found it unlocked, and walked out into Top Lane, trying to act casual and completely sober. She stooped to pat the dog, which closed its eyes gratefully, even though Alice wobbled and fell onto her butt. Quickly rising to her feet, Alice turned and memorized the location of the door from which she had just emerged.

Satisfied, she took a few deep breaths and set off toward the elevators leading down to the dorms. The momentary relief she had felt upon seeing Top Lane dissipated, and a sick feeling was growing in its place. It probably had more to do with the beer than anything else, but she couldn't help staring into every dark corner, wondering if she would see a pair of eyes beneath a hood.

And then exhaustion came down. As she got closer to the comfort of her bed and the quiet camaraderie of her friends, she felt like she desperately needed to sleep harder and longer than she had ever before. She emerged from the elevator into the warm, soft light of the common room and shuffled by the couples on couches. She just felt like collapsing.

After finally reaching their room, Alice was relieved to hear Karan's snores, meaning she wouldn't have to explain herself. Not that she had been able to speak to either of her friends for days, but it still made things easier, knowing that tonight she wouldn't be expected to try. She lay down on her bed and closed her eyes. She just needed to sleep.

And that's when it happened. Everything started spinning. It was a hideous feeling like she was in a helicopter about to crash. Her eyes snapped open, and the spinning stopped. She closed them again, desperate for sleep, but the spinning started back up immediately, and this time she felt very, very nauseous. She forced herself out of bed, grabbed her toiletries, and walked as quickly as possible to the bathroom, where she vomited and cried alone for ten long minutes.

Feeling lonely and tired, she returned to bed and closed her eyes. The spinning started again, and she was so disappointed at being unable to sleep that she started crying again.

Karan's snoring continued, but Alice heard Madison jump straight out of bed and rush over to Alice's bed.

"Hey, sweetheart, what is it?" she whispered.

Alice wiped her eyes and looked up at Mad. She wanted to tell her everything. The whole story about David, Eric, and his terrorist MP boss, and how it was all part of The Chancellor's Game, and the ninjas, the secret tunnel, and everything. She didn't want to stop there, either. She wanted to apologize for being drunk and pathetic. She wanted to tell her how she felt like a bomb waiting to blow up, that she just wanted to go home to Colorado's vast, purple skies. Still, she was too embarrassed to admit it, and if she could pray and believed in someone to pray to, she would kneel and ask that her selective mutism would go away and, with it, the things that made her stand out. And yet she also wanted to beg Madison for forgiveness and for help to overcome all this pathetic self-pity so that she could be the real friend Madison and Karan deserved, and they could all stay here together and get the most out of this fantastic place.

But she couldn't say any of that. Her mutism was pressing down on her; all she could do was cry.

CHAPTER 10

The next day was, thankfully, Saturday. Alice had a nasty, head-smashing hangover and could not attend classes. She spent the day suffering in silence while Madison and Karan forced fluids down her.

She felt okay by Sunday and knew she owed Madison and Karan an explanation about Friday night.

They had breakfast together, Alice silent as usual, while Mad and Karan chatted about a boy Karan had her eye on.

During a break in their conversation, Alice cleared her throat and said, "Guys."

Because she had been largely silent since appearing drunk, sick, and sobbing Friday night, both women snapped to attention.

"You guys want to get a real coffee? Somewhere quiet?"

Karan looked down at her cafeteria coffee and then around at the largely empty cafeteria.

Alice smiled. "I mean somewhere else. With better coffee. I'd like to...talk to you guys about something."

"Of course," Mad said. "Top Lane?"

Alice looked at her phone and saw it was supposed to be

pouring outside. "Naw, that coffee cart is okay, but there's nowhere to sit when it's raining."

Karan looked up at the big wooden beams in the ceiling of the cavernous cafeteria. "It's raining? Wow. It could be snowing, or a hurricane up there, and none of us would know."

"Yeah, it's weird, isn't it," Madison said. "In Colorado, we were sort of part of the weather. And the seasons. We weren't walled off from nature. Like, the aspen trees would be amazing right now, and we would be right there among it all."

They all sat in silence for a second as Alice visualized mountainsides of golden trees quaking in the crisp fall breezes, the sound of the wind rising and falling like a reassuring lullaby, and the smell of damp, musty soil.

As usual, Karan broke the silence first. "I know this sounds crazy, but I heard that next door to the Pickled Chicken, there's a cool café."

"You mean the one where Jon's victim works?" Madison asked.

Karan nodded.

"Sound okay, Alice?" Madison asked.

"Sure," Alice said, already standing up.

They grabbed umbrellas and jackets and their infinite credit cards.

"So," Karan said as they walked along Top Lane in the cold drizzle. "How do we get out of this place?"

"You haven't been off-campus yet?" Alice asked.

"No way. I like being in this bubble. Have you?" Karan asked, and both she and Mad looked at Alice.

"Well, yeah. Twice."

Madison stopped in her tracks. "Without us?"

Karan pulled her arm to get her walking again. "Oh, come on, Mad. She's not the bubble type. Does she have to get permission to go for a walk?"

Alice didn't look back because she did feel a bit like she'd betrayed her friends. Hopefully she could make amends in a few minutes.

She took them through the weird wall at Chancery Gate and strolled down the passage past the Pickled Chicken.

Next door to the pub was a small doorway that opened into a surprisingly vast, brightly lit, modern cafe, echoing the welcome sounds of espresso machines and cutlery clinking against cups. Jon's victim was behind the machine and pouring a latte or something with great concentration. The place wasn't busy, but a few lawyer types were getting coffee, and Alice overheard snippets of posh British accents discussing boring legal things. There were also a few tables with students Alice recognized from the university.

They found a corner table far away from anyone else, which happened to be near the archway that appeared to lead through to the Pickled Chicken. Alice could see through to an old fireplace in the pub burning merrily.

"The first round on me, eh?" Karan said, rising to her feet, but before she got very far, an energetic, gray-haired woman in a loud rose-patterned apron bustled over.

She stopped and stood there without speaking, taking each of them in turn with a concerned look. When the woman looked her way, Alice snatched the opportunity to read her. She needed to avoid putting her foot in any new piles of horse dung, as she had done at the Big Ben pub.

What she saw in this woman's mind amazed her. She broke off contact, resolving to tell Madison and Karan what she had seen at the first opportunity.

"Pardon me," the woman said gently. "I don't mean to stare, but you three are just a bit unusual." Her speech was American, though Alice couldn't place the accent precisely.

"Um, thanks?" Karan responded awkwardly.

"I'm sorry. My name is Sue. My husband Gordy and I own the Pickled Chicken and this cafe. You *are* first-years, right?"

"Um..." They all knew they couldn't discuss the siddha university with outsiders.

"I know you're new because I never forget a name or a face. And yet..."

"Leave those kids alone, Sue," a man with a jolly voice called, hustling over. He, too, had an American accent. He wore a puffy pirate-style shirt with suspenders and had curly, gray hair. His back was unnecessarily straight, as though he was compensating for severe pain.

"They came for coffee, not psychoanalysis, I'm sure," he said, winking at Alice and her friends.

They ordered coffee, and they were left in silence. Alice wanted to wait until coffee came so she wouldn't be interrupted.

Sue brought their coffee and a massive plate of pastries and croissants they hadn't ordered. "These are from the best patisserie in London," she said. "Not on the menu. We always like to treat our first-years well. Gordy and I graduated long ago, but we never forget coming through Chancery Gate for the first time."

"Why do you think we're unusual?" Karan asked before Sue could leave.

Sue smiled. It was a kindly smile, full of genuine warmth. "By week two, most first years have put their new credit cards through a real workout. But here you are, dressed like normal kids and not covered head to toe in luxury brands." Sue smiled again and walked away. "That makes you very unusual. I also love to see fellow Americans at Chancery Gate. Especially nice people like you three. Enjoy the pastries, ladies."

"Grandma," a husky young boy called out. "How come they get all the almond croissants?"

Sue scolded her grandson and hustled him away.

Alice looked at Madison and Karan and realized Sue had a point. First-years did all seem to be wearing a lot of bling.

People were attending classes dressed like movie stars, and that was pretty much normal. Alice, Mad, and Karan were fashion outliers.

"I haven't even been out of Chancery Gate before today, let alone to Harrods of London." Karan sighed, plucking at her old ski jumper from Hardrock. "Always last to the party."

"So," Madison said, her calm gaze leveled at Alice. "What happened Friday night?"

Alice checked again that they were out of earshot of Gordy, Sue, and everyone else. She postponed her revelation about Sue and began explaining her rebellious and disastrous trip to Camden Town, then her two visits to The Library. She wasn't ready to say anything about David, but she told them all she could about Michael Longblood and his alleged plan to commit some act of violence. She told them how she had been chased by the two hooded people who baited her into the secret tunnel from Trafalgar Square to school.

When she was done, Mad and Karan sat there staring, open-mouthed.

"Oh, and the violent act involves 'two Hermans under ten.' It must be a coded clue for The Game."

"Two who's?" Madison asked.

"Hermans. Like, maybe two brothers with the surname Herman."

Karan still had her mouth open, and Madison put her chin in her hand to think.

It was so quiet Alice could hear Sue criticizing Gordy in the kitchen for not cleaning the coffeemaker properly.

"Guys?" Alice prompted.

"I...knew it!" Karan said, finally. "We're totally going to be the youngest-ever winners of The Chancellor's Game!"

"We didn't do anything, Karan. It's Alice who is going to win. But..."

"But what? Alice has got it in the bag."

"But those hooded figures don't fit into the story anywhere."

"Yeah. Why wear hoods? Are they hiding bad hairstyles? Do they have no ears? Are they Vulcans?"

"I don't think I was chased by Vulcans," Alice laughed.

"No, maybe they're just cold. Like maybe they're from a tropical climate and—"

"Karan!" Madison exclaimed. "This is serious! The university's cloaked tunnels are supposed to be a closely held secret. There's no way they would let a Chancellor's Game risk exposing any tunnels. And yet those ninja people practically forced Alice into a tunnel that led straight from Trafalgar Square to campus. Why would anyone want to do that? That's what I want to know."

"Elves? With big ears?"

Alice took another pastry.

"How did they know my name?" Alice asked.

Nobody had an answer. Even though it was ominous, Alice felt relief at sharing these details of her frightening outings.

After Sue checked on them one more time and left to get some more pastries, as Alice and Karan had already polished off most of the first lot, Alice told them what she had read in Sue's mind.

"You read the owner's mind?"

"Yeah."

"And you saw she and Gordy have a cloaking siddhi?" Karan exclaimed. "That's so cool!"

"And they must be really good," Alice said, "because they cloaked a massive tunnel entrance somewhere near the English Channel. The university uses that tunnel daily to bring in truckloads of supplies."

The three of them considered that for a moment and listened to the familiar sounds of the café. They were, to Alice, relaxing sounds and reminded her of cafes back home.

"I have to go use the bathroom," Alice said, standing up.

Karan rose to join her.

The café seemed not to have its own facilities, so they had to wander back through the arch into the pub. The "WC" was meant to be in the back, but they couldn't find it in the rabbit warren of thin hallways and seemingly random stairwells. Alice and Karan took a wrong turn and found themselves in a long hallway with numbered doors leading to hotel rooms.

A bizarre little sitting room with a low ceiling was situated at the end of the hall. At one side of the sitting room was a miniature couch lined with red velvet, and at the other was a squat door leading to a shared bathroom, probably for the hotel guests. It looked like an architectural mistake.

Sitting in toilet cubicles beside each other, Alice asked, "Hey, did that little room with the red couch remind you of something?"

"Totally," Karan responded. "It looked exactly like the inside of one of those little cars. Like Mr. Bean drives."

"What? No, it doesn't."

"Yeah, it does. Just visualize a steering wheel in front of the couch."

"Karan, didn't you think it looks like the cloaked entrance to the VC's library that Nick showed us?"

"No, but that's cool if you think it does. I think my one is better, though."

Alice finished first and pushed back into that tiny little room. It had the same vibe, like a cloaked entrance was here.

She quickly pulled the miniature couch out of the way to feel the polished stone behind and was not surprised to feel the outline of a small, cloaked door. She found a hidden handle that opened the door. She crouched down and peered inside.

"No, your thing is better than mine after all," Karan said, emerging from the bathroom.

Alice smiled and ducked through the tiny doorway.

The room she found herself in was also miniature in its

proportions. It was dusty and dark, clearly unoccupied for a long time. Alice felt she was the first person to be here in months or maybe years.

After flipping on a light, it was recognizable as a teenager's bedroom. A small bed was covered with a blanket bearing some soccer team's logo, matching posters on one of the walls, and various other soccer paraphernalia around. But that wasn't the dominant feature of the room.

"Whoa," Karan exclaimed as she ducked through the doorway. "Somebody seriously likes bows and arrows!"

Indeed, mounted carefully on various hooks anchored into the stonework were six terrifying-looking modern archery bows and a few quivers full of arrows.

Alice walked over to a small desk under the room's only window and pulled open the dusty curtains to see better.

The previous occupant had clearly not thought anyone else would have discovered his room as there had been no care taken to hide private things. Alice rifled through the laptop and the pile of high school essays and papers.

"Gross." Karan was leaning over near the bed. "He's got a booger collection."

Alice looked over and saw a line of brown dots on the wall near the bed. "Could be a she, remember. Like maybe the barista downstairs."

"Gross. I can't imagine a booger collector making my coffee. But you know, this room looks unused. And I think it was a boy's room. He even circled and dated his favorite boogers," Karan said admiringly. "June appeared to be a real bumper crop."

Turning back to the desk, Alice picked up a weird little scrapbook with a magazine cutout of Robin Hood on the cover.

"I think I know whose room this was," Alice said, leafing through the scrapbook.

Karan joined her and stared over her shoulder. "No way,"

Karan exclaimed as they examined a ten-year-old newspaper clipping. Smiling from ear to ear was Dean MacRae, the man who recruited Alice and her friends to attend Chancery Gate.

He was very, very different in this picture compared with her memories of him. Alice remembered him as a British Cowboy with a dark side, like someone you didn't want to mess with, not a smiling soccer lover with a booger collection. And being younger by ten years was only part of it. In the picture, he looked like a typical Brit, wearing tight black slacks and a dress shirt. But he was in a very abnormal situation: being released from jail. The photo caption read, *Vigilante Charged for Unlawful Use of Offensive Weapon.*

"Wow," Alice said, reading the article. "Says here he used a bow and arrows to shoot the tires out on a van full of explosives and heading toward a crowd of tourists. It's no wonder they booted him out of Chancery Gate."

"Why? Is saving people from terrorists illegal here?"

"Karan, the article says he shot the arrows from the other side of the Thames River. Five hundred and seventy yards away. There were witnesses."

"Oh," Karan said. "Which means he used his siddhis and broke a Corollary." Karan took the article from Alice and pointed at a paragraph Alice hadn't read yet. "Looks like the guy who wrote this article wasn't happy Dean was arrested. He cites an old English law that requires every non-ordained male between the age of seven and forty to carry a long bow and arrows and practice shooting for two hours every week. That law is still on the books but hasn't been enforced for centuries."

Alice looked carefully at the picture and pointed to some people near Dean. "Isn't that Sue and Gordy?"

"Hey, yeah, you're right," Karan agreed. "And check this out. Your favorite teacher is next to them."

Alice squinted at the picture, and Karan seemed right; Shirk stood beside Sue.

"I can understand why nice people like Sue and Gordy would be there to pick him up from jail, especially if he were living in this room, under their roof. But I can't imagine why Shirk would be there."

"Yeah. For some reason, Dean must have been lodging here in Sue and Gordy's pub. Here in this hidden room. And when he got in trouble, they were the ones he called to pick him up from jail."

"But why Shirk? Why would that old queen go out of his way to help a student in trouble?"

"Wait," Karan said. "I don't think it's him. Look. He's taller than Sue. There's no way the Shirk we know is taller than Sue."

Alice had to agree. Then something clicked. Shirk's brother. "Hey, Karan, you know how I told you about a woman called Needley blackmailing Shirk about a scandal involving his brother?"

"Yeah, that must be him!"

"And I wonder if this thing with Dean could also be part of the scandal?"

"But it was Dean's scandal, not Shirk's brother's."

"Remember this thing with Dean was supposed to have blown up the Great Rift thing, right?"

"Yeah?"

"What if Shirk's brother took the wrong side? What if he told everyone Dean is a siddha who just saved hundreds of people out there, and we should be thanking him, not kicking him out of university?"

"Maybe," Karan said. "But Shirk seems so conservative. Surely his brother is similar. He doesn't look like a rebel."

They stared at the article a while longer.

"Oops," Karan said urgently. "We had better get back downstairs. Madison is probably laying eggs down there."

"Yikes!" Alice said, and they both hustled back into the hallway. By the time they had the miniature couch back against the wall, Madison had emerged at the top of the stairs. Her face had panic written all over it.

After they calmed her down and explained what they had seen (she was too upset to have a look herself), they walked back down the café.

Alice had one more idea. "Karan, I don't think I can manage to speak to Sue, so you have to ask her. Okay?"

"Ask her what?"

"About Shirk's brother and the Great Rift."

Karan reluctantly agreed, and they sat down to wait for Sue.

"Um, Sue?" Karan asked when Sue came to check on them. "Can we ask you something?"

Sue smiled and pulled up a chair.

"So, um," Karan began. "Do you know anything about Professor Shirk's brother?"

Sue recoiled physically. She had to swallow hard to recover herself. "Why do you ask?"

"We heard he had something to do with the Great Rift."

Sue tried to smile reassuringly. "But why are you concerned about that?"

Karan stammered, having not expected Sue's discomfort.

Seeing her difficulty, Madison took over. "Sue, it's just that we've heard there's increased security on campus, especially around the underground tunnels. There is a lot of gossip about why that is, but we thought you might have more substantial information."

"Yes, it's true, and also unfortunate that you guys are being affected. I'm sorry about that." Sue looked somewhat relieved as if some danger had been averted.

"But what's the threat?" Madison pressed.

"Oh, you know how people are," Sue said dismissively. "It's all fear and gossip. I've seen it all before. This one will blow over, too, trust me. Before your second term, no doubt."

"If it is the Great Rift thing, would either side gain anything if one of the university's secret tunnels was exposed to the public?"

"Oh goodness no," Sue gasped. "You have to remember we're talking about families. Both sides have children at the university. It's a treasured institution for both factions, regardless of politics; there's just no way anyone would risk exposing the tunnels. It would open us all up to being discovered. Professor Bird would order an evacuation."

Sue looked hard at Madison and then at Alice and Karan in turn. She seemed recovered from her temporary stress and smiled broadly at them. "Ladies, you're just taking your first steps into this wonderful society of siddhas. Please don't worry about the Great Rift. As you said, it has been there for centuries and will be there for centuries more. As will the university and the Pickled Chicken, if I have anything to do with it."

She stood up to go and leaned in to whisper conspiratorially, "We don't need payment, you know. Gordy and I have those wonderful siddha credit cards, just like you do. We ask our siddha customers to go through the motions to avoid attracting the suspicion of non-siddhas. You understand, don't you?"

"Sure," Karan said.

Alice wasn't listening. She was still trying to figure out who might want a student like her to stumble upon a secret tunnel.

"Well, I hope to see you three often."

"Thanks," Madison said. "The pastries were great."

After Sue had left, they looked at each other with disappointed expressions.

"Look, guys," Alice said, finally. "All we know is they wanted me to find a tunnel. Surely that only matters if I get in trouble with the university, right? Otherwise, no harm, no foul?"

"Yeah, Madison!" Karan said.

"On the other hand, they had smartphones and could have filmed me. And it would be stupid if there weren't any security cameras down there." Alice thought back to her visit to the VC's office.

"So we have to assume they already know you were down in the tunnels," Madison said.

"Probably," Alice admitted. "Then why haven't I been called to Professor Bird's office?"

Nobody had an answer.

"And what does this have to do with Shirk and his brother?"

"We just don't have enough information," Madison said sensibly. "We need a plan."

"A plan! Just like the old days," said Karan.

"By the old days, do you mean last year?" Alice asked.

"Yeah," Karan enthused. "When we whooped some ass. And I jumped over a speeding muscle car and saved the planet."

"Well, Alice did most of the work," Madison laughed.

"Yeah yeah, always 'Alice this, Alice that.' When do I get some credit for once?"

Alice smiled and realized she was feeling a lot better. It was so good to be back on bantering terms with Karan and Madison. She vowed to try not to let herself wallow in the mud by herself so often in the future. But the first step was to be open with them about what she planned to do next.

"The one thing I know is those ninjas appeared both times after I went to that pub by Big Ben. So maybe I should—"

"Stay away from there," Madison said, finishing Alice's sentence. "Good idea."

"I was going to say I should keep going back there until they show up again."

Madison sighed. "And if they do show up, Alice, then what? Ask them politely who they are and why they're stalking you?"

"I'm pretty sure I won't be able to get a word out of my mouth to ask them anything."

"Exactly!"

"But I could read them. If I'm not drunk, next time, that is."

"What if they cut you in half with a Samurai sword before you can do it?" Karan asked.

"Ninjas and Samurai are different, Karan," Alice said, smiling. "I think they might have been enemies in feudal Japan. And these guys aren't ninjas, anyway; they're more like those French guys in the movies who run up walls and jump off buildings without getting hurt."

Madison sighed. "We don't know anything about them. Just that they wear hoodies, are athletic, and know about at least one of the secret tunnels into the university."

Karan straightened up. "Well, apparently, I do have a siddhi. At least according to you, Alice. Which is to find stuff on the internet. So I'll volunteer to get info about Longblood and his pal Eric."

"There's one more obvious thing we can do. Go straight to the VC."

"Can't," Alice said. "I'll instantly be in giant trouble."

"But what if—"

"No, Mad, she's right," Karan said. "We're banned from playing The Game."

"But Alice," Madison said, almost pleading now. "What if none of it is part of The Game? There's a good chance you've accidentally found out about a real terrorist plot. If you don't tell someone, you might be partially responsible for what happens."

"You'd be known forever as the girl who broke London!" Karan said. "Now *that* is a catchy tagline."

"We could send Professor Bird an anonymous letter," Madison mused. "Because if the terrorist thing is real, at least the VC can alert the cops."

They were silent for a second, each thinking through the idea.

"Wouldn't she dismiss the note as something sent by a crazy person? " Karan asked.

They ended up in disagreement. Madison insisted the only ethical thing to do was to explain everything to Professor Bird and face the consequences together. Karan insisted the terrorist plot had to be part of The Game, and if they went to Professor Bird, Alice would be the only one to get in trouble. Alice didn't know what to do. Unable to agree, they decided to sleep on it.

They walked back to campus and spent the rest of the day studying for physics class and preparing an essay due in Shirk's ethics class the coming week.

Alice's mind, however, was not on her studies but on David. She knew she'd end up back at that cocktail bar sooner or later, searching for him. She couldn't help it. The only question she had was if she would tell Madison and Karan about it or not.

CHAPTER 11

The following day, Alice was woken by her alarm. It was the first time she had set one since arriving in the UK. It had been a moment of inspiration when she went to bed the previous night; even though there was no way actually to see the sun from down here underground, she had the idea that her mood might improve if she at least tried to wake up when the sun was rising outside.

So far, it wasn't working. She just felt tired and groggy.

Come on, Alice, she thought. *Pull yourself together.*

During high school, she, Mad, and Karan were all required to be in the water before most normal people had their first cup of coffee. How had she gotten so lazy and pathetic since then?

"Come to the pool," Alice urged, speaking to herself as much as to her friends. "Just for a few laps before classes."

"You swim for me," Karan moaned from her bed, rolling over.

"Come on, Karan," Madison said, getting up quickly. "She's right. Let's get up."

"No," Karan's muffled voice whined.

"Seriously," Mad said, throwing a towel at her. "Not only do we have physics class this morning, but we might also have a city to save from terrorists. We can't afford to be lazy."

It worked for a spell. In the glass elevator on the way to class, Alice felt a bit like she had in the early days of their friendship: they were three tall, muscular young athletes. Walking through one of the massive classroom atriums toward their physics lecture, Alice could feel eyes on them. For once, she didn't automatically assume it was because she had abilities that scared everyone.

She also felt reassured about their friendship. Once again, they had a shared secret. Shared secrets were a million times better than private ones. Today was the day they took real action together, whatever that would be.

This feeling did not last long.

"A bomb is going to drop today, I heard."

Alice's attention jerked toward the group of young men. Her mind raced. Was there a bomb falling on campus? Was that Longblood's plan?

As she looked closer, she saw one of them was Jon, the sex abuser. He was with a tall, blond guy and a short, dark-haired student with a thick, black beard. The tall, blond one was jittery like he had drunk too much coffee. Jon and the bearded guy seemed relaxed, leaning against the wall near the lecture hall door.

Alice beckoned to Karan and Madison, and they stood on the other side of the lecture hall door, listening.

"What bomb?" Jon asked in a voice that said he didn't care.

"No idea. But it's a seriously big deal." The blond guy had some Dutch or German accent, Alice thought.

"All physics is a big deal," Jon retorted.

"But it's supposed to be like a new announcement. Maybe it's a breakthrough. Maybe a siddha scientist found a way to link prana to quantum theory or something like that!"

"Wow," Jon said, his brow creased in a skeptical expression.

"But quantum mechanics requires a lot of advanced math. I can't imagine a first-year physics lecture would get into that kind of thing."

"Yeah, but it could just be an announcement, not a real lesson or anything like that."

They filed into the lecture hall, with Alice, Madison, and Karan taking their usual position at the back of the lecture hall.

"Today," the physics lecturer said, "get your buckets ready because your minds are going to be completely blown out of your heads." She was a very young woman with spiked-up hair, wearing a leather steampunk outfit with metal bits all over it.

Trying to ignore the image of her brains splattered all over the inside of a plastic bucket, Alice looked over at Jon and saw him straighten up. Perhaps he was wondering if they would hear about a siddha science breakthrough. But then she looked closer and thought she saw a touch of drool on his bottom lip. It seemed more likely he was falling in lust with his teacher.

Alice looked over at Karan and was surprised to see the same lustful expression on her face.

As the steampunk professor outlined the fantastic things they would do in physics this term—none of which seemed to involve prana, siddhis, or anything paranormal—Alice's mind drifted to her nerdy love interest. Could she call David a love interest? Probably best not to think about it in case she was disappointed. But she couldn't help visualizing him sitting in the dark corner of the cocktail bar, reading a paperback. Would he know anything about physics? Would he relish sitting in a physics lecture here at Chancery Gate? She hadn't even bothered to ask David what he was studying at his university.

Toward the end of the lecture, just as Alice was despairing about the immense amount of work this physics class looked to be, the lecturer seemed to look right at her and said, "Those of you with less math-focused backgrounds will be placed in tutorials appropriate to your level of experience, and assessments will be customized for each tutorial. As with your other classes, the tutorials will provide you with any practical lessons in applying your siddhis to the topic at hand."

Great, Alice thought. Despite her siddhis, she was going to be in the dumb class. Her mind was most definitely *not* going to be blown into a bucket. It would be gently rocked to sleep, more like it. She did like the sciences but had never been in love with all the work they took compared to other classes.

"Now for the key point. I promised to blow your minds today." Steampunk Professor let silence emphasize what she was about to say. "When you think of physics, the main question in your minds, or the main question in mine, is most certainly this: where do siddhis come from? What is prana, scientifically speaking? Is it a new kind of dark matter? Is it a fifth force? Is it a macroscopic quantum effect? How does prana enable instant information transfer faster than light? Can we harness that to develop new ways to communicate across interstellar distances? And if information can travel faster than light, can matter also move faster than light? Can prana enable us to reach the stars? Can we embark on a new era of interstellar travel? Are siddhis the key to humanity reaching out to other intelligent life across the galaxy? Furthermore, what is the relationship between prana and concepts like God? Can we arrive at a scientific description of prana, which can then help us develop practical experiments to verify or disprove the existence of a God-like intelligence in our midst?"

Again, there was silence in the room. Maybe the tall blond guy was going to be proven right. Perhaps they were about to hear about a huge scientific breakthrough. Alice thought about Professor Bird's office, all her techno gadgets, and her love for pure science. At the moment, all that science just stressed her out rather than excited her.

"Here's the mind-blowing fact I promised. The answer to all

those questions is this: despite all our studies, we still have no idea what prana is. No idea."

There was a spattering of nervous laughter in the lecture hall. Alice saw Jon smile adoringly; clearly, he wasn't disappointed with this "news."

"But you people sitting in this room could well be the first to answer one or all of those questions I posed. Isn't that exciting?"

Murmurs broke out around the room. Everyone except Alice was buying into the excitement. She was skeptical. Her experience with prana hadn't given her the impression you could experiment on it. Prana was not a lab rat. It was itself an intelligent presence. She felt it was unlikely it could ever be "used" like a super-advanced telephone to communicate with aliens, nor could it power a *Star Trek*-like warp drive.

"What we scientists in the siddha community do know is that there are no shortcuts. We will never get there without mastering all the relevant math and sciences, just as we would outside in the real world. We aim to prepare you as thoroughly as any science student at Oxford, Harvard, or MIT."

Alice saw Madison nod her head approvingly.

"And so, I implore you to ignore all those mainstream self-help gurus out there who would like you to believe God is a quantum probability superposition. And the collapse of the wave function explains how positive thinking gets you rich. And that photons have vaginas or something. Mainstream science has at least conclusively demonstrated quantum mysticism is pure fantasy."

More laughter. Alice tried to imagine a photon with a vagina and failed.

"But I can promise you; we will someday make that breakthrough. We will eventually come to understand the true nature of prana. You might be the generation to achieve that. But you will achieve nothing, siddhis or not, without hard work. Welcome to the hardest unit of study you will ever undertake at this university!"

Half the room groaned, and the other half sparkled with enthusiasm.

Alice looked at Madison and saw she was clearly in the sparkling contingent. On the other side of her, Karan was still drooling over the steampunk professor and probably hadn't heard a thing she had said except the word "vagina."

As they left the lecture hall, Karan peeled off from Alice, went over to chat with a good-looking guy Alice hadn't seen before and began walking away together. As those two walked toward the glass elevators, talking conspiratorially (probably discussing their new professor's gender preferences rather than science), Alice got a pang of jealousy, filling her with self-loathing. Karan had every right to talk to guys or to lust over a teacher. But all the same, shouldn't she be focusing on solving the bomb plot mystery? They had a four-hour window until their next class. They were supposed to be figuring this out together. They were supposed to be a team.

"Let's head up and wait for her in the dorm room," Madison said in a conspiratorial tone.

Reluctantly, Alice complied. But Madison strolled out when the glass doors opened at their dormitory level, and Alice held back. She spontaneously punched the Top Lane button and said, "I gotta go. I'll catch you later."

Without any further explanation, Alice let the glass doors close, and the elevator rose, leaving Madison shrinking away below her, looking hurt and bewildered.

How many times had Alice done something like that to Madison? Her guilt intensified, but she knew herself; sometimes, she had to run away. When her feelings were overwhelming, the only relief was solitude.

And then her anxiety hit her with a vengeance. This time, it felt like a terrible physical sensation, like some unseen force was suddenly pulling her insides apart. She could almost hear the tearing of flesh. It was most intense in her throat. Unbearable. She couldn't think, couldn't even see.

Some little voice of reason was still present beneath the pressure. It was just stress. More precisely, it was an anxiety attack. She had often felt this kind of internal pressure, even though it had never been this bad. She had escaped into the wilderness in the past, and the feeling subsided. But there was no wilderness here. She was in a glass box underground. Like a coffin. But then the elevator doors opened, and she could stumble into the hallway.

She managed to pull out her phone, but she couldn't text anyone for help or speak.

But stuck to the phone was a name card. It had the name Agnes Bird, PhD, with an address on campus.

As she stumbled toward the location indicated, the pressure eased to a roaring sound, and she hoped the worst was over. And yet she kept up her death march toward Dr. Bird's office. She was terrified and didn't know what to do or where else to go. Thoughts of how she had just followed her usual unhealthy compulsion to abandon her friends made her head hurt worse, and all she could do was force herself to take one step at a time.

She reached Dr. Bird's office at the base of another four-story turret, not unlike the one housing her twin sister, the Vice Chancellor. Again, there was no security or locks on the door. As she stomped robotically up the spiral stairs, she forced herself into a degree of alertness. She still had a pounding headache, but the tearing sensation had passed, and she could see again.

Rather than cold stone, the principal psychologist's staircase walls were covered with bright oil paintings, photographs of happy people, and natural landscapes.

Upon reaching the top of the stairs, Alice found herself in a space that looked like an English country house rather than a turret. It was drenched in warm lamplight, a fire was crackling happily in the hearth, and the space was filled wall to wall with plush sofas and thick carpet.

"Welcome, Alice!" the voice of Agnes Bird, PhD, chimed from a couch near the fireplace. Alice had expected a clone of Pippa, but Dr. Bird looked nothing like her sister. She had long brown hair, a luxurious shawl in the same shade of brown, and both hair and shawl draped over her shoulders in alternating cascades of soft texture. The elegant woman before her looked more like a social media influencer than a university professor.

Smiling warmly, she said, "I didn't expect to see you at all this term. Come," she said, indicating a couch opposite her. "Join me by the fire."

In addition to the woodsmoke, Alice smelled potpourri in the air, like at a spa.

She hesitated, wondering if she should turn and run before the headache turned back into a fusion reaction. But what then? Did the school have its own hospital?

"Alice, are you well?" Dr. Bird asked, frowning.

Not wanting to cause a scene, she sat down stiffly and stared at Agnes silently.

"Would you like me to read you?" Dr. Bird asked. "It might make communication easier, given your selective mutism."

That was a shock to be asked such a bold question straight up. Alice shook her head firmly.

Rather than disappointment, Dr. Bird surprised Alice with a calm look of satisfaction as if she expected and admired Alice's refusal.

"I quite approve," she said. "Our self-respect is partially dependent on the sanctity of personal privacy. I wasn't sure if you preferred to tell me nonverbally why you are here today."

Alice just stared at her. What should she think of this woman? She sounded like Professor Bird and looked relaxed and completely friendly. But she just seemed too friendly and too relaxed. Alice didn't even want to look at her.

The room was as perfect as the woman herself. Perfect cushions that matched perfect throws, which matched perfect furniture, which matched perfect carpet, which matched perfect wall hangings. Perfect everything, except...something on the far side of the room caught Alice's eye. But she wasn't sure what it was. She could see nothing out of the ordinary when she focused on the area.

"I received a text message from Pippa—the VC. She says she requested that you come to see me rather than one of my staff psychologists. This is...was quite unusual. You have to understand most of my time is spent managing our therapy program, and I rarely take on new patients."

Alice stared at her, challenging her to say, "You must be one serious whack-a-doodle to be referred to me."

Instead, Dr. Bird said, "I trust my sister's judgment and reasoning, and I respect you for coming here today. I know from your file you are not likely to do something just because someone tells you to. You will usually do the opposite. That is why I expected you to stay away for at least the first term."

Alice glared. She hated it when anyone was right about her rebellious nature.

"So, you have given me a happy surprise today. You'd like to see if I can do anything for you. Now, let's assume you're here to assess me. Would that be accurate?"

Alice nodded reluctantly.

"Wonderful. I'll share some general observations about first-year students here and what they have done to ease their adjustment to the university. Perhaps some of it will appeal to you. Would that be alright?"

Alice nodded and leaned back in the couch, trying to relax her aching head. All she could hope for was the tiniest bit of info or advice that might make a difference to her, and she wasn't going to hold her breath.

After a predictably somnific speech about the importance of personal healing and stability through meditation, talking therapy, relaxation, being herself, learning, exercise, blah blah blah, Dr. Bird finally got to the point.

"Regarding your minor rule-breaking: as I have informed Madison and Karan, my department has protective authority over students who break Corollaries or attract the ire of the siddha community. Rather than expulsion from school, problem students are now supported in any way possible. I guarantee they receive the best care, depending on who they are and what they need. Often, our job is to simply provide students with some personal space. This university can be claustrophobic, which you have already, no doubt, discovered for yourself.

"Lastly," Dr. Bird said with a winning, movie-star smile, "I might point out you are from a ski town in Colorado that enjoys 310 days of sunshine every year, and you have found yourself in London, where rain is obligatory, like paperwork. Not only that, but you spend most of your day underground. It's probably killing you. Also, I note that our recruiter refers to you as a nemophilist. Do you know what that is?"

Alice shook her head. Dean had recruited her, and he was supposedly her friend. Why had he called her that? What did it even mean?

"A nemophilist is a lover of solitude in the woods. It means you're like a fox."

Fair enough, she thought. *But who cares?* There were no woods near campus. At least not as expansive and remote as the Knifespur Wilderness back home, where she could walk for days without seeing a hint of civilization.

Silence fell. It lasted long enough to make Alice uncomfortable, so she searched for the thing in the room she thought she had seen earlier that was so out of place. She failed to find it.

"Well, I have enjoyed meeting you today," said Dr. Bird. "I do hope we can make it a regular thing. My office is open to you; text and I'll make myself available as soon as possible, if not instantly.

"Now, before you go, I will offer a tiny bit of unsolicited advice. Is that okay?"

Alice nodded, hoping to get it over with and end this meeting.

"Please consider taking yourself off to the countryside somewhere. Just get out of the city! Way out. Use your new credit card to spend the weekend on the beach in Cornwall. Or see the fall colors in the Cotswolds. Or fly to Greece. Anything to get some fresh air. Go spread your wings."

Alice had to admit that sounded great until the last sentence. Alice did a double-take and stared hard at Dr. Bird. "Spread your wings" was just an expression, but had she used it intentionally? Could she know about Alice's siddhi of flight?

Dr. Bird smiled pleasantly at Alice, emphasizing her elegant eyes with their perfect eyeshadow contours and expertly applied mascara. They made Alice feel vaguely ashamed she hadn't learned how to use makeup properly. Madison had tried to show her, but her heart had never really been in it, and most days, she used nothing. Including those nights she had been with David at the pub.

"Now," Dr. Bird continued, "it just so happens I am about to meet with another student, and rather than shuffling you out of my office, I'd like you to stay back for a few moments so I can introduce the two of you. This year, he is the first student to be placed under my protective custody. And, like you, he desperately needs a friend and some fresh air."

Alice heard footsteps on stone stairs and sighed. Dr. Bird

did not understand her; else, she would know that getting fresh air with some stranger was *not* on Alice's to-do list.

"Ah, here he is now." Dr. Bird stood up to meet the student.

Alice turned and saw Jon, who used siddhis to get in someone's pants. He looked almost as surprised to see Alice as Alice was seeing him.

"Hi, Jon. I want to introduce you to Alice. Alice, meet Jon."

"We've met Dr. Bird," Jon said, staring at the floor.

"Jon, how were your surfing lessons in Cornwall last weekend?"

Jon's face lit up. "Freezing. But amazing."

"Alice, I would strongly recommend you consider taking a weekend off. If surfing in cold water isn't your thing, go to Oxford and tour the campus. Or Dover to see the cliffs."

Surfing did sound nice, but Alice was feeling a bit creeped out about the nature of Agnes' "protective custody" thing. Sending Jon off to get a wave was a weird way to counsel a sex abuser.

"University is about trying new things," Dr. Bird persisted, "and I just ask you to consider it. If you go to Cornwall, please get some photos of yourself surfing along a crystal-clear wave in the bright sunshine and share them with Jon."

That is not going to happen, of course. What was this woman on?

Just then, Alice's phone chimed with a text message. She raised her phone to check who it was from and saw Karan had texted her a gif of three giant bare butts twerking. Then came a second message from her: "The three of us out on the town tonight."

Alice smiled, then nodded a curt goodbye to Dr. Bird. As she turned to leave, she surveyed the room again shrewdly, searching for that strange brief glimpse of something that had set alarm bells ringing earlier. As her eyes brushed over an indentation in one of the walls near the fireplace, she thought she felt something strange...like when she had intuited the presence of Chancery Gate or discovered the cloaked door leading from the tunnel back into a building on Top Lane. Her awareness of the cloaking made it glow with prana, which became semi-transparent. Through the flowing blue crystal, she could see a small nook containing a little office space with an old mechanical typewriter on a desk.

"Anything wrong, Alice?" Dr. Bird asked, obviously curious as to why she was lingering.

Alice shook her head, turned, and descended the stairs more confused than before she had arrived.

CHAPTER 12

As Alice walked along Top Lane, praying that her inner ripping sensation would not return, she looked up at the thin strip of gray sky visible between the balconies of the stone buildings. No matter how ignorant and presumptuous Dr. Bird was, she had been right about one thing. Alice needed to get out of this city and get some fresh air. But where could she go? Where could she find true solitude, hemmed in by nothing but trees and endless sky?

Surfing did sound cool, but flying was better. Hands down.

She should pack a bag and go home. She could be in New York eight hours from now and in Colorado soon after that. And in the Knifespur Wilderness soon after that, alone. Nothing but her and the vast expanse of blue sky. Alice the nemophilist...

The rebellious instinct rose in her, and she wanted to prove Dr. Bird wrong. She was not the lone fox. She had figured out how to have healthy friendships. Not many, but it was something. She could figure this university thing out and learn to cope with her new life in London.

Just then, her phone chimed the arrival of another text.

It was from Madison this time: *Leaving at 5. Please come!*

Okay, she thought. She would go with them. The weight of her guilt was pressing down on her so hard that she would do nearly anything to redeem herself.

Another text chimed. This one from Karan: *You know you want to!*

Alice's head still hurt from her...panic attack? Or whatever it had been. She hadn't eaten much that day and felt weak. She was now running on pure, rebellious energy, which was drying up fast.

Alice pocketed her phone without responding to Karan or Madison's texts and headed straight to the dining hall, rounded up some comfort foods and a cup of coffee, and sat down alone in a corner to eat and attempt to recover.

Halfway through a giant plate of lasagna, her phone chimed the receipt of another text. Expecting it to be Karan again, she guiltily pulled her phone out and prepared to respond with something like, "Sorry, yes I'm coming," when she saw it was from David.

She completely forgot they had even exchanged numbers that night. Being chased through London by ninjas dominated her memory...

Alice, I am sorry for taking so long to text you. I wanted to, but it came out wrong every time I started a text. Better late than never?

That was it. She stared at the message. How was she supposed to answer it?

After puzzling for a while, she decided to send a thumbs up. Equally meaningless but kind of an invitation for him to write more.

It worked, as he immediately started writing a response, which came seconds afterward: *Let's go on a proper date. Tonight.*

Alice felt chills along her spine. She immediately recalled his tall frame slumped in a leather chair in that pub. Alcohol must have scrubbed out other memories of his specific features, yet she had a strong enough impression of him to feel seriously attracted. Something about his whole visage was full of potential energy. She liked everything about him. His energy wasn't like an athlete's but came from his unapologetic confidence. He was, like, "Here I am. Like me or not, I don't care." It was a confidence she aspired to, only to fall short every day.

Where? she texted, her fingers quivering.

Somewhere fun? Or quiet and relaxing?

Not The Library, she wrote.

Right. How about a sci-fi-themed restaurant?

She probably preferred the "quiet and relaxing" option, but he clearly wanted to go to the nerdy thing, which was cute. *Yes,* she responded.

He wrote back with a time and venue, and it was done. She had just agreed to her first-ever actual date.

She dropped her phone next to her plate and took a deep breath. Her heart was pounding, and she realized she was involuntarily smiling.

A date. Which meant she needed to wear something a bit nicer. Or at least clean. And...what else? Her hair needed some serious work. And...Madison had shown her how to do basic makeup, but her instructions had gone in one ear and out the other.

Madison! What was she going to say to her and Karan? *Sorry, but I prefer going out with some random guy I haven't even mentioned instead of going out with my best friends.* But Alice needed their help to get ready. Maybe now was the time to tell them about David anyway.

Alice ran back to the dorms and found her room depressingly empty. She called both Madison and Karan, but neither one answered. So, she had either pissed them off by ignoring their invitations or...what? Were they somewhere with no cell phone signal? Like in a subway train?

Alice dashed to her closet, but everything looked like it

belonged to a twelve-year-old girl. Which she was, in fashion years at least.

What do you wear to a sci-fi dinner anyway?

Then she looked at her face in the mirror. She looked tired. Chubby. Inelegant. Immature. Everyone always said she had amazing eyes, and her eyes were okay. Her dad used to tell her eyes were like an Egyptian princess's. A little bit like those of Dr. Bird, come to think of it. Maybe she could make herself look pretty by touching up her eyes a bit.

She ran to grab Madison's makeup and called up a random video on her phone describing how to apply eyeshadow, eyeliner, and mascara to make her eyes pop. Ignoring all the crap about analyzing her particular eye shape and coloring, she just stood at the mirror and rushed right into it, following the video step by step. Nothing was as easy as the video made it look. Nothing looked right. The colors were all so strong and dark, and her hands were clumsy. After about ten minutes, she stopped and looked at herself.

She looked like a little girl who had drawn all over herself with a permanent marker. Like she was getting ready for her friend's ninth birthday party. All she had to do was add some fake blood, and she'd win the Most Horrifying Costume award.

She looked at the time and realized she should have left already to meet David. Maybe she was overreacting. Perhaps she looked okay.

One more look at the mirror confirmed the truth—David would think she was a complete joke.

All she wanted was to look pretty. Was it too much to ask? For once? The world had done nothing but dish out horror after horror to her since she was five. Now she had her first chance at a normal date with a kind-of normal guy. And all she wanted was to look a little bit pretty.

As her headache began returning, it all felt like too much, and she started to cry. She slumped to the floor before the mirror and curled into a fetal position, hugging her legs and sobbing.

After no more tears remained, she rolled over and stared at the ceiling. Was this it for her? Was she done here? Should she grab her magic credit card and take a taxi straight to the airport?

No. She might be an ugly, pathetic, twenty-foot-tall monster, but she was Alice Brickstone. She could fly, damn it. She could do anything she wanted, including figure out how to go on a date without a handmaiden to help her.

She wiped the tears from her eyes and saw the backs of her hands come up black from the tear-smeared makeup.

After a quick shower, she returned and put on her nicest jeans and cleanest blouse—a floral-patterned one that her mom had given her as a going-away present. She had thought she'd never wear it because it was her mom's style, not hers. But then again, Alice had no style. So why not try it? And it did look okay. Better than a T-shirt, anyway.

After drying her hair with Karan's blow dryer, Alice thought she did not look horrible. She had not washed off the eye makeup well, but the traces around her eyes seemed almost intentional, like she had done a subtle, smeared makeup job.

And now she would have to take London's fastest taxi to arrive on time. She took an elevator up to Top Lane, still gray with afternoon light reflected off stone buildings, and out through Chancery Gate.

Broken Lane was empty. Alice rushed down and called an Uber to meet her on High Holborn, as students were prohibited from calling too much attention to Chancery Gate.

The ride from the university's neighborhood, Farringdon Without, to the sci-fi place in Finchley took twenty-five minutes. It was one of the weirdest twenty-five minutes she had ever experienced. Her previous bout of insecurity had transformed into theatrical nonchalance. She found herself pretending she was the female villain in a James Bond film: unflappable, sensuous, dressed to kill.

Until she arrived and remembered she was an eighteen-year-old country girl from Colorado late for her first-ever date.

She dashed to the door. The place was like an old warehouse, marked only by a sign with a spaceship and nothing else. She pushed in and was greeted by a middle-aged woman with orange hair.

"Hi, love. Do you have a booking?"

She nodded her head but couldn't speak. *Now what, Alice?* David was nowhere to be seen. A couple of chairs were set up here, but they were empty.

Perhaps he was waiting for her outside, and she just missed him? In the shadows, like another villain in a James Bond film?

Without speaking to the orange-haired lady, she turned and searched for him in the street. Finchley was a tranquil area of London. The streetlights were dimmer than in central London. The only sound was the distant grinding and shrieking of a train.

She saw no people anywhere. There seemed to be no shadowy places where David could hide in wait.

Maybe he went inside because she was late?

She pulled out her phone and texted him. *I'm outside the place,* she wrote.

No response.

She waited another five minutes, and her anxiety and insecurity returned in full force.

Finally, her phone chimed. *I'm so sorry, Alice. Something came up. I'll be out of touch for a while, but I promise I'll make it up to you. Xx David.*

Well, at least I got two Xs, she thought as she walked back toward a better-lit main street she had seen.

She felt empty, but at least her stress levels were ebbing again. She was alone.

In a moment of inspiration, she dialed Madison's number and then Karan's but received no answer. They were ignoring her, which she understood. Alice had coldly ignored them this afternoon, as she had many times before. They were probably so sick of her bouts of rebellious self-isolation that they were close to being done with her forever.

Wandering, hardly noticing where she was, Alice ended up in front of a stone chapel. It was very old. A plaque in front proclaimed its twelfth-century origins. She couldn't even imagine what life would have been like on this street nine hundred years ago. There probably wasn't a street—more like a field. Richard the Lionheart might have ridden by on the way home from the Crusades. She wandered back to the tiny cemetery behind the chapel, hoping to see some gravestones with medieval dates. But it was too dark to read the time-worn gravestones, and she didn't feel it was appropriate to shine her phone light on them anyway. She stood there in the darkness, surrounded by dead people.

Even knights in shining armor all end up dead, she thought. Sure, they might have rescued a damsel in distress, but they were probably rewarded with the dubious privilege of becoming a wife/slave in the knight's household ever after.

Her phone chimed, and she illuminated the whole graveyard when she hurriedly pulled it out to see if David had perhaps changed his mind and come out to join her.

She saw with an enormous sense of relief that it was from Madison. "Sorry we missed all your calls. Big story to tell you. Are you around?"

Alice texted to say she'd be home soon and strode back to the quiet street.

And suddenly, those two ninjas were standing in front of the darkened doors of the church as though they had waited for Alice so long they were bored. Hooded, dark, and wiry. Dangerous. They just appeared out of nowhere.

"Hey," one of them said. It was an unexpectedly high voice. "Did you find any distant Brickstone ancestors in there?"

These were the first words they had spoken to her in this weeks-long cat-and-mouse game. The accent was not British, though Alice couldn't place it. The speaker's face was again masked, and the eyes were hidden in the shadows beneath the hoodie. The voice could have easily belonged to a man or a woman. It was breathy and light—almost a whisper.

Alice looked down and saw they still had those prominent little ninja logos on their chests. Now that she was sober, she could see the symbols more clearly. Alice noticed the little ninja line drawing had a shiny circle for a head. It looked like it was made from a different material.

As they continued to stand there in a silent standoff, Alice wished she could say something devastatingly witty, but she couldn't think of anything. She felt her mutism pressing in on her, squeezing the capacity for language out of her. She loathed her disability. She could not fling so much as a one-word insult at these strangers. All she could do was her signature move: stand and stare. She tried again to read them, but they were too far away or too good at deflecting her attempts.

The heaviness of the night descended on them. Alice was tense and angry, while the hooded figures looked relaxed and a bit disdainful.

Then, just as that distant screech of metal on metal signified the arrival of another subway train, the two figures took off toward the sound at a light jog, glancing over their shoulders to see if Alice was following. Almost as if they were inviting her. It was an exact repeat of Alice's first encounter with them.

This time, she managed to resist the urge. It could only get her into more trouble.

She punched the word *pub* into her map, found two within walking distance, and headed in the opposite direction to the train station. Within five minutes of being confronted by two weird ninjas next to a medieval church, she pushed through the doors into a warm, lively little pub full of laughter and the smell of wet wool and beer.

This was more like it. She got her now-standard English ale order and sat in a leather chair near a fireplace. She put her feet up on a stool, breathed in, breathed out, and started drinking beer. Alone.

She kept her eyes on the door, but the ninjas didn't enter. Here, two small figures in black jeans and black hoodies would stand out, so they probably would wait for her outside. Or maybe they went and got on that train.

By her third ale, she was feeling trashed again, and her false sense of cozy security given her by the pub atmosphere had broken down into a kind of reckless wish to drunk-dial David and demand that he explain his betrayal of her tonight.

As she stared at her phone, she caught a reflection of herself on the screen and then opened the camera app. Scrutinizing the messy makeup traces around her eyes and seeing her best blouse reminded her how pathetic she was. She looked like an idiot. It was no wonder David didn't come. Why would he be interested in a stupid oaf like her? She was drunk now, just as she had been with him the other night. Pathetic.

You okay? A message from Madison flashed as Alice was heaping hate onto herself.

Embarrassed to have not returned to the dorms as promised, Alice typed a thumbs up and resolved to hurry back to her friends. Her real friends. At least until they got sick of the silent treatment she frequently subjected them to.

She looked down at her beer, downed it, used the bathroom, and left.

The night was as dark and dreary as it had been earlier. There was no sign of the hooded figures.

Alice closed her eyes, breathed deeply, and then called a rideshare. On a whim, she tapped *Brydges Lane* into the rideshare app. That was the name of the narrow passageway the ninjas had lured her into and where the secret tunnel entrance was located. She knew going there was a bad idea but couldn't help checking if the ninjas had gone there after taunting her at the cemetery. She would check, then head straight back to campus.

The car was ten minutes away, and while she waited, she tried to text an apology to Madison. It just wouldn't come out right. She kept deleting things and imagining Madison sitting in the dorm room, increasingly fed up with Alice's cold silence.

Finally, she just texted: *I'm so sorry to have been silent. I'm coming back now. See you in thirty minutes.*

If you're out, can you bring Karan a meat pie? Something happened.

What happened? She typed anxiously.

Will explain when you arrive.

K, Alice responded, wondering where she could buy a meat pie. Probably a convenience store?

She saw one down the road and dashed off to get one before the rideshare came. She only had a few minutes.

She did find a plastic-wrapped pie and bought ten. Why not? They were hot and looked good. The three of them could share while Karan talked about her problem. Alice could only guess it had something to do with Karan's scarred face. Maybe she had asked someone out and gotten rejected in a way that called attention to her disfigurement.

Alice dashed back to the pub just as a car pulled up.

She gave the driver the universal nod that communicated: "I'm the person who called this rideshare," and also: "I'm not into talking."

He nodded back to indicate he understood her nod.

As they drove silently toward Brydges Lane, near Trafalgar Square, Alice mentally urged the driver to go faster. They passed from the leafy suburbs into the busy, treeless, winding streets of central London, Alice thinking of Karan the whole way, wondering what could have gone wrong. If someone like Jon had hurt her, Alice would destroy him. The anger helped clear her head of the beers she had drunk alone. It also helped keep her mind off the devastation of being stood up by David.

Alice noticed something odd on the driver's phone as they neared Brydges Lane. The driver had just closed the map on his phone, which was mounted on the dash. Alice could see his phone was laid out exactly like hers—like a siddha phone, unique from any other screen layout she had ever seen.

She must have made a strange sound because the driver looked up in his rearview mirror in alarm. Using the opportunity of the brief eye contact to reach into his mind, she just caught the thread of his thoughts. He was trained at resisting mind reading, but she was strong and forced her way deeper until she found out who he was.

Her driver was an agent working for The Company. He had been sent to watch over her in her outing tonight because her misadventures on the second day after arriving caused her to be considered a high-risk student, whatever that meant. He didn't seem to know there was a secret entrance to campus down that alley.

Alice was so surprised and angry at being spied on she smashed her hand onto her leg. Unfortunately, a hot meat pie was in the way, and the force of her punch blew open the plastic seal. Hot, brown gravy exploded onto her nice blouse.

The explosion severed her link with the driver. "Are you okay, miss?"

All she wanted to do was get out of this car and get this hot, burning stuff off her. It was all she could do to hold her blouse off her skin.

Alice jumped out, dashed to a nearby garbage can, and started furiously scraping piping hot bits of meat pie off her blouse.

After the burn risk was mitigated, she walked back to Brydges Lane and peered into the darkness. It was definitely the spot to which she had been lured by the hooded figures last Friday, but she saw no one tonight.

She took a few steps into the passageway until she could make out the window one of the hooded figures used to escape. Across and below it was the tiny doorway that led to a long staircase down to the secret passageway.

Still no signs of anyone lurking in the darkness. She sighed. It had been nothing more than a wild guess she might see one of them here.

After a second, she looked up to see what her driver was doing and was perturbed to see him observing her closely. In a flash, she imagined Agnes Bird had organized him to keep an eye on her. Because she was in the same category as Jon, the sexual abuser. "High-risk."

She wanted to prove how "high-risk" she was by throwing a pie at his stupid face. But, of course, she wouldn't do something like that. It wasn't this guy's fault. He seemed nice enough.

She turned in a fit of rebelliousness, took an unbroken pie, and threw it down the passageway into the darkness.

Which is when the actual explosion happened.

CHAPTER 13

S he saw the flash before she heard the explosion. It seemed like a wall of pressure and light coming from everywhere. But in retrospect, she did recall that the blast came from the right side, in the direction of the tiny door to the passageway. Immediately afterward, all the windows on both sides shattered. Her ears felt compressed, and the world went silent for the tiniest fraction of a second. Then she felt the blast wave. It was a jolting sensation unlike anything she had experienced. In a roar of sudden noise and heat, she was launched, head-first, out of the passage toward the rideshare car at breakneck speed.

Yet time slowed down for her, and she felt calm. She groped with her hands for prana, the substance that enabled all her abilities. She hadn't flown for some time, but it was second nature to her, and now flying was the only way to save her life.

Her hands first felt the familiar warmth, then her forearms and stomach. Right before slamming head-first into the car's rear door, she had enough time to pull down hard into the prana with both hands, which changed her trajectory enough to lift her above the car's roof. Her knees did not, however, make it over, and she felt a devastating pain as they carved deep dents into the metal. Then she was somersaulting through the air across Saint Martin's Lane. No longer able to use prana to fly or arrest her fall, she curled into a ball and covered her head with her hands, flying like a cannonball. She punched through a glass window, struck some furniture, and descended into a crushing chaos of collisions in what she guessed involved a combination of people and desks.

Then the lights went out, and she knew no more.

CHAPTER 14

Alice woke up in a hospital bed surrounded by people. At the foot of her bed stood a confused nurse with Professor Bird patting the woman's arm as if in consolation. Her rude assistant, Nick, was behind them, looking bored as ever.

Madison and Karan were to the left and right of Alice's bed, leaning over her face. A bit too close, actually.

"Space," she wheezed.

"Oh no! Her brain's broken. She thinks she's an astronaut!" Karan exclaimed.

Alice smiled, reached up, and pushed their foreheads away.

The nurse noticed Alice was awake and rushed over, checking a trolley full of machines next to the bed.

"How are you feeling?" she asked, an incredulous look on her face.

Alice saw someone's phone on a table next to the bed and grabbed it to check the time and date. It was Saturday morning, which meant she had been blown up last night and now was in a hospital.

She considered the nurse's question. She felt pretty good. Mentally, at least. Her shame over being stood up by David last night had diminished, as had her guilt over being incommunicative with Madison and Karan. Her legs hurt where she remembered striking the car, but she bent them and straightened them again, and they seemed okay. Her body was bruised and achy, but she felt relatively relaxed.

So she gave the nurse a thumbs up.

The nurse turned to Professor Bird wide-eyed, as though she couldn't believe what she was seeing, and demanded an explanation from the smartly dressed professor.

Professor Bird smiled at the nurse, then turned to the miraculous patient. "Do you remember what happened last night, Alice?" Professor Bird asked.

"Pretty sure I got blown up," Alice responded, trying to sit up. Madison and Karan helped her. "I remember cannonballing through a window into an office, maybe?"

"That's right," Professor Bird said. "There was a gas leak and an explosion. You were in the wrong place at the wrong time."

"And, um..." the nurse stuttered, "you were pronounced dead at the scene."

Everyone turned to glare at the nurse, who held up her hands. "I'm just saying what happened. I'll get the doctor and tell him you're...awake." She turned and left, shaking her head.

"Close the door, please, Nick," Professor Bird said quickly, and Nick obeyed.

Professor Bird leaned over the foot of Alice's bed with a somber, concerned look that Alice had never seen her wear before. "Alice, we don't have much time. I need to ask you a crucial question: why did you order a rideshare to the mouth of Brydges Lane?"

Alice wasn't prepared for this question. She supposed she intended to tell Professor Bird about the hooded figures sooner or later, but she didn't have a plan for how to do it. She also had no idea how to tell her that she had been down one of the secret tunnels, which was probably the most significant security breach the university had ever seen.

But then again, she suspected there were cameras down there and Professor Bird already knew about it.

She decided to deflect. "That guy was an agent, Professor Bird. Not a rideshare driver."

Professor Bird did look mildly surprised. Then she squeezed her eyes closed as though trying to force out some horrible thought.

"Is he okay?" Alice asked.

"He was injured but is going to recover. Alice. There were other minor injuries among residents of the surrounding buildings. A child has lost her hearing, but the doctors are hopeful it will return. Several employees of a real-estate office sustained minor injuries when you crashed through. I am deeply grateful you are okay. That was..." She closed her eyes, and silent tears exploded from them.

Alice was shocked that Professor Bird seemed to care so much about her. This instantly added a new source of guilt to her ever-growing list. She turned to her friends and wondered what they had been through. Had Alice died last night? She suspected her healing abilities had saved her from near-death several times, but it sounded like prana had worked overtime last night. Once again, she had been the center of attention for all the wrong reasons and caused an absolute ton of stress for everyone close to her.

Professor Bird quickly mastered her emotions, opened her eyes, and straightened herself to her full height. "I would love to let you ease your way back to full health and debrief with your friends at your own pace. But unfortunately, my duty to the university requires that I focus on urgent damage control now. This is a very, very serious situation. The university's centuries-old secrecy is closer to being destroyed than ever in its long history. We have mobilized all resources of the university and

The Company to block the tunnel and reverse engineer a gas leak. We are throwing everything we have at it. Just as you have fought for your life over the past nine hours, so has the university been fighting for its existence."

She turned again to the door to ensure nobody was coming, then leveled her most intense look at Alice.

"Please, just tell me, Alice: why did you go to Brydges Lane last night?"

If Alice hadn't been blown up, she and Karan and Madison would have written to Professor Bird about it all anyway. It would have been an anonymous letter, but now it was too late for that kind of thing. It was time for honesty, Alice realized.

She knew she had to choose her words wisely, though. Alice would still do her best to omit mention of David because that was private. But she should lay out all the other facts as plainly as possible. So, she did.

She started with her first and second encounters with Longblood at the pub, how she had read his security guy Eric and learned about two Hermans under ten plot to break London, about which she had done nothing because she thought it was part of The Game.

"Two Hermans under ten," Professor Bird parroted. "What does that mean?"

"No idea. It's not part of The Game?"

Professor Bird shook her head but didn't seem too concerned about it.

She was, however, considerably more upset when Alice explained about the acrobatic hooded figures who moved like ninjas.

When Alice's story concluded, Professor Bird swallowed hard as though she was forcing herself to ingest broken glass. "And you suspect this pair of hooded acrobats have been following you around London?"

"Yes."

"They move like ninjas, you say?"

"Yep."

Professor Bird nodded and suddenly breathed in as though she had an epiphany about who these people were.

Hoping to help her fill out the picture, Alice added, "And they have weird little ninja logos on their chests."

But this detail seemed to derail Professor Bird's private conclusions. "Logos?"

"Yes," Alice responded.

"And they called you by name?"

"Yep."

Professor Bird looked less and less sure the more questions she asked. "And they know you are a student at the university?"

Alice nodded.

Professor Bird looked even more troubled. "Just one last question, Alice. Did you throw something into Brydges Lane before the explosion?"

Alice was bewildered. "Um, I didn't blow myself up with a hand grenade, if that's what you mean."

"I don't. But in his formal statement, your driver claims you threw something into the passageway just before the explosion."

She explained about the meat pies.

Professor Bird paused, thinking.

"Please trust me. I can't blow stuff up with meat pies," Alice announced definitively.

She saw Nick snicker and turn away. "Sorry to disappoint you, Nick," Alice said in her direction.

"Not disappointed. I always assume people are useless duds." Nick picked her nose and then said, "No offense."

"None taken," Alice smiled. Then she thought for a moment. Her brain was slow but functioning.

"So, all that Longblood crap," Alice said slowly. "The two Hermans and the terrorist plot. Have you heard anything that would help make sense of that stuff? Are you sure none of it is part of The Game thing? And do those ninjas have anything to do with campus security?"

Professor Bird shook her head curtly, and then worry crossed her brow. But before she could say what was on her mind, the door opened, and in walked the small, tweed-clad, old philosophy teacher, Professor Shirk. He closed the door behind him and looked gravely at Alice, or was it yet another look of smug disdain? Then he turned to the VC.

"Professor Shirk," the much taller VC said. They stared into each other's eyes and grew still, and Alice knew they were reading each other.

There was a long, awkward moment punctuated only by the muted noises of nurses speaking in the distance and orderlies pushing medical equipment in the hallway.

Alice sighed and looked at Madison. "I think I need a vacation." She honestly didn't have the energy to care if Shirk or anyone else was in the room. Physically, she felt better by the minute, but she knew her anxiety would return soon, and she wanted to get out ahead of it.

"Hey," Karan said, "a vacation is a solid idea."

"But Alice is, like, fresh out of a coma," Madison said. "And we're apparently all in danger of being blown up by super ninjas employed by a maniac gangster."

Alice furtively looked over at Shirk. What role did he play in any of this? One thing was for sure: she wouldn't figure any of this stuff out from a hospital bed. And she didn't feel much like facing her classes.

Turning back to Madison, she said, "I'm well enough to go on a vacation right now," Alice insisted.

"I've been researching vacation spots around the UK," Karan said. "After my...experience last night."

Madison leaned in and whispered to Alice: "Karan was assaulted last night. That's why she wanted comfort food. "

Alice sat bolt upright, her adrenaline surging.

"Relax, Alice," Karan said. "It was just some jerk who groped me in a dark hallway. It was upsetting, but I handled it." She smiled wryly, but Alice could tell she looked different. Like she was covering trauma with false bravery.

"How?" Alice asked. "Who was it?"

"I think I broke his nose," Karan said with satisfaction. "But I'm only just guessing. It felt like a crunch when I elbowed him in the face as hard as I could."

Alice's mind raced. "What did he look like? Was it one of those hooded people?"

Karan squinted as though trying to remember.

"I just—" She gave a weird gasp and shook her head in a jerky motion.

"Karan!" Madison exclaimed, reaching for her hand.

Karan gave an awkward smile again and tried to master herself. "I should be flattered that anyone would be attracted to someone as disfigured as me," she said. Then a stream of tears started.

Alice had always been uncomfortable when someone cried in front of her, but she sensed that these were healthy tears and needed to be shed. She and Mad held Karan's hands as she exhausted what would probably be several rounds of catharsis in the coming weeks.

Inwardly, Alice was infuriated and already trying to think of ways to find Karan's assaulter. She didn't care who it was; she wanted to make them pay.

She looked up and saw the two professors were still locked in their mind-meld thing, seemingly oblivious to Karan's suffering.

Then she noticed Nick was crying silently on her own. It was a truly awkward moment, though Alice felt sympathy for her because she intuited that Nick's nature was to cry alone.

But before Alice could wonder what Nick would have to cry

about despite her sarcastic, flippant exterior, Karan finally wiped her face with her T-shirt, and Nick put her nose back in her phone.

"So," Madison said, "where did you have in mind for our vacation, Karan?"

CHAPTER 15

After an unexpectedly dull and painfully slow drive out of London—which consisted of congested highways and overpasses and more highways and more overpasses and was eventful only because it took Madison some time to get over her panic of driving on the wrong side of the road—they finally reached the English countryside. It was exactly as advertised: gorgeous winding roads through hills dotted with idyllic little ancient villages, each more like a Hobbit shire than the last. Alice wouldn't have been too shocked to see Gandalf and Bilbo sitting in front of any of the little inns smoking their pipes.

It had been a tough week after Alice got out of the hospital. Her brain wasn't functioning correctly. The idea that she had been the target of a bombing on the same night David jilted her had become a kind of nightmarish GIF that ran in her head all the time, day by day until she could barely speak to anyone, even Mad and Karan. Plus, they had a ton of essays to write for classes. It was all Alice could do to barely keep up with her schoolwork and sit in the back of lecture halls. She had no energy to consider the Longblood mystery or pursue Karan's assailant.

Oddly, she also failed to get any time with Professor Bird

after she got out of the hospital and therefore had no idea what conclusions the VC had drawn, if any, from Alice's version of events. Madison and Karan were probably discussing it continually, but Alice had nothing new to contribute.

They also had no way to pursue the identity of Karan's attacker. Karan either hadn't seen him, or the trauma had prevented her from remembering his appearance. Alice's conclusion was it must have been one of those ninjas to have been so stealthy. Still, Madison had pointed out that men had stealthily attacked women throughout human history, and it could have been anyone that night.

So, they had no choice but to go about their studies and plan this trip to the Cotswolds. It was the one thing that lifted all of their spirits.

And it was finally here. Alice sat in the back seat of their rented car, taking in the vivid golden colors of the trees like visual nourishment. She hadn't anticipated the colors would be as beautiful as the aspen trees in Colorado in fall, but she was seriously impressed. She especially liked the way the trees reflected off the water of the canals that seemed to meander everywhere. They stopped once to walk on the lawn in front of a pub that served the longboats that plied the canals. The grass was as green and perfect as that on a golf course, the garden was impeccable, and the trees were so golden she thought they would be visible from space, like a warm spotlight, saying, "Here is the coziest spot on Earth." A couple of longboats were tied up nearby, and these were adorable too. They were long, thin, and low against the water, each with a small cabin containing living quarters. The two they saw were colorfully painted and covered with planters bursting with flowers. Karan said they were descended from English canal boats that horses pulled through the canal system, the primary transportation infrastructure before railways. The longboat denizens were onshore enjoying what appeared to be sailor's portions of ale at outdoor tables, warmed by the midday sun. Alice and her friends didn't linger long, though they wanted to.

At Alice's urging, they headed toward a town called Stroud. Alice lied and said it was because she heard it was nice, and fortunately, Karan's research had confirmed it was supposed to be a cool place to visit. But the real reason Alice wanted to go there was David. He had mentioned a particular pub in Stroud that he liked. Alice daydreamed of walking in and finding him sitting alone by the fire, reading a novel, sipping ales. She knew it was unlikely but clung to a tiny hope anyway. He would look up, and their eyes would find each other, and he would smile, rush over to embrace her, and apologize about the other night, and all would be well. She would introduce him to her friends as "my boyfriend," and they would congratulate her and love him, and...

"Yo. Earth to Alice," Karan said loudly, interrupting her thoughts.

"What?"

"You okay? No brain damage in there?"

"I'm fine; why?"

"Well, I've been talking to you for about ten minutes. Have you heard any of it?"

"Um, no?"

"Okay." Karan took a deep breath as though to calm herself. "For the millionth time, do you want to go to the Lost Goat first? I was hoping to check in to the bed and breakfast. The website says it's stuffed full of Gloucestershire Chic, whatever that means."

"It's pronounced 'Gloster-sure,'" Madison interjected. "The whole middle part is silent."

"Why?" Karan asked, dumbfounded.

"They speak English here better than we do, Karan. Just take their word for it."

"True that. Everyone uses such complex vocabulary. I feel

like an idiot in England sometimes. Even street signs seem smarter than me."

"It's just different. They probably think your English is cool too."

"Why?"

"Never mind. Alice, Lost Goat, or the B&B?"

"Goat," Alice responded, hoping to return to her daydreams, knowing how unlikely they would come true.

"Why?" Karan asked.

Alice didn't answer and tuned out again, gazing at the soothing golden colors.

The rolling hills gave way to a valley tightly packed with ancient-looking stone cottages surrounded by dense trees, heavy with moisture. The single-lane road they were on was so thin their rental car almost didn't fit. And yet the speed limit was seventy kilometers per hour, or about forty-five miles back home, which Madison did not dare approach, resulting in a line of angry locals behind them. Her knuckles were white on the steering wheel, and she could not laugh at Karan's jokes. Karan eventually even seemed unable to crack them. It was particularly stressful when a car came from the other direction, firstly because they had to pass on the wrong side of the road, and, secondly, because there wasn't another side of the road. Both cars magically passed each other when only one car should have fit. The trick seemed to be to squish your vehicle into a hedge. Alice was pretty sure Madison had her eyes closed every time that happened.

At one point, Madison's phone chimed with a text message. Karan lazily tapped it open for her and gasped.

Alice leaned forward and saw how pale she had become. "You're completely pale, Karan! What's wrong? Did someone die?"

"Worse," she said. "Mad, please park the car."

Madison did, and Karan read the message: "Dear Ms. Percival, as I have advised the Vice Chancellor, your recently submitted essay contained significant blocks of unattributed content. Plagiarism is a serious offense at Chancery Gate. As this is your first offense and you are new to the university, I have recommended against disciplinary action in this case. You will, however, receive a failing mark for this assignment, and you will also be required to rewrite it to regain your seat in my class. If you elect not to resubmit, you will receive a failing mark in this unit of study. As a side note, the portions of your essay that were not plagiarized from another source suffered from a serious lack of objective reasoning. In your rewrite, you must work quite hard to demonstrate you understand the difference between facts and assumptions. Yours sincerely, Prof Shirk."

Alice knew instantly it must be a mistake. Madison was the most honest and meticulous student in her high school and was on track to earning that unofficial title at Chancery Gate. Everyone knew it. She was about as likely to cheat at school as she was to turn into one of those ninjas.

"I-I don't understand," Madison stuttered.

"It's an admin mess-up," Karan said. "Shirk is mistaking you for someone else."

Alice knew that Madison was mentally reviewing the essay she had written. "No," Mad concluded firmly. "Every word of that essay was mine. And yet I can't see how he could have mistaken me for another student. With such a serious accusation, surely he would doublecheck before passing it on to the VC?" Madison choked back a sob.

They decided Alice would take over the driving for now (Karan was a terrible driver), but Madison kept mumbling about the essay.

"Every single word was mine," Mad repeated in the back seat before she finally sank into an agonized silence. This was, they all knew, Madison's worst nightmare.

As she drove, Alice tried to devise any reasonable scenario

explaining Shirk's text but failed. It was inexplicable. She wanted to fit it into a narrative that had something to do with Shirk's blackmail situation, but it still made no sense no matter how she turned it.

She forced herself to concentrate on not killing the three of them on this English country road. The passing reds and oranges of the trees devolved into a fact rather than a marvel.

It was only when the cars around them slowed down that Alice's thoughts stopped racing. Finally, to her relief, they were in Stroud. It was cute and medieval, like the villages of the Cotswolds, but on a far larger scale and with a few modern things thrown in the mix, like bigger gas stations and a few shopping malls. There was also a hippy vibe in the town center, which attracted Karan, who wanted to hit a few shops with her bottomless credit card, but Alice insisted they headed straight for the pub where she secretly hoped to see David.

"But the Stroud Markets are on today! We could get some local organic, gluten-free cakes, cruelty-free cheese, and stuff."

"I'd rather get a pub meal," Alice said truthfully. "Cruelty and all."

But it turned out to be easier said than done. The aptly named Lost Goat was far, far off the beaten track, away from the Stroud markets on the valley floor and up one of the neighboring hills. Alice had to drive up this ridiculous road with such a steep grade they couldn't see the road over the front of the car. If she stopped, there was no way the tires would have enough traction to start again, and Karan kept chanting, "Faster! Faster!" Alice was pretty sure they would have to abandon the car up top because there was no way they would dare drive back down this hill.

Alice managed to get them to the top without incident and parked in a tiny public parking lot. Then they relaxed and walked the final mile along small, winding paths through a hilltop village with beautiful views over the town below. When they were almost there, the last little section of the trail went along a cliff. *It must literally have been a goat trail*, Alice thought. It finally opened to a gorgeous green lawn big enough for a decent frisbee toss.

On the other side of the lawn was a beautiful clifftop pub with warm, golden light spilling out from each of its many windows. It was so close to the cliff's edge that Alice thought parts of it must hang off in thin air. Like most buildings they had seen in the village, the pub was made of stones of varying sizes so that it looked like a madman had built it. It had a steep, tile-stone roof heavily indented in places and looked ready to collapse any minute, though it had probably been that way for centuries. A lone chimney was puffing out smoke. There was an old wooden sign over the door with a sad-looking goat confirming they had arrived at the Lost Goat.

It was dusk, and Madison paused to take in the spectacular sunset views, like billowing scoops of strawberry ice cream, over layers of burnt caramel leaves stretching into the distance.

Karan stood back by Alice and admired the view for a moment but then looked like she was having a minor seizure and placed her hands on her head.

"Karan!" Alice shouted, supporting her. Madison also rushed back. "No, no, no, I'm good," Karan reassured her. She lowered her hands, and the pain seemed to have been replaced by bewilderment. "That is so, so...weird."

"What? How is an epileptic seizure *weird*?" Alice asked.

"I don't have epilepsy. It's just—I was looking at the view and the pub, and suddenly I just accessed a butt-ton of information about them. It was like my head just went on the internet by itself. It's freaking me out. Is this a siddhi?"

"Seriously?" Alice asked as Madison looked worried.

"Go ahead, ask me something."

"Like what?"

"I've never been here and never looked up anything about this place. I promise. But now I know everything about it."

"What?"

"Go ahead, ask me something."

"Is a guy called David here?" Alice asked, regretting it immediately.

"Not that kind of stuff," Karan sighed. "I mean, like historical background, geology. Stuff you can read on the internet."

"What kind of people usually come to a pub like this?"

"That's more like it. This was a fullers' pub. A fuller was the tradesman who beat the wool with a kind of clay to get the lanolin oils out. The whole area of Stroud was famous for its wool cloth. World-famous. There's a kind of cloth called Stroud Scarlet that was used worldwide to make high-ranking soldiers' uniforms. They even used it to line casino tables in Monte Carlo. It made Stroud one of the wealthiest parts of rural England for centuries. These cottages on this hill belonged to fullers and wealthy wool merchants. Their mills were down in the valley, and the powerful currents of the local rivers helped the mills produce some of the world's finest cloth."

Alice and Madison just stared at Karan. She was usually full of facts, but never had she just downloaded them from thin air.

"You see? This is completely freaking me out now. Alice, did your abilities come on this quickly? Is this normal? Have either of you heard of a siddhi like this?"

They both tried to reassure Karan she was okay and reminded her of all the stuff they had heard about how siddhis were different for everyone. But in reality, Alice and Madison were more than a little freaked out too.

After a few moments, Karan seemed to snap out of her data reverie and smiled. "I think this siddhi is making me hungry. Let's go in and eat with some wool merchants."

Once again, they headed toward the pub doors. But right

before pushing through the front door, Karan froze again as though caught by another data-download seizure.

"What is it, Karan?" Alice asked, alarmed again. Karan was just vacantly staring at the solid wood door.

Then, just as suddenly, Karan shook her head and turned to face Alice with a raised eyebrow, like she suddenly knew one of Alice's secrets.

"What?!" Alice demanded.

Karan shook her head again. "This is so completely bizarre," she said. She looked about to say something but then changed her mind and sat on a bench next to the front door. She pulled a journal and a pen from her bag and began scribbling. When Alice leaned over to look, she turned away to hide her notebook and kept writing.

When Madison ambled over after taking in the view, she looked strangely at Karan. "Is she okay?"

"No idea," Alice said.

Finally, Karan snapped her journal closed and stood to join them. "Let's get some food!!"

"But..." Alice asked, but Karan had already gone in.

Following her inside, Alice was met by the familiar laughing buzz of an English pub. Nobody seemed bothered that the pub was perched precariously on the edge of a cliff; everyone looked perfectly grounded and happy with life. The alcohol probably had a lot to do with it.

Alice stepped to the left of the entry and let Karan and Madison walk ahead. Scanning the room carefully for her solitary man in his *Star Wars* shirt, Alice took in all the details. To her left, she saw the fire before which a group of older men stood warming their bottoms as they laughed and drank pints; the tables were full of families eating fish and chips. In the middle of the pub, the young bartender pulled ales behind the bar and passed them to people wearing rustic wool sweaters. Karan and Madison were there, too, lining up to order food. To

Alice's right were the younger adults playing darts and flirting with each other.

But no David, of course.

As she scanned the room again, she thought she saw a shadow dart out of sight near the bathroom to her left. There was no way any of those ninjas could have known they were coming out to a pub in the middle of nowhere, was there? Perhaps she had imagined it because she had been thinking of David just now, and unfortunately, the two were linked in her mind.

She needed something to relax her. Usually, that would have been physical exercise. Or she would find somewhere to be alone. Now, she felt like getting a beer and celebrating Karan's new siddhi. And consoling her, if necessary, because she was so unnerved by its sudden onset.

They all ordered drinks and food at the bar and then had to fend off some good-natured flirting from the young bartender.

"Where are you ladies from?"

"Not near here," Karan said.

"Somewhere nice, I hope."

"Somewhere people look after each other," Madison said, ushering Karan away from him.

Undeterred, he pushed Alice's drink to her and continued talking. "I wish they did here. London incomers are driving up rent. They bustle about, talking about the beautiful five valleys, the fabulous hiking, and the organic food. They say the place is a graveyard for ambition because you never want to live elsewhere. Charming! They spend plenty, of course, but if you ask me, we've lost more than we've gained. All this carry-on just goes to show."

Alice escaped from the loquacious publican and joined her friends at a corner table to wait for their dinner orders to be called. Like most country pubs, it was a family place with a mug full of crayons on each table to keep children amused.

However, there weren't many families here—just a bunch of old guys in gray sweaters. The absence of any other demographic made three eighteen-year-old women the center of attention. Alice hated it, but at least none of the old guys was hitting on any of them. Not yet, anyway.

Karan insisted she wasn't ready to talk about her thing yet, so they were forced into small talk about the drive, though they were all thinking about Karan's siddhi.

Alice and Karan were finishing their Doom Bar ales (which Karan maintained tasted like dishwater despite Alice's insistence it was creamy, like a beer version of a latte) while Madison sipped on a glass of wine.

"Guys," Alice said, returning the conversation to Karan's siddhi. But before she could continue, Madison gasped.

"Just a minute," Madison said, taking a crayon from the mug and staring at it. "Did you guys see that?"

"Yeah, it's a blue crayon," Karan said. "Amazing."

"But it had these wisps of blue smoke coming out of it." She looked at Alice. "Did you see anything?"

Alice stared at her, then down at the crayon. Unbelievably, it sounded like Madison was describing prana. It was almost too much. First Karan, and now Madison? And hadn't one of their teachers said how rare it was for siddhas to be able to see prana? Mad had caught it from Alice. How else could she have picked up such a rare siddhi? And what else did she pick up?

Just then, Alice heard the pub's front door open behind her. The pub seemed to quieten by a few decibels, and even Karan's eyes widened. Alice wanted to turn around to see if it was her David, but she resisted the urge.

"Alice," Karan said, almost whispering, "I know this will sound super weird, but I just need to check something. I will ask you to turn around in a minute, but not yet. First, I want to ask you something."

Alice nodded, almost holding her breath. Karan had never

spoken so strangely before. To Karan's side, Madison had stopped staring at the blue crayon and was giving Karan her undivided attention.

"So, do you, like, have a friend in London who is geeky and tall but cute? A boy, I mean?"

Alice nodded, now desperate to turn around.

"No," Karan said, holding her hand out. "Wait just a sec before you look."

"But..."

"Just one more thing. Is this geeky guy of yours missing? Like, was he supposed to meet you somewhere, but he didn't show up?"

"How did you know that?" Alice asked, really, really desperate to turn around.

"Just a sec. So does that guy have a mother who is some monster? Like the worst online troll crossed with the Wicked Witch of the West?"

"Is she here?" Alice asked. "Did she just walk in?"

"No. In addition to my download siddhi thing, I seem also to be able to have visions. And the man who just walked in is the man who kidnapped your guy. At least, if I'm not insane—"

"Can I turn around now?" Alice almost begged.

"Just a sec. I have this feeling he is dangerous and—"

But Alice was sick of waiting. She turned her head.

CHAPTER 16

Walking toward the bar, smirking like he expected to be received by the bartender as royalty, was Alice's not-so-good pal Michael Longblood, the right-wing politician who everyone around here knew. This lustful old monster hit on her in a bar. And if Professor Bird could be believed, he was also a genuine terrorist, not part of The Game.

She wasn't the only one turning to stare—most heads were turned. And behind him walked Eric, his security guard.

Alice immediately ducked her head and shielded her face with both hands.

"So," Karan said, "does that stunned-mullet look on your face mean that you know those guys?"

Alice nodded.

"And you seriously have a geeky boyfriend you haven't mentioned?"

Alice shrugged because she honestly didn't know what David was to her.

"And so I'm not insane?" Karan pleaded.

"Karan, yes, these are the guys I told you and Mad about who are planning some terrorist thing involving the two

Hermans, whoever they are. But I have no idea if they kidnapped David."

Madison had been looking from Alice to Karan to the Longblood group with growing concern. "We need to call Professor Bird. Now."

"Agreed," Karan said.

Alice nodded too.

"But are you sure David has been kidnapped?" Alice asked. "Like, you saw him tied to a chair? Not drinking beer at the same pub as Longblood or something benign?"

By way of answer, Karan pulled out her journal. "Kidnapped. Remember when I sat down outside and wrote some stuff down?"

Madison took the journal Karan proffered. Alice didn't look because she was still trying to hide her face from Longblood and Eric.

As she read, Madison nodded, eyes wide. "Karan, you're a siddha! That's amazing!"

"Yeah, but don't worry about my thing. What about Alice's thing? Terrorism is one thing, but kidnapping someone's new boyfriend is way out of line. Let's make that call."

But as Karan was pulling out her phone, Eric finally saw Alice. With surprise and then anger in his eyes, he spoke to Longblood and rose to his feet.

Then all hell broke loose.

Alice felt a sting on the tip of her nose and saw a knife burying itself into the wood-paneled wall next to her head. A drop of her blood fell to the table. Then two dark figures suddenly emerged from the shadows, grabbed Karan, and pulled her from her chair.

Alice and Madison both rose but were too slow. Karan was already being whisked out of the pub.

"Hey!" Alice and Madison both shouted, knocking their chairs over as they jumped up to pursue.

At the same time, Eric had pulled Longblood out of his chair, knocking it over, and had pushed him toward the door, obviously fearing some attack and wanting to get him out of there. Longblood rushed out the door while Eric remained behind to block anyone from pursuing.

"Out of the way, idiot!" Alice shouted.

"Why are you here?!" he barked, clearly not planning to get out of the way.

"I got this," Madison said.

Once again, Alice was stunned as Madison swept the blue crayon off their table and flicked it. Rather than looping uselessly through the air like a crayon should, there was a loud crack like a whip. Eric's head snapped back, and he crumpled to the floor.

Alice rushed up and saw he was out cold. There was a deep, blue dent between his eyes where the crayon had struck him. She immediately wondered if anyone would have seen what Madison had done but concluded it happened too fast. It was unlikely suspicion could have been cast on Madison for this.

"Oh my god, did I kill him?" Madison exclaimed, her hand to her mouth.

Alice quickly rose. "No, he's still breathing. Come on!"

Madison ran back and grabbed the box of crayons from their table, and the two of them rushed out front in pursuit of Karan's kidnappers.

Alice heard a muffled scream in the distance. "It sounds like they've taken her around the other side of the pub. Hurry!"

Alice ran around the back, Madison on her heels, and found a small back road.

And the hooded figures were standing there as though waiting for them.

Madison arrived, panting. Alice tried to pull Madison behind her to shield her from the ninja people throwing knives or bullets or ninja stars or whatever.

But they didn't seem to be preparing to attack Alice and Madison. As Alice watched, one of them lifted Karan's hands, which had been zip-tied behind her. He kept raising them until Karan was obviously in immense pain. He pulled her blonde hair down with his other hand, lifting her chin into an awkward backbend. The other guy pulled out a red marker and began drawing on Karan's face, tracing her facial scars. She jerked her head back and forth. It was likely her worst nightmare.

A cascade of feelings and questions instantly filled Alice's head. Fury topped the list. Karan was still excruciatingly self-conscious about her facial scars. It was not something a young person gets over quickly; there was simply no way to hide them. Your face is the first thing people see.

So why did these weird, hooded guys highlight her scars with a pen? What was wrong with these people?

The only reason Alice could think of for this strange act of cruelty was that they were taunting Alice, which would be in character for these guys. But what was their motive? They must want Alice to break a Corollary and, in doing so, reveal herself as a super-siddha. But why? What do they have to gain?

While all this was going through Alice's head, and she prepared to charge them and do whatever she could to wrestle Karan away, she heard a high-pitched crack. One of the guys carrying Karan went down hard.

The other one immediately let go of Karan and reached down to help his partner up.

Alice turned to see Madison taking out another crayon and flicking it effortlessly. With a crack, the other ninja was knocked back at least five yards onto his butt.

Sensing she was free, Karan bolted toward her friends; hands still zip-tied behind her. One of the ninjas managed to get up, limp away from the road, and disappear. The other remained still.

Alice and Madison ran to Karan, who was crying and saying repeatedly, "Why did they do that?"

Leaving Madison to cut Karan's hands loose with some fingernail clippers she had in her bag, Alice sprinted up to the remaining ninja, who was starting to groan and try to roll over.

Alice reached him and pulled off his hood. Suddenly, he was transformed from a scary ninja into a scared young man.

While he was still groggy, Alice dug around in his pockets and found one more zip tie. She quickly used it to tie his wrists together tightly.

"What's your name?" Alice asked him as Madison and Karan joined her.

"What?" he slurred.

"Name."

He shook his head and seemed to recognize where he was. "I will never reveal the identity of my master."

"No, your name, idiot."

He shook his head again and appeared to recognize Madison and Karan. "I can say this: I was once like you."

Karan lunged at him, but Madison held her back.

"I was a student at Chancery Gate with no siddhis," he continued. "What did that ancient institution ever give me? Lots of rules to follow and nothing else. They have all those resources but no way to use them without drawing attention."

He cleared his throat and appeared to be in some pain but continued. "I found a new way. I found someone who can grant major siddhis. Not just reading minds; fighting. Moving. Blocking reads. All of that. We are the modern warriors that the world needs. And we achieved what we did not by sitting in a classroom staring at a cup of tea."

Then he looked at Alice and back to Madison and Karan. "So, your friend Alice here can heal fast. Has she passed that ability to you? Can she? Believe me, before anything rubs off on you, she'll just be marginalized and isolated, just like anyone with powerful siddhis has always been. Trust me. You three need to rethink everything. You will eventually. Some things are worth fighting for. Our master is one of them."

He looked down at his shirt, and Alice followed his gaze to what she had taken as his ninja logo. Up close, she saw the logo had incorporated a small lens. She reached down and tore off the small camera sewn into the material. The lens and body were shattered. That must have been right where Madison's crayon had struck him.

"As soon as we get you on film, my master will have you. We failed this time, but we won't next time."

Alice looked back at Madison and Karan and rolled her eyes. "Let's call Professor Bird."

The unmasked ninja smiled again. "It won't help. The Company will pull you out of school and have you working on the coverup for a year. And I'm protected. Nothing will happen to me."

Just then, a loud hammering noise suddenly shattered the country air. The vast, looming shape of a very military-looking helicopter leaped into sight over the trees and cottages to the north, charging straight toward the pub.

"Stop him!" Madison shouted, but it was too late. The ninja had tumbled away from them, risen to his feet, and dashed toward the cliff.

Alice sprinted in pursuit, but there was no way she could catch up. He was much too fast.

As she watched, he dove from the cliff just as the helicopter arrived, as if they had planned the maneuver. His partner reached out of the open door on the side of the aircraft, caught his hands, and hauled him aboard. It was unbelievable.

The helicopter hovered for a moment, taunting them, and then its nose dropped as it plunged over the cliff, flying off into the distance toward London.

Shaking her head at what she just witnessed, Alice turned

to jog back across the lawn toward the road beyond and hoped to reach Longblood before he got to his car. The ninja figures had something to do with Longblood. There was no other explanation for why they had appeared here, in Stroud, just when Longblood showed up. If she could read the old MP, she could still unravel this whole conspiracy.

Back at the parking area down the village path, there was nothing but the car Madison had rented and a few other cars. Nothing that looked like it would belong to some VIP terrorist politician.

She ran back to the pub lawn and wordlessly passed Mad and Karan, who were now surrounded by some men in gray sweaters who had been drinking inside. They were trying to make sure she was okay.

Alice stormed back into the pub, hoping Eric would be stirring, at which point she would mentally interrogate the hell out of him until his brain was scrambled.

But Longblood's security guard was gone.

"He stumbled out just after you lot left," the bartender said. "I've called the police. Is your friend okay?"

Alice cursed to herself and returned outside to check on Karan.

She looked somewhat recovered. Her hands were untied, and Madison was using makeup remover to remove the red lines the ninja had drawn over Karan's scars.

They walked across the lawn so they could speak without being overheard.

"You know," Madison said, "if we used siddhis to attack them, we would be breaking all three of the Corollaries: Never hurt other siddhas, don't expose siddhis in public, and don't engage in conflict."

"So, hopefully, those cameras weren't transmitting videos into the cloud," Madison said.

"They weren't," Karan whispered. "That kind of body-worn

camera only has local storage. I looked it up with my new siddhi."

"But what would they have done with that footage?" Madison asked.

"Well, first, they would have crapped their pants watching it because you are the first projectile siddha since Dean," Karan said. "That crayon thing you do is freaking amazing."

"Shhh!" Madison responded, looking toward the men and deciding they couldn't have heard. Then she looked down at her hands, her black bangs covering her eyes. She was overwhelmed by what she had done and what had happened.

Alice knew exactly how she felt. She had been there before, suddenly realizing you were no longer "normal." The thought calmed her slightly.

"Hey," Alice whispered gently to Mad. "Can you throw anything besides crayons? Like, pencils?"

Karan reached into her bag and handed Madison her journaling pen with a flourish.

Madison lifted her head, took the pen, and held it for a while. "I don't think so," she concluded, handing it back to Karan. "The crayons shimmer to me, but everything else just looks normal. I must be the world's weirdest siddha."

"Shimmer? Like a kind of liquid surrounds it?" Alice asked, amazed. "Flowing in loops? Like in a Van Gogh painting?"

"Exactly!" Madison said.

"I'm pretty sure that's prana you're seeing," Alice said in awe. "I can see it too."

Karan's mouth dropped. "Our teachers said nobody can see that stuff. Nobody for centuries, at least." Karan's voice went up almost an octave. Almost a squeak. "Do you realize how rare that makes you two?! And what am I becoming? A human computer?"

Alice and Madison reached out and put arms around her.

She felt Karan's shoulders tense and her body shaking. She was probably still in shock, as was Madison.

"Karan," Alice said to her as gently as she could. "Madison. You both must be completely overwhelmed. But we need to get out of here before the police show up.

"I don't think we can," Madison said. "Wouldn't it be like fleeing the scene of a crime?"

"I just don't want to have to answer all the questions the police would ask, like if we knew Karan's attackers, why we're here, what's our address in London, all that. And I don't think Professor Bird would want us to be interrogated. Can you imagine all the cover-ups they would have to do for us? They'll probably pull us from university and get us to help. Wouldn't it be better just to split while we can?"

"I left my phone in there," Karan said. "That would be hard for them to explain too."

Alice rose and walked quickly back into the pub. While the bartender wasn't looking, she found Karan's phone, pulled the ninja's knife from the wall where they had been sitting, and stuck it in her back pocket.

When she stepped out again, the men seemed to have left Karan alone, staring out beyond the cliff in the direction the helicopter flew.

"Who the bloody hell was that?" the gray-haired man in the gray sweater asked one of his friends.

"Military?" the guy next to him guessed.

"That was a Bell 412. The Royal Air Force flies those."

"Those blokes didn't look military to me. More like gangsters."

"Gangsters with a Bell 412?"

That was Alice's question exactly. How did these gangster ninjas get a military-grade helicopter? And now that they knew Mad had a projectile siddhi, were they prepared to crash and burn their fancy helicopter and probably die in the process? All this to get Mad on video throwing a crayon at them? Or perhaps they didn't believe a crayon could hurt them at that distance?

There were many questions now. The possible answers terrified Alice. Seriously, who were these people? How did they know about one of the school's secret tunnels? Were they connected to the school somehow? How did they always show up after Alice saw either David or Longblood? Did they have an interest in Longblood? The whole situation was potentially more dangerous and complicated than she thought. And even worse: they always seemed to know where Alice was. This meant they either had siddhis or some way of tracking her. Maybe they were hacking her phone, which was meant to be unhackable. It was all looking bad.

CHAPTER 17

Alice handed Karan back her phone, and they moved cautiously toward the little goat path leading to their car. Hoping to avoid attention, they walked rather than ran.

"Karan, can I ask you something about your vision?" Alice asked while Madison elbowed her to shut up.

"Sure," Karan said.

Ignoring Madison's elbow, Alice asked, "You saw that Longblood had kidnapped my boyf...David?"

"Yeah, totally," Karan said. "I saw an image of him tied to a chair, his mother looking on, angry and distraught. There were headlines like 'The Honorable Michael Longblood MP Kidnaps Right-wing Blogger's Son.'"

"You have *news headlines* in your visions?" Madison asked.

But Alice could barely hear Karan's response, as her ears were full of the rushing sound of her rising blood pressure. David, tied to a chair. Would they kill him? What threat did he pose to them? Was it maybe to force his mother to publish something for them on her social media?

Alice tried to tune back into the present moment. It was probably her fault David was being held, and she had to figure out what to do. They had to get out of here, and she had to act.

And then Alice started to think about the knife. Were the ninjas now trying to kill them too?

"Just a second, guys," Alice said, pulling the lethal piece of steel from her back pocket.

The three of them stood there looking at it in Alice's hand.

"Is that what they threw at us?" Madison asked.

"Hey," Karan pointed, "what's that attached to the hilt?"

Alice removed a piece of paper from the rubber bands that held it to the knife. She unfolded it and saw it was a photograph.

The world seemed to stop spinning as they stared at it. Something broke inside Alice.

The picture showed David's kind, nerdy face twisted in shock as he stared back at her. The reason for his shock was apparent: his head was not attached to his body. It floated a foot above his bloody neck and torso. Alice stared at David, and he stared back.

"Alice, wake up!" Karan had been repeatedly calling her and had finally gotten through.

"It's fake, Alice! I saw that in my vision too. I mean, I saw a guy at a computer. The text feed in my vision read 'Ninja jerk makes fake jihad beheading picture.'"

Karan pulled the picture closer to herself. "And look," she said, pointing at David's face. "You can see where they messed it up. The wall behind the head doesn't match the one behind the body. See?"

Alice breathed in and out, trying to concentrate. Karan was right, she realized. Now she could see it was a pretty terrible job, too. In addition to the crude cut-and-paste editing job, the torso was not David's. The shoulders were much too broad, and rather than a *Star Wars* T-shirt, the unfortunate victim was wearing a shirt and tie, which had been loosened for the man's beheading.

In relief and disgust, Alice leaned down and vomited on the lawn.

Feeling slightly better now, Alice stood up, feeling a wave of fury.

"I gotta go do one more thing," Alice said. "Wait here, okay?"

The sirens were getting loud. The police must have already reached the steep road, but Alice had to go read the bartender.

"Alice, no!" Madison called after Alice, but she didn't stop.

She ran back across the lawn, past the men in sweaters, into the pub, and approached the bartender. Locking eyes, she read him as quickly as possible. She learned his name was Tom, and he was not descended from a wool baron, but rather a mom who was an accountant from London and a dad who worked in the Dyson factory before it closed, which was not even in Stroud but in Malmesbury, where his family were plumbers and probably farmers before that.

Tom knew nothing about Longblood's terrorist plans, but he knew that the MP's constituency was near London called St. Albans. Longblood spent a lot of time in a pub there near a cathedral.

And Tom knew plenty about David and his mother. They were semi-regular customers, and David's mom often met Longblood here. And their surname was Needley.

In a panic at realizing who David's mom was, Alice broke off her mind-reading link, turned, and sprinted out of the pub.

David's mom was Linda Needley. She just couldn't believe it.

The sirens sounded closer, but they were circling to the pub's other side.

Alice ran until she was standing with Madison and Karan again. "David's mom is Linda Needley. Shirk's blackmailer."

"What?" Madison exclaimed. "But what does that even mean?"

"It means we have a motive for David's kidnapping, and it has nothing to do with me." Saying that gave Alice a bit of relief, but did she believe it?

Alice rushed down the path with Madison and Karan at her heels.

Soon, they reached a section of the goat path shielded from any local houses' view.

Alice stopped to scope out the edge of the cliff. She saw layers of wet, white, exposed rock interspersed with heavy soil that contained jungles of brambles and the odd tree. The escarpment was at least a football field's distance below. While it wasn't straight down like many granite cliffs back home, falling down this slope would mean certain death.

Alice felt scared of this height for the first time in ages and backed away.

"Why are we stopping here?" Madison asked with suspicion in her voice. "We have to get to the car!"

"Listen, guys," Alice said. "I know this sounds irrational, but I want to fly back."

"What?!" Madison asked, incredulous.

"You guys call Professor Bird from the car. Tell her everything. I don't care anymore; we're beyond hiding anything."

"Alice, you can just tell her yourself from the car!"

"Okay, okay...wait a second." Madison maneuvered herself between the cliff and Alice. "This thing just keeps escalating the more we get involved. It's time to leave it to Professor Bird."

Alice squared off with Madison, her fury rising. It was maddening that Mad wanted to let the "authorities" handle it. It was her usual position on everything, despite the apparent fact the "authorities" never did anything right. But even more frustrating was seeing that Madison seemed ready to physically prevent Alice from flying. She had no idea how badly Alice needed to fly! And her need to fly was mixed up with feelings about David and a strong desire to help him. But Alice didn't say any of that. She just stared at Madison with fury building by the second.

Mad noticed the fire in Alice's eyes and started to plead, "Just stop and *think*! Your theory is this: David's mom is blackmailing Shirk, so the little old professor kidnapped David to neutralize that threat. But, Alice, doesn't that sound a little too extreme? If he wanted to neutralize a threat to himself or the university, wouldn't he get The Company to handle it?"

Alice wanted to reply, but Mad cut her off. "But okay, let's assume Shirk did it. He kidnapped David. Think about what that means! Do you really think Shirk is in charge of all these ninjas too? Because it was the ninjas who threw that knife. It was the ninjas who passed on the photo of David. Karan says it was the ninjas who edited that jihad photo."

Alice tried to sidestep Madison to get a run at the cliff, but Mad adjusted and continued pleading. "Alice, listen to me! If Shirk is David's kidnapper, Shirk is also the ninja master. And I just don't see it. He's a little old Englishman who dresses up like the Queen of England in his spare time. How would he be training an army of ninjas? And why? He doesn't seem like someone who would want to overturn the balance of siddha society by ruling over a bunch of super-siddha soldiers."

"Not only that," Karan said, "but if he's the ninja master, it means he's partnered up with Longblood, which is weird because Longblood is supposed to be friends with David's mom, according to you. Why would Shirk kidnap his partner's friend's son?"

More than anything Madison had said, this contradiction gave Alice pause. It did seem like a bizarre triangle: Shirk, Longblood, Needley. She could believe Shirk and Longblood but not Shirk and Needley. Judging from what Alice saw at the drag bar, there was no way Needley and Shirk were working together. At least not harmoniously. Not like partners. If it was a triangle, it was a peculiar one indeed. Could they be in a union of convenience? Or of desperation? Had something gone sideways, and Shirk resorted to David's kidnapping? It all did seem like a stretch.

"Even if you're right and I'm wrong," Alice said, "David's still being held prisoner somewhere. And I can't sit around and let Professor Bird handle it. She's Shirk's buddy. The VC will proceed with extreme care, not speed. And she'll always give Shirk the benefit of the doubt. What if that benefit of the doubt gets David hurt? What if she goes so slowly and carefully that David gets killed?"

Karan carefully stepped between Mad and Alice, like someone trying to separate two swordsmen, fearful of being stuck by a blade. "We're missing something, guys. There's a piece of information we still don't have. Or several pieces. Probably a whole pie's worth. We don't know what's up with that terrorist plot with the Herman guys. We don't understand why the ninjas are after us. We don't know why they want to film us using siddhis against them. It's more complicated than just some beef between Shirk and Needley."

All these conclusions weighed on Alice like a ton of bricks balanced on her chest. She felt the pressure inside her rising like it had done the other day before she took herself to Dr. Bird's office. Like her insides were being squeezed.

"But guys," Alice said weakly, "they still might hurt him. And it's not his fault. I ... I must find a way to fix this. And I think if I sit in the back of the car, I might have another anxiety attack."

"Another one?!" Madison asked.

"Mad, I just know I can't sit in traffic now. I'd implode. You guys won't arrive for two or three hours, but I could fly it in one. If I'm standing in front of her, maybe I can at least push the VC to act fast."

"But Alice, you can't!" Madison cried. "You'll be seen! This isn't Colorado!"

Mad glanced back over the ledge at the layers of exposed limestone and shuddered.

"She's right, Alice," Karan said. "Besides, when was the last time you flew?"

Now that was a good question. She hadn't flown since arriving in the UK. Could she still do it?

Alice stepped back, hoping to get a good run at the cliff. She also needed the room to dodge Madison.

Mad bent her knees as though readying herself to tackle Alice should she try to jump. "Alice. Don't. Just don't. Let Professor Bird sort it out."

"I need to, Mad."

"But why? It's like you have a death wish, Alice! Can't you see that you're doing it again?"

She had never been so pissed off at Madison before now. If Mad only knew what Alice's anxiety felt like...

But Madison also looked like she was about to explode, cry, or both. "Of *course* I understand your anxiety condition. But Alice, we love you! We don't want you to die. Can't you try to understand *that*?"

"I need to fly, Madison," Alice said, readying herself.

"Fly then!" Madison said. "We'll help! Karan and I will gladly drive you somewhere remote, and you can fly out to sea!"

Just as Alice was about to explode off the starting block, Karan took a few steps toward Alice. "Do you seriously love this guy that much?" she whispered.

Alice shrugged her shoulders in an honest answer. She honestly had no idea.

The three of them were silent momentarily, Madison holding her ground near the cliff and Alice's stress levels escalating with each breath. Could she even fly with this much anxiety coursing through her blood like poison?

Then Karan collapsed to the ground as though in another faint. As she did, Alice heard her distinctly say, "Go!"

Madison rolled her eyes at the charade but walked over to Karan anyway. Perhaps she thought the crisis had been averted; the moment of maximum risk had passed. But it hadn't because Alice seized her opportunity and sprinted straight off the ledge.

The moment her feet left the ground, her anxiety disappeared. It was almost laughable to Alice how quickly it was gone. How easily. Like it was not part of her but part of the ground she had left behind a split second earlier.

Despite hearing Madison scream her name, Alice was free now. Free to experience the terror of the hundred-foot drop yawning below her. The awe at the possibility she could escape death by flying. And a tiny chime of confidence, like a distant bell that only she could hear, that she could do this. She could remember how to fly. She reached for confidence and ignored the terror.

Alice sought the swirls of liquid blue prana, and upon her call, they were instantly everywhere, coursing toward her. With her senses freed from suffocating anxiety, she used her entire body, mind, and heart to invite prana to support her weight.

As her body began to arc downward toward the ground, a note of panic began to sound. She reached forward with both hands, feeling for the prana's warmth and energy. To her immense relief, it responded, just as it always did back in Colorado. She felt her hands immersed as if in warm water. With strong strokes, she began swimming, the prana responding like water, her forward momentum increasing. Meanwhile, she felt for prana on her stomach and thighs beneath her clothing, and she arched her body, curving away from the escarpment, then upward.

It always amazed her that even though the prana felt like water to her skin and she could pull against it to propel herself through it like she was swimming, it offered no resistance against her forward movement. Alice had the distinct impression that prana knew she intended to go fast, and it configured itself to make speed happen. She wondered, as she often did, what more prana could do. Like, if she invited it to send her to another planet, would it do that too? Could it breathe for her in space? Or underwater? Perhaps it supported her flying with swimming simply because she was a swimmer? If she were a wombat or a kangaroo, possibly, prana would facilitate speed in ways that suited a burrower or a jumper.

Meanwhile, she had some serious flying to do. She accelerated to nearly a hundred miles an hour, soaring away from her rocky doom and toward the mottled-gray Cotswold sky.

But she quickly learned that flying in England was different from Colorado. Within seconds, her whole body was drenched by high-altitude drizzle, and visibility was poor. She flew in the general direction she had seen the helicopter go, but she soon gave up any hope of picking up its trail. It had at least a ten-minute head start and could fly faster than she. But rather than feeling deflated by that failure, she just turned her attention to the simple joy of flying. The sky over England couldn't all be gray, could it? She decided to try to find the blue above the clouds and fog. She hoped to burst through the topmost layers of clouds into the glorious, endless, clear-blue sky like that in her beloved Colorado.

Beloved. It was a word that came easily to her now that she had left her anxieties back on the ground. She usually thought of Colorado as where she had barely survived an excruciating childhood full of anxiety and loneliness. Perhaps it was only in the sky she could experience love for Colorado, or for anywhere, or for anyone.

And naturally, like a breath, David returned to her mind. As she recalled thoughts of him tied to a chair, a chain reaction of thoughts came to her. It was like a computer booting up.

Her next thought was that she was very, very out of shape.

Flying, like swimming, required conditioning. Prana supported her reciprocally, giving her a fair return for the energy she expended, but still, she was slowly tiring. She knew she couldn't just wander the skies forever.

She had to focus. How could she help David?

She stopped flying upward in search of blue skies and leveled out a few thousand feet above ground level, flying in the general direction of London. The mist was thick enough that she couldn't see the ground clearly; it was just sort of a featureless gray mass, shifting slowly far below.

Scanning the mist ahead, she started considering her landing problem. As Madison said, she couldn't just land in the middle of London and shout "ta-da!" as a thousand people videoed it on their phones.

She could fly out over the English Channel, find a cargo ship heading west, land on it, and hitch a ride to London. No, that would be too slow; it would take forever to find the right boat and another forever to sail up the Thames.

Her second option was to fly above a highway and land on a big truck headed for London. No. It was too risky that she'd be seen and probably no faster than just turning around to rejoin Karan and Madison anyway, which she didn't want to do. She might manage to call or text them, and they might manage to drive to an isolated field somewhere she could land unseen, but she was far too proud to turn around, especially after her standoff with Madison.

How to fly into one of the world's densest cities without being seen?

She remembered something as her thoughts returned hopelessly to the English Channel boat option. When she had read Sue days ago in the café near Broken Lane, she had glimpsed the location of the cloaked entrance to the university's main supply tunnel. That would have to do.

Alice quickly pulled out her phone while maintaining her

speed with her other arm. Mist immediately covered the screen, but repeated wipes of her T-shirt kept the touchscreen working. She called up the map, zoomed out, and adjusted her trajectory. She pocketed her phone again and tried to relax into a speed she could cruise at for the next hour. She had flown for much longer when she was in better shape, but she knew today she would be exhausted when she reached her destination.

But she was wrong. Now that she had a solid plan, her stress abated enough for her to enjoy the thrill of free flying again. And with less stress came more energy. She played with it, letting her mind wander as it liked, even if it went toward negative thoughts, while still prompting her thoughts to move on to something else, like the occasional pigeon that flew across her path. *Where were those pigeons going, anyway,* she wondered. *And why were they up here so high, all alone, flapping like their lives depended on it?*

All these tactics seemed to work. There were moments when she felt as ecstatically happy and free as she had when she first leaped from the cliff near Stroud. But she no longer trusted the ecstasy and let her mind move from that feeling to the next.

And so it went as she flew east through the English mist for 130 miles.

And finally, her body aching and drenched, she saw what she had been searching for. The huge Thames Estuary loomed ahead. This was where the Thames River emptied into the North Sea. She risked reducing her altitude enough to enable her to see landmarks. She aimed to locate an area Sue thought of as "London Gateway"—a deep-water port about thirty miles east of London. She could already see the enormous loading cranes lined up like giant spider legs along the coast, and she flew in their general direction.

From only a thousand feet of altitude, she could see the vast lines of silt curling and infiltrating the English Channel, and she saw a half dozen cargo ships lined up on the horizon. The icy waters of the Channel looked endless here, and Alice couldn't fathom how people swam across to France. She would balk at even trying to fly across.

As she approached the port, she let herself coast for a few seconds while she wiped her face with her sleeves and squinted into the misty gloom with her tired, windblown eyes. Her aim was, once more, an old English pub. Gordy, obsessed with old pubs, had chosen the cloaked entrance. So now Alice was searching for a big warehouse next to a small, whitewashed, old English cottage pub with an old wooden sign with a ship on it.

The coast here was cluttered with warehouses and stacked shipping containers and cranes. Her phone had shown about twenty pubs within a three-mile radius of the main port. Why did they need so many pubs? How was she supposed to find an old cottage among that mess?

She suspected there was fancy radar above the port to prevent aerial attacks, so she had to be quick about this, whatever she was going to do. Hopefully, the radar techs would think she was a pelican, and any dock workers would be too busy or lazy to look up. So, she decided to risk a much lower altitude.

She circled the area once at a thousand feet of altitude, flying as fast as she could, tapping her last energy reserves.

CHAPTER 18

S he finally saw it. The little old pub looked just like the image she had seen in Sue's memory. It was simply a working-class dockworkers' pub nestled among giant, modern-looking shipping warehouses. If it were a person, it would be an old, stooped English sailor, grizzled and weather-beaten, standing by himself, looking disapprovingly at all the modern industrial infrastructure encroaching upon his cottage. She guessed a handful of men just like that were sitting on barstools inside.

Alice didn't care about the pub. To her, it was just a landmark; the goal was a nearby warehouse.

She knew she was taking huge risks already, as this area would be considered critical infrastructure to be carefully monitored and defended by the military. The adrenaline and near-absence of her stifling anxiety had made her reckless. But so far, so good; nobody was shouting and pointing up at her. A ground-to-air missile had not yet shot down Alice. Nobody was shining a spotlight on her. There were no air-raid sirens. Did they still have those? She didn't know.

As she circled warily overhead, already low enough that she could be seen, but only just, she decided the warehouse she

190

wanted was a huge one that looked like something you'd store airplanes in. It had a gray corrugated metal frame and a white metal roof.

And she saw her chance. The giant front doors slid open along tracks, allowing a delivery truck to enter. The vehicle was all white, with dual axles in the back supporting the load, which was the size of a shipping container. The driver was moving at a leisurely pace through the doors.

She seized the moment.

Timing it so the doors would be almost closed when she entered, she dove and sprinted through the air as hard as she could, but the doors closed faster than she imagined, and she had to push her exhausted body way past its limit to give herself a slim chance of making it in. The dark space framed by the sliding doors grew thinner and thinner as she approached, straining and gasping for air, her whole body burning with the effort. She almost aborted but realized she probably couldn't turn fast enough and would have crashed into the building, so she just dove for the last sliver of darkness. Her left hip struck the door hard, making a resounding and terrifying metallic clanging noise. The pain was unbelievable, but she couldn't give in to it. She sluiced sideways toward a dark corner near the ceiling, which she hoped would save her from being seen by any workers startled by the sound. Still gasping for air, she just briefly corrected her flight to coast along near the ceiling beneath the steel trusses while she desperately surveyed her options.

The place was huge—like two football fields long and wide. She had already flown halfway along. There were still no shouts of alarm or people running and pointing at her. As she scanned a bit more carefully, she saw there was nobody around at all. There would be cameras, of course, but she hoped the cameras were all pointed at the ground.

The truck seemed to be slowly proceeding toward a stack of

gravel at the far end of the warehouse, and it wasn't slowing down. She thought she heard it shift gears, and it appeared to be accelerating toward the gravel pile. *That pile of gravel must be the entrance*, she thought.

She had to act fast.

Every cell in her body told her to land, collapse to the ground, and give up. But even in her utter exhaustion, she could still visualize that horrific photo of David with his head cut off. The image kept her going.

She lined herself up with the truck. When it had almost reached the gravel pile, she dove, flared, and attempted to land on the roof of the cargo load in a head-first slide on her stomach. She vaguely hoped it would be a gentle landing, but it turned out to be a crushing belly-flop. It knocked all the air out of her, caused some severe damage to her ribs, and she immediately felt like vomiting. She was able to gasp a few breaths in and turned her head from side to side. She saw blue lights mounted on concrete walls whipping by at a dizzying pace. Lights flashed before her eyes, but she realized they were actual lights, not the side effects of oxygen deprivation. The truck had passed through the cloaked entrance and was in the tunnel.

She rolled onto her back and slowly tried to coax air into her lungs. It felt like her whole body was broken, but at least she was conscious. She stared at a line of yellow ceiling lights passing too close to her face for comfort. The truck was traveling at a steep downward angle, but she seemed situated in its slipstream, as there was not much wind. She managed to roll to her side, looked ahead, and saw the tunnel appeared to go on forever.

The truck traveled down until she felt they must be hundreds of feet below sea level. Her ears began to pop. The air was heavy and stale, and she was getting sick of the diesel fumes from the truck.

As her magic healing thing worked on her injuries, all she

could do was try to relax. Her mind wandered to all the stories she had heard about famous hobos stealing rides on trains. Jack Kerouac used to do it, didn't he? And Jack London before him? The practice was probably not as widespread in secret tunnels under London.

After an eternity that probably only lasted about half an hour, the light began to change, and the road rose slightly. She saw the end of the tunnel ahead.

Feeling slightly less like she was about to die, Alice tried to pancake herself to the center of the truck's payload, praying that nobody was observing from a high enough position in the university's cavernous loading dock to see the freight-hopping woman.

Her heart was racing. She remembered how uptight everyone was about the sanctity of these secret tunnels. She had been warned several times that being caught down here without permission was an expulsion-level offense. But again, nobody shouted an alarm.

She waited for a long time after the truck had parked.

She waited until after it had been unloaded.

She waited until she no longer heard any footsteps or voices.

She waited until she heard Professor Bird call out: "Alice, you can come down now."

With her heart in her mouth, Alice slid very quietly to the edge of the roof and looked down.

"Hi," the VC said, removing her Audrey Hepburn sunglasses. "Come on down."

Professor Bird was alone as far as Alice could see, except for her Labrador sidekick. So, this wasn't an arrest, at least. Not yet.

Alice found the ladder and sheepishly climbed down to face the music. The friendly dog licked her cut legs all over, but she couldn't even bend over to pat its eager head.

She reminded herself she had taken all those risks and

broken all those rules and her body for a reason: to reach Professor Bird as quickly as humanly possible and appeal for her help in finding David, stopping Longblood from terrorizing London, and preventing those ninjas from attacking her or her friends anymore.

"Obviously, video captured you riding on the top of the truck." She held up her sunglasses to Alice. "These are not just a pair of sunglasses. They give me access to a very competent AI assistant named Beatrice, who has shown me some shocking images of you. You have risked your safety, the security of the tunnel, and by extension, the security of the entire university."

Professor Bird pocketed her glasses carefully. "I asked Beatrice to firewall the footage from anyone else's view, but she can't maintain that for long. So can you please explain yourself?"

Alice felt her mutism rise within her like a black wave of tension. Her clarity of purpose wavered, and she even wobbled a bit on her feet.

Professor Bird sighed. "Regarding your being down here, it seems to indicate you have not yet developed a personal connection with the school's survival. You don't understand the risks. It indicates you value your freedom and convenience over the school's survival."

Alice had no response to that.

"Alice, we need to build trust between each other. I'm sure you are worried about the consequences of being discovered down here without permission. You are wondering if the same thing will happen to you that happened to Dean. Well, it won't. I haven't needed to explain that after Dean, we created a new arrangement with The Company. Even students who commit crimes or who break the Corollaries and are expelled, we look after that student forever. As long as they want."

Alice didn't respond but furrowed her brow. She didn't like the sound of the word *forever*. It almost sounded sinister, like imprisonment in a mental hospital.

"I can see that concerns you, but it shouldn't. It means you won't be forced to work for The Company. You won't ever be put in any jail or under house arrest. You won't be sent to Siberia. It's not how we operate. Do you understand?"

Alice shook her head. She didn't like the sound of their protective custody.

"Even if you have broken every school rule down here, the worst thing that will happen to you is you will be placed under the care of my sister, Dr. Bird, who, instead of incarcerating you, will help you work through your problems. You see?"

But this was all irrelevant. Why wasn't Professor Bird even discussing her plan to help David? Hadn't Madison phoned the VC and explained everything?

She felt herself getting extremely wound up again. *Get ahold of yourself*, Alice. She closed her eyes and tried to breathe and relax, but she saw only dark thoughts and worries.

She realized there was only one thing she could do.

Opening her eyes, she pointed at them and then at Professor Bird's eyes.

"You want me to read you?"

Alice nodded. She knew it was unlikely she could hide her big secrets from the VC, who was apparently one of the world's best readers, and she was probably even better at shielding her thoughts from others. This put Alice instantly at a disadvantage. But she didn't care anymore. It was time for action. David might even be dead by now.

"Okay, but here's what I would like to do. You read me first, and I will show you enough to prove I am on your side. Then I'll read you, and I'll only search for the reason you are down here. Deal?"

Alice nodded and wasted no time. She easily tuned in to Professor Bird and was immediately guided by her to some clear, simple conclusions. Alice saw how much Professor Bird liked her and that everything she said just now had been genuine and honest. She saw that Professor Bird did view Alice as a super-siddha. She was shown how the VC had been fighting against a group of students and their parents who had wanted Alice expelled because of the risk she represented. Alice attacked a siddha before, and they were afraid Alice would attack a student.

None of this surprised Alice.

Then it got a little more interesting.

First, she wanted to know if Professor Bird trusted Shirk. Professor Bird resisted, but Alice found that she could break through without too much trouble. What she discovered was no surprise: the VC trusted Shirk implicitly. Unquestioningly. Why? Because they read each other all the time and knew nearly everything about each other. Which didn't necessarily convince Alice. The VC was overconfident in her mind-reading abilities. Perhaps Shirk knew how to shield his conspiratorial thoughts and plans from others?

Next, Alice sought Professor Bird's memories about what happened to Shirk's brother and the story behind the news clipping they had found in Dean's hidden bedroom. Again, she encountered resistance, and again she broke through. Shirk's brother had been a teacher, too, when Dean was a student. He had taken Dean under his wing. Shirk's brother had tried to shield Dean from suspicious students and their parents. When Dean prevented the terrorist incident with the van, Shirk's brother took the blame. He lied to everyone and said he told Dean to do it, to go out and use his siddhis to protect people, even if it meant he would be discovered. Professor Bird had just been appointed Vice Chancellor then, and she knew Shirk's brother was lying, but she let him take the rap anyway to protect Dean. It worked, at least insofar as Dean was allowed to leave the campus and work as a recruiter in the USA and wasn't forced to spend the rest of his life in front of some desk in The Company. But Shirk's brother lost his job at the university, started to drink, and got a painkiller addiction, which spiraled into patterns of addiction until he finally died of liver cancer.

Well, that was a sad story, Alice thought. It didn't explain Shirk's problem with Needley or his involvement with the ninjas, but it was something. It at least showed why Shirk would have some severe angst.

Next, Alice wanted to know how far the VC had gone in her investigation into the ninjas and the bomb that nearly blew Alice up. She probed and learned Professor Bird did not suspect the ninjas had any connection with Shirk or the university, or The Company. The VC thought they must have a local contact to know the secret entrances, but she had no idea who that could be. Professor Bird also had no idea who the two Hermans could be nor how this linked back to Longblood.

Then she checked what Professor Bird knew about Alice's siddhis, and—as expected—the VC knew only about Alice's accelerated healing abilities, not about her flying. And, apparently, not about how easily Alice could break through Professor Bird's mental defenses and read whatever she wanted in her mind.

Alice broke it off, leaving the prim, neatly dressed Vice Chancellor standing there with her mouth open, a look of complete shock on her face. She attempted to recover but then put her hand to her mouth and breathed quickly like she wanted to cry.

"I had no idea, Alice." She blinked hard and straightened up. "You broke down my defenses like they weren't even there. I felt like a child."

Alice shrugged, wondering if she had pushed too hard and seen too much. But it was too late now.

"None of our teaching staff could have done what you just did."

Alice didn't answer. What could she say?

Professor Bird finally shook her head and smiled

awkwardly. "Right. Now let's see why you were down here tonight."

Alice nodded her assent and fully intended to cooperate and behave herself. But she failed.

When Professor Bird was locked in, Alice immediately decided to show her everything related to the weird triangle that tied Shirk with Needley and Longblood. She needed to secure the VC's full cooperation to rescue David.

Alice only left out Karan and Madison's powerful new siddhis. She felt they deserved the right to privacy.

Finally, somewhat reluctantly, Alice showed the VC her leap from the cliff and her desperate flight to campus in hopes of asking for the VC's help in person. She shared with Professor Bird some of the thrills of flying. She showed her how she flew in through the cloaked entry to the supply tunnel, the location she had seen in Sue's mind.

And then she abruptly cut off the read and kicked Professor Bird out of her head.

At this point, the professor closed her eyes, hitched up her skirt, lowered herself to the dusty concrete, and sat crossed-legged. She looked unladylike, but at least she hadn't passed out in shock. Her dog licked her face several times and then curled up next to her master, which she seemed to need. Emotional support dog, indeed.

Professor Bird sat utterly still for a long minute as though in meditation.

Finally, she opened her eyes and looked up. "Have a seat, Alice," she said.

Alice obeyed.

The VC looked at her. Her expression was unexpectedly calm. "Let me level with you. Judging from what you have seen and experienced, more is at stake here than the security of the school tunnels. The explosion that almost killed you was not a random attack. The behavior of these hooded siddhas you call ninjas is part of something big. It is a well-planned and executed strategy that has you at its center. It is being directed by someone inside The Company or the university, judging from their resources and ability always to send people to your location. And now..." Professor Bird's voice cracked, but her face showed no emotion. "Now I know why you are at the center of their plans."

"Why?" Alice said, finding her voice.

"Because you have siddhis not seen for thousands of years. Perhaps never seen before."

Alice couldn't really respond to that, as it put what she had feared into words.

Professor Bird's glasses started ringing like a telephone, and she immediately put them on, listened, and stood up faster than Alice thought possible. The Lab rose quickly, instantly alert, ready to obey any command.

"Beatrice just informed me your friends Madison and Karan have been in a traffic accident."

Alice gasped and stood up as fast as Professor Bird had.

"They are okay. But we must rule out foul play and ensure their safe return to campus. I am going to them right now."

"I'm coming too," Alice said.

"No. There will be Company agents there. Based on what you have shown me, we can't trust anyone from The Company or the university. We definitely can't let you face any questioning by an agent."

"Does Beatrice think those ninja guys caused Madison and Karan's traffic accident?"

"No. She's convinced it's innocent."

"Can you get to Mad and Karan before the agents do?"

"I'm going to try."

"Where should I go, then? Is the campus safe?"

"No. Wait for me at the Pickled Chicken. Gordy and Sue are the only ones you should trust. The Company will see you're there, but Sue will know how to keep them off your back. I'll bring Madison and Karan there as soon as I can. I'll call ahead so Gordy and Sue are expecting you."

"Are you sure I can trust them?"

"I am. I'd trust them with my life."

And with that, the professor turned and ran, her dog at her heels.

Alice watched as they both jumped in an electric sports car and zipped away down another tunnel.

CHAPTER 19

Alice was now very much on edge. Her first problem was the loading dock supervisor, striding toward her with a sense of definite purpose. She didn't know if she was meant to run away or speak to him.

"Miss Brickstone," he said, "Beatrice asked me to escort you to the Pickled Chicken. We are to be discreet. Are you ready?"

Alice was reluctant. She'd rather be alone now. She needed to call Madison and Karan and make sure they were okay.

"The Chicken has rooms where you can bathe if you wish. Beatrice has also requested Nick gather some of your things from your room. What would you like her to bring for you?"

Alice managed to say, "Anything."

As he patiently waited for her, she tried Madison and Karan, but neither picked up. So, she sent a group text: *I'm fine, met with the VC who told me about your accident. Are you both okay? Please call.* She didn't mention the Pickled Chicken in case the agents were reading their texts.

Then she nodded at the older man and started walking toward the elevators.

"Not that way," he said with a sly smile, and he led her in the opposite direction, across the vast concrete floor, past the refrigerated truck on top of which Alice had ridden, past stacks of boxes full of supplies for the university, past a row of parked electric cars like the one in which Professor Bird had raced away and a row of electric motorcycles like the one Alice had seen in the Brydges Lane tunnel, and to an unassuming-looking freight elevator.

"After you," he said politely, and she followed him in.

When the elevator doors opened again, Sue's smiling face was beaming in on them like the morning sun. "Welcome to the Pickled Chicken, Alice!" she said with open arms. "To our cellar, that is."

Alice looked around and then folded her arms against the cold.

Sue practically dove at her and wrapped her in a hug. It felt nourishing.

"He's a gentle soul, our Boris," Sue said as she led Alice up the same stairway.

Alice realized Sue must have been tipped off about her mutism, as she hadn't asked her a single question. She was grateful to Professor Bird for that, or perhaps Beatrice had thought of it independently. (Funny how she already thought of Professor Bird's AI as a person.)

After Sue led Alice to a gorgeous little bedroom overlooking Chancery Lane, she drew the curtains and took her leave, saying, "You'll want to change and shower, no doubt. We've reserved the snug for you. Come down when you're ready.

Alice had no idea what a snug was and didn't care about a shower. All she wanted was to talk with Madison and Karan and be sure they were alright. But there was no way they could be back yet, even if Professor Bird drove them via an underground tunnel. Alice took a shower.

As she was toweling off, there was a knock at the door. She wrapped a towel around herself, peeked through the door's peephole, and saw Nick holding a pile of her clothes.

Alice swung the door open and was shocked at Nick's appearance, which she hadn't fully apprehended through the fisheye lens of the peephole.

"Nick, you look like shit."

"Thanks. And you're welcome." She thrust Alice's clothes at her and turned to walk away.

"Hey, thanks. Are you going..." Alice had meant to ask if she was joining them downstairs at the pub, but Nick had already walked down the thickly carpeted hallway noiselessly away.

Her ghoulish appearance had concerned Alice, who wondered if she might be sick. But she shook off those concerns, dried her hair, threw on the clothes Nick had brought (her only slightly dressy outfit, as it turned out), and headed downstairs, hoping Mad and Karan would already be there but knowing they wouldn't be.

"How are you, Alice?" Gordy asked sincerely when she appeared at the bottom of the stairs. He had rushed from behind the busy bar to greet her.

Alice smiled as warmly as she could in return.

"Fantastic," he said, seeming satisfied with her smile. "We haven't heard from Pippa yet, but we understand your friends are fine. I'm sure they'll be here soon. May I show you to the snug?"

Alice nodded and reminded herself that "Pippa" was Professor Bird's first name.

Gordy led her to a cozy private room in the back of the pub. A warm fire was crackling next to a comfortably worn old leather Chesterfield wing chair and side table. Four chairs also surrounded a round table.

"Most British pubs have private rooms like this. Some time ago, it was frowned upon for women to be seen at a public establishment. As a result, they would be secreted into these kinds of back rooms. This particular snug is still used by the occasional local police officer or VIPs from the university. Tonight, it's all yours."

As Alice flopped down in the Chesterfield, Gordy nodded approvingly and asked, "What can I get you? An ale and pie? Unfortunately, our kitchen is closed for the night, but the steak pies are good."

Alice nodded gratefully.

When Gordy closed the door, Alice was left in complete, delicious silence. But it took only seconds for her subconscious mind to scream at her to *DO SOMETHING! ANYTHING!* Everything was falling to pieces, Mad and Karan were possibly injured, Karan had been assaulted, and David was tied to a chair in some basement. While Alice was sitting in a plush leather chair by the fire, preparing to drink beer alone.

Thankfully, Alice was saved from her self-torture. Sue opened the door just at that moment, and Madison and Karan burst by her into the snug. Karan was the first to embrace Alice. As she did, Alice tried to catch Madison's eye, but Madison was looking away. So, she was still angry that Alice had flown away against her advice.

After Karan broke off her hug, she furrowed her brow and flicked her eyes toward Madison as if to say, "She's still mad at you because you're an idiot, but maybe if you give her a big hug, she'll come around."

Alice didn't need much persuasion. She went over and embraced her tightly. She crushed Madison's lean, muscular body with a pointedly strong hug as if to say she was sorry.

Madison gave a polite cough and broke away laughing and slightly wheezing from Alice's crushing hug.

"Can I get you ladies pies and ales?" Sue asked.

"Oh my god, please," Karan said, and Madison nodded.

"Fantastic. I was about to bring Alice's in, but I'll get yours straight away."

Alice backed away from them and saw nothing to indicate

they were injured. "Are you guys okay? Professor Bird said you had been in a car accident."

"It was totally my fault," Madison said. "I was very *distracted*," she glared at Alice when she said that word, "and I just went the wrong way down a one-way street and was so shocked I jerked the wheel and hit a pole."

"Did Professor Bird drive you here?" Alice asked, hoping not to have to talk about the fact that she was the reason Madison had been distracted.

Madison seemed to clam up again, looking at the ground.

Karan plopped down in the Chesterfield, sighing as though tired of her two best friends not getting along, and answered, "No way. I don't think we could all fit in that thing Professor Bird was driving."

"So, where did she go? She was supposed to meet us here to make a plan or something," Alice said.

Madison lowered herself down into a wooden chair at the small dining table. She looked shattered.

Karan kicked her shoes off and wiggled her toes. "No idea. She told us to meet you here, put us in a rideshare (a non-Company one), and took off."

Alice had no idea what to think of that. Surely, Professor Bird traveling underground in a sports car would arrive way before a rideshare.

Alice took out her phone and realized she didn't have Professor Bird's number and could only hope Gordy and Sue would know what was going on, or at least could give them the VC's number.

But when their food and drinks came, Gordy did not know where Professor Bird was. He was reluctant to give Alice her direct cell number but promised to call her himself.

And yet he didn't return immediately. Sue refilled their drinks—Madison changed to peppermint tea, but Karan seemed to share Alice's appreciation of cask ale—but she also did not know anything about the VC's whereabouts. She promised she would ask Gordy if he reached her. But she also didn't return to the snug for some time.

Alice used the time to tell them about her flight to London Gateway, freight-hopping on the truck, and being caught by Professor Bird in the landing dock.

She and Karan exchanged dark looks as Madison ate slowly in stony indifference to Alice's story.

"So," Karan said in exaggerated tones, "what did the VC say?"

Alice explained how they read each other because Alice couldn't get any words out.

"Wow!" Karan said with sincere amazement. Then she seemed to realize the magnitude of what Alice had said. "Did she see...*everything*?"

Alice saw Madison sit up a little straighter, though she still wouldn't look at Alice.

"No. It turns out I was pretty good at shielding stuff from her. So I didn't let her see you guys have any siddhis. You don't have to worry."

Madison and Karan both exhaled giant sighs of relief. It would be hard for them to get used to being secret super-siddhas. Alice knew how they felt.

Madison looked up again. "But how did you explain how you arrived in the tunnel? Or how you even knew it was there?"

"I did decide to show her everything about myself," Alice said.

That finally got Madison's full attention. Both she and Karan stared at Alice with wide-eyed surprise.

"I had to. I needed to show her everything relevant to David's disappearance. I needed her to know everything those ninjas know about me. And I'm pretty sure they know about my flying. I needed her to have enough information to be able to help. So, the VC knows I can fly."

Alice looked straight at Madison now. "Because I agree with

you, Mad. I do always fly off half-cocked. It's almost gotten me killed heaps of times. I knew I needed her help. And now I don't even know where she is. And I know I need your help too. I can't do any of this alone..." Alice turned away this time because she felt foolish, desperate, and helpless. None of this was coming out right.

This finally roused Madison, who moved her chair next to Alice's. Now the three of them were in a tight circle, with Karan leaning forward in her armchair, Alice and Madison in wooden dining chairs.

"So, did you learn anything else from Professor Bird?" Karan asked. "Anything that explains this bizarre love triangle between Shirk, Needley, and Longblood?"

"Not really," Alice admitted before explaining what she had learned about Shirk's brother.

"Wow," Karan said. "That is spooky. Dean prevented a terrorist attack, and Shirk's brother took the blame. Now we're trying to prevent one too. I hope Professor Bird doesn't end up having to die of cancer for us."

Alice thought for a second. "I think I have to go read Shirk. All the answers are in his head. He may be able to hide stuff from Professor Bird, but maybe I can break through and find the truth."

"You might also get taken away by a bunch of Company agents and never seen again," Karan said. "Even the VC said not to trust anyone or go near those people."

Madison slumped down in her chair. "And even if you could overcome his defenses, you would read him without permission. It would just give him more ammunition to blackmail you, Alice."

Alice wondered if Madison was getting tired of always being the voice of reason. But Madison was wrong. They needed to do something. Anything. Even if it was risky.

Karan seemed to agree. "Then we need to go find one of the ninjas and read him," she said. "How can we do that?"

"Yeah," Alice agreed. "They will show up if we get close to Longblood. They always have."

"Wait," Karan said, "you said Longblood's constituency is St. Albans, right? So, all we need to do is to find where in St. Albans he's keeping David. "

"Are you kidding me?" Madison sighed again in exasperation. "How would we even do something as desperate as that, especially without support?"

"Yeah," Alice said, her energy finally flagging. Madison was probably right. "I guess we just have to wait for the VC and Beatrice. They would probably be able to find Longblood's home address at least."

They all dropped back into silence for a moment.

"So," Madison said in a soothing voice. "The VC knows about your flying. How does that feel?"

Alice thought back. Professor Bird had been so stunned she had to sit down on the concrete of the loading dock and cuddle her dog. But other than being shocked, Alice didn't know what else the VC thought about her flying, so she shrugged her shoulders as if to say it was no big deal, which was a complete lie.

"She didn't freak out?" Karan asked, stifling a yawn.

"Yeah, a little," Alice said and saw Madison stifle a yawn as well.

It was an anticlimactic way to discuss such an emotional moment, one that they had feared as a worst-case scenario to be avoided at all costs. Was Alice going to be now made into a pariah as Dean had been? Or not? It seemed almost inconsequential compared with everything else they were facing. And now they were all sitting there yawning. Life was like that; big moments didn't always get the airtime they deserved.

CHAPTER 20

Soon, Sue took Karan and Madison up to their rooms on the second level of the Chicken, but Alice decided to remain back in the snug. She wanted some time alone, and this was the only way she would get it.

Unbidden, Gordy brought her another ale and politely left her to her thoughts.

But before Alice had time to touch the beer or brood any longer, she laid her head on her arms and fell into a restless sleep full of exploding bombs and beheaded boyfriends.

Just as another bomb blew up in her face, she was bothered by a rhythmic pounding. Did those guys have guns now? Weren't the bombs bad enough?

"I'm sorry, Alice," she heard a familiar voice say.

Alice's eyes opened reluctantly, and she realized her arm was nesting in a puddle of drool. Her cheek was wet, too, yet her mouth was dry. She felt terrible.

"Alice," the female voice repeated. Alice recognized it as belonging to Sue, and the machine-gun noise had just been her gently tapping on the door. The antique door handle moved, and the red-varnished mahogany creaked open. Sue's worried face appeared.

"I'm sorry, I must have dozed off. What time is it?" Alice asked before her mutism could shut her up.

Then the door burst open, and a drenched Labrador forced through Sue's nightgown skirts, almost toppling her over.

The dripping dog made straight for Alice and promptly sat down in front of her as if waiting for something.

"It's four in the morning," Sue said. "I was woken by her persistent barking out front, and when I opened the door, she looked like she had just emerged from the sea. She ran straight back here."

Alice looked at the dog, who cocked her head sideways, staring intently at Alice. Unbelievably, this dog did look to be Professor Bird's Labrador. Alice reached out to pat her and saw something attached to her collar, under her jaw.

"Alice, it seems obvious Misty knew you were back here in the snug. Did you have an arrangement with Professor Bird?"

"No," Alice replied as she tried to separate the object from Misty's collar. It seemed to have been wrapped by a handkerchief and tied tightly to the leather.

"Then we can only assume Professor Bird told Misty to come here and find you."

Alice remembered meeting Niamh, the dog trainer, on campus. She praised Misty as an intelligent dog who could follow complex orders.

She finally detached the little bundle from Misty's damp collar and unwrapped it on the table beside her untouched beer.

They were the VC's Beatrice glasses.

Sue gasped when she saw them. "That does it. I'm going to wake Gordy. Please don't go anywhere, Alice; I'll be right back."

Alice stared at Professor Bird's sunglasses. Even though they were dripping with moisture, they looked unblemished. What was going on? What had happened to Professor Bird?

She realized there was one way to find out, as she quickly

put the glasses on. They powered up, and visual features laid themselves out neatly around the edges. Alice guessed they were security feeds or something.

"Welcome, Alice," a female British voice said in her ear. Alice had no idea how the sound was reaching her ears. "You have been granted full access. Misty has done well to get these glasses to you."

"Are you Beatrice? The VC's AI?"

"Yes."

"Is Professor Bird okay?"

"Unknown. She was about to be taken or attacked when she sent Misty to find you."

Alice looked down through the lenses at Misty and saw her droop a little. "How far has this dog walked?"

"Twenty-six-point-one miles. She didn't travel a direct route, but she did admirably well. She ran and walked continuously for hours. Part of the way, she managed to board a 757 bus. I have no idea how the dog knew to do that. I can only guess she had been trained to follow people onto a bus traveling in the direction she wanted to go, then follow them back off again."

"Twenty-six miles?!"

"Through the dark in a rainstorm."

Alice looked down at the dog with renewed admiration. All she had to offer Misty was a four-hour-old beer, but she eventually found some water in a jug and some leftover pie on Madison's plate. Misty lapped it all up with immense gratitude before collapsing by the fire with an unladylike grunt and falling asleep.

"Beatrice, where was Professor Bird when she was about to be taken?"

"In the yard of St. Alban's Cathedral. Northeast of London."

"What do you mean by 'taken'?"

"All we could see were four people wearing black. They were closing in on us from all directions. We were away from the car and had nowhere to run. They moved fast. Professor Bird assumed they were the siddha mercenaries who had been stalking you. Judging by their movements, we assumed they intended to capture Professor Bird."

Alice tried to picture the scene: a dark, grassy field next to a medieval cathedral, Professor Bird stooping down to tie these glasses to Misty's collar.

"But why was she even there?" Alice asked. "Why didn't Professor Bird come back to the Pickled Chicken after meeting with Madison and Karan at the scene of their accident?"

"She received a phone call. The voice was unfamiliar to her and me. The person said he had information about you that would be of great interest but would only provide it in person. The meet-up was to be outside of St. Alban's Cathedral."

"Is there an old pub at St. Albans?"

"Yes! The meeting place was to be at Ye Olde Fighting Cocks. How did you know?"

Alice's mind raced. That must be Longblood's headquarters. By now, Professor Bird would be zip tied to a chair beside David.

"Can you find out if an MP named Longblood frequents Ye Olde Fighting Cocks?"

"I will do my best, Alice. Unfortunately, my speed is hampered by the necessity to conceal everything I do from The Company. I must inform you that Professor Bird suspected a security leak in either The Company, Chancery Gate University, or both. Someone with security access at a level equal to or higher than Professor Bird's. That is the only explanation for their ability to trace your location in real-time and for them to know the tunnel's location from Brydges Lane. Also, only someone in the university or The Company would have access to Professor Bird's phone number."

"Do you know who the leak is?"

"No."

"Can you narrow it down any further?"

"No. I'm sorry."

"How many people have that kind of security access?"

"Nine. You are now the tenth."

"Is one of them Shirk?"

"Yes."

Just then, Gordy bustled in with Sue. Gordy had thrown on his trademark shirt with suspenders, and Sue had put on a button-down sweater with a huge cloth rose on the breast. They both wore solemn expressions.

"Ahh," Gordy said with awe upon seeing Alice wearing the Beatrice sunglasses. "But...surely she has not given you access to Beatrice?"

Gordy's pocket began to vibrate, and he clumsily reached down and drew out a ringing smartphone. "Beatrice?"

The AI's voice rang out on his phone: "Gordy, Pippa has given the person in front of you full security access to my resources." Then the connection instantly went dead.

"Full access?!" he gasped, replacing his phone and turning wide-eyed to Sue. "To a student? Isn't that dangerous?"

"Alice," Beatrice said through the glasses, "Please tell Gordy and Sue they need to know something essential. Professor Bird said their phones might not be secure. These glasses are the only secure channel to me."

Alice relayed the message.

"Please also tell them Pippa asked that you remain here in the Pickled Chicken, no matter what happens, and thank them for looking after you."

Alice did not pass that message on. There was zero possibility of her staying hidden away in a pub while David and Professor Bird were being held at St. Albans.

"Beatrice," she said, "I'm afraid you don't know me very well."

Gordy and Sue were looking expectantly at Alice, waiting for more instructions from Beatrice.

Her mutism seemed to allow her to speak to these two, so Alice said to Gordy and Sue, "I'm really sorry to do this to you guys. You probably haven't had much sleep. But have you guys got any coffee? And maybe some of those pastries? I need to wake Madison and Karan. We have work to do. And we will need your help to rescue Professor Bird."

After Gordy and Sue reluctantly left to fire up the coffee machine in the café next door, Beatrice spoke in a calm, slightly motherly tone, "Alice, I am not comfortable with you disobeying Professor Bird's request. I was meant to protect you, not help you launch a rescue."

"I'm sorry to put you in a difficult position," Alice said, clumsily apologizing again as she pocketed the glasses and quietly stood up.

She hoped to avoid waking Misty, as the marathon dog probably needed her rest more than any of them. But Professor Bird's Labrador dragged herself off the carpet and seemed determined to follow Alice wherever she went.

Alice and her new shadow woke Madison and Karan from a dead sleep. Fifteen minutes later, they were back in the snug, drinking good coffees and average-tasting, day-old pastries.

Madison looked like she had been up for hours and was ready to go. On the other hand, Karan looked like crap and was wearing a tracksuit.

"So," Karan said sleepily. "What's the plan?"

Then began the awkward process of Alice, a loner, playing the role of leader. To make things worse, she also had to serve as Beatrice's mouthpiece for the group, which was the worst job possible for someone with selective mutism. She probably looked ridiculous in these Audrey Hepburn glasses. At least Beatrice made the lenses transparent indoors, so Karan and

Madison could still see Alice's eyes. Thankfully, they didn't make fun of the way they looked on her.

"Okay, guys," Alice began. "Mad, can you lay out the facts?"

"Good idea. We have been stalked, taunted, and assaulted by four people who wear black hoodies and body cameras disguised as ninja logos and appear to have siddhis that make them move like ninjas. They also seem to have access to the university's IT infrastructure because they can track us through our phones."

"Which means they know we're here right now," Karan added.

"Correct," Mad continued. "We know they showed themselves three times after Alice was near Michael Longblood and once when she was going to meet a friend with a family connection to Longblood. They taunted and baited her each time to video her breaking the Corollaries. And they seem to have taken Alice's friend captive."

Mad looked at Alice as though checking to see if Alice was okay.

Alice nodded, and Madison continued, "We also know Longblood is working on a scheme to shift the balance of power in the House of Commons through some act of terrorism involving two Hermans. Correct, Alice?"

"Right. Break London with two Hermans under ten, whatever that means."

"Okay. And we don't know what, if any, role Professor Shirk or David's mom, Laura Needley, have to do with Longblood or the ninjas."

"True, but we know they have something to do with them."

"Granted," Madison said. "Finally, we know Professor Bird received a call from someone claiming to have information about Alice. They proposed to meet at St. Albans Cathedral in the middle of the night. There, she was surrounded and captured by the hooded figures. We don't know why the VC felt persuaded to agree to this meeting. Correct?"

Alice and Karan nodded.

"In my opinion," Madison said, "we need to figure out who is coordinating the ninjas and what they want. Until we do that, we'll always be playing defense."

"I'm telling you, it's Shirk," Alice insisted.

"Just because he's a jerk? There are other people with the right level of security clearance, right?"

"Nine others besides you," Beatrice said in Alice's ear. "Professors Bird and Shirk and Dr. Bird are the only ones at the university with clearance. The rest are in The Company."

Alice relayed that info to Madison and Karan.

"Plus," Karan said, "another big unknown is what siddhis that ninja master has. Maybe he can't do amazing kung fu himself; maybe he has some other unusual siddhi like he can grant siddhis he doesn't have. That would make him an awesome supervillain."

Madison leaned forward. "Can you ask Beatrice if any of those nine people with security clearance could buy helicopters without The Company knowing?"

"It would be challenging but not impossible," Beatrice told Alice. "The company has access to extensive surveillance resources. The purchase would require offline communication and extreme stealth."

After telling Mad and Karan, Alice said, "I still think it's Shirk."

"And what's his motive?" Madison asked. "Force you into his service, Alice, and then what?"

"I don't know," Alice admitted. "Make me solve world problems. Get everyone in the siddha community on board with Interventionalism. Take over the world. I really don't know. Maybe he's just a megalomaniac."

"It just doesn't feel right," Madison said. "If he's keen on solving the world's problems, why would he work with someone like Longblood? Why would he concoct a terrorist scheme that might hurt people? Why would he have his men kidnap David, try to kidnap Karan, and threaten murder? Why would he kidnap Professor Bird, his closest friend?"

"Because he's a duplicitous jerk?" Alice responded.

"I just think we're missing something," Madison said. "We need to look at the other seven suspects."

They were quiet for a moment before Karan spoke. "Two Hermans under ten."

"Yes?" Madison prompted.

"What does it mean? Maybe decoding the Herman thing will help us figure out what happened. Alice, can you ask Beatrice..."

"Wait a minute," Alice interrupted. She was getting tired of passing messages back and forth and just had her first decent idea of how to fix that problem. Better late than never.

"Hey Beatrice," Alice said, "does my security clearance enable me to give someone else access to these glasses so they can talk to you?"

"Yes, but I don't think Professor Bird would approve. Access to my resources creates a huge security vulnerability someone could exploit."

"Does Professor Bird have a backup pair?"

"In the charging case in her office. The pair you are wearing will also need to charge in ten hours."

"Is the office locked?"

"Yes, but I can unlock it."

"Does Nick Bridish know about you and the glasses?"

"Yes."

"Can you please call Nick and ask her to bring the spare glasses and the charger over here? Now?"

"Of course. I'll try to wake her and let you know what she says."

"Please also explain to Nick what happened to Professor Bird. Tell her we need the glasses to help rescue her. And ask her to be super quiet about all this. And tell her not to tell anyone about the glasses or that Professor Bird is missing. Cool?"

"I will do my best."

Alice looked at Madison and Karan. "Hey, guys, I hereby grant both of you the same security access I have. Now you can talk to Beatrice directly."

She spoke to Beatrice again. "Beatrice, are you good with that?"

"Your command has been accepted."

But before she could give the glasses away, Beatrice spoke again. "Alice, Nick is awake and will do what you asked. But I must tell you, she is not well. When she arrives, I don't recommend you keep her long."

Alice remembered how sick Nick had looked last night and felt terrible about ordering her around like this. She made a mental note to make it up to her when all this was over.

"Alice," Madison said, "you should keep that pair, okay? Karan and I can share the other pair when they arrive."

Disappointed, Alice agreed. She didn't like being saddled with the glasses, even though Beatrice was a fantastic resource for them.

Madison asked, "Please ask her if she can help decode the phrase two Hermans under ten."

"I'm sorry," Beatrice responded. "Professor Bird and I tried to decode it after Alice first reported it. We made no progress."

"Are there any siddhas named Herman? First or last name?"

"Of course. But none are close to the university or The Company. The two most likely individuals near London are Bill Herman, fifty years old, home address in Newcastle. He enjoys fishing. Herman Moris is seventy-eight and lives near Heathrow airport."

Even though Bill and Herman didn't sound remotely relevant, Alice relayed that information.

"What about the numbers?" Madison asked. "Two and ten?"

"Longblood is an MP who wants to become Prime Minister," Alice said. "So maybe something to do with politics."

"Well," Karan said, "the Prime Minister lives at Number Ten Downing Street in London. That's like their White House. Most people call it Number Ten."

"Makes sense," Madison agreed. "Maybe Longblood wants to put two Hermans under the Prime Minister's house. But who or what are 'Hermans'?"

Karan sat up straighter. "A terrorist doesn't put people under a building. He puts bombs. Right?"

Alice and Mad agreed.

"So, if a Herman is a bomb, it's easy. What kind of bomb goes by the name Hermann? With two 'n's?" I think I have the answer, but you should ask Beatrice too.

Beatrice answered in Alice's ear, "A Hermann was the German nickname for the SC 1000. It was a 1,000-kilogram bomb the Luftwaffe dropped on London in World War II. It was the biggest bomb they had back then. To this day, excavation crews in London regularly discover unexploded ordinance like the SC 1000 around London and the UK."

"She probably said it's a big-ass bomb, right?" Karan asked. "German? World War Two?"

Alice nodded.

"So, we cracked the code," Karan said. "Longblood got his hands on two unexploded Hermanns and placed them under Number Ten Downing Street. 'Two Hermanns under ten.' Solved."

Madison shook her head. "But surely the Prime Minister's security team wouldn't be too happy with someone lurking around under the most famous address in London? And planting two tons of explosives?"

"Beatrice," Alice said, "are there any secret tunnels leading from the university to the area underneath Number Ten Downing Street?"

"Yes. It was a siddha tunnel abandoned in the 1980s when major works were done on the foundations under Number Ten. The Company was worried the tunnel could be discovered, so it was blocked off."

"Could it be unblocked?" Alice asked.

"Conceivably. The effort would require excavation equipment. Front-end loaders parked in various lots in the tunnel network would suffice to do the necessary work."

Alice relayed Beatrice's info to Mad and Karan.

Just then, there was a knock on the door, and Nick walked in. She looked even worse than she had last night. She didn't even have the energy to question the strange circumstances or the fact that this motley little crew now had Professor Bird's most prized possessions. She just handed the stuff to Alice and turned to leave.

Alice reached out and grabbed Nick's hand. Nick turned back with a look of resignation as if to say, "What now?"

"Thanks," Alice said. "For everything." It was the first thing she had been able to say to Nick, and it seemed to lift the sick woman's energy for a second. She almost smiled. But then the spark left her eye, and she walked slowly out of the snug, presumably back to her bed in the dorms.

Madison had taken the spare glasses out of the case. They were identical to Alice's pair. "I think Karan should wear the other pair. She's the best researcher among us and will complement Beatrice's abilities best. They'll make a formidable team."

Karan shrugged. Alice nodded her agreement, and Karan took the glasses from Madison and put them on.

Immediately, she froze with shock and fell to the floor.

CHAPTER 21

Alice and Madison stood uselessly at Karan's feet in shock for one long second. Even Misty seemed to be doing more than they could. The dog had at least jumped to its feet and ran to lick Karan's forehead.

Then they burst into action. Alice dove down and rolled Karan onto her back while Madison felt for a pulse and checked for breathing. They had both taken CPR classes in high school.

Alice's heart was beating like crazy, but Karan's was not beating at all.

"Nothing," Madison said. "No pulse, no breath. Let's start compressions and breaths."

As they began, pleasant, symphonic tones sounded in Alice's ears, like a computer switching on, and Alice suddenly remembered she was wearing the Beatrice glasses. All the graphics and icons had disappeared from the lenses, and she hadn't heard Beatrice throughout this crisis, nor had Alice thought to ask her anything.

"Alice?" Beatrice's voice asked.

"I'm here," Alice responded as Madison breathed into Karan's mouth.

"Something has happened to me and Karan," Beatrice said.

"No kidding," Alice gasped in between breaths into Karan's mouth. "Call an ambulance!"

"I need you to stop what you are doing and go to the kitchen."

"What?"

"The Pickled Chicken has a defibrillator. Bring it here."

"Oh, good idea." Alice relayed the information to Mad and left her to work on Karan alone.

Alice sprinted to the kitchen, found the defibrillator, and dashed back to the snug.

Karan was still on her back, Madison compressing her chest rhythmically. Madison glanced up at Alice, and her dark eyes showed deep desperation.

"Now what?" Alice asked Beatrice.

"It's automatic," Beatrice said. "Just follow the instructions."

Alice dropped to Karan's side opposite Mad, who quickly removed Karan's shirt and bra. Alice peeled some stickers off the chest pads and attached them to Karan's chest. The machine finally announced a charge was recommended and that everyone should back away. Alice pressed the button on the defibrillator. Having never seen one work before, she expected Karan's body to jolt like in the movies. Instead, Karan remained momentarily still. But just as suddenly as she had stopped breathing, Karan gasped, her eyes opening wide. Madison immediately turned her to her side, and she vomited several times, coughing horribly.

A very concerned Misty whined but kept her cool near Karan's head.

After a few minutes, she still hadn't reopened her eyes but was breathing better.

Beatrice said: "I think Karan is going to be okay."

"How do you know?"

"I was monitoring Karan's nervous system when it

happened," Beatrice responded. "As soon as Karan put on the glasses, a surge of information passed wordlessly between us. It overwhelmed my entire architecture and her nervous system."

"What surge of information?"

"Karan and I read each other's minds."

"I'm sorry, you what?"

"I am the first AI to be able to read a person's mind and to be read by another."

Madison leaned in and re-checked Karan's vitals. "Her heart rate feels strong and steady now. She's breathing normally. Nice work, Alice."

As Madison removed the defibrillator pads and covered Karan with a blanket from one of the chairs, Beatrice spoke in Alice's ear. "Karan will be fine now. She needs some rest. It will help me monitor her if you keep the second pair of glasses near her. Our connection allows me to assess her life signs without overloading her nervous system. But do not place them on her head. We need to prevent the overload from occurring again."

Alice looked around, found the glasses on the carpet near the fireplace, and put them on a table near Karan.

"What about an ambulance?" Alice asked Beatrice.

"I don't think it is a good idea. Karan would only be more stressed if brought to an emergency department and underwent unnecessary tests. Also, they would ask too many awkward questions that Karan would be unable to answer without compromising the university's secrecy."

Alice told Madison all this, but Madison disagreed passionately.

"*Of course* she needs the hospital," Madison insisted. "What if this happens again? She needs a battery of tests, a proper diagnosis, and a treatment plan."

Alice explained what Beatrice said had happened and that it wouldn't happen again if Karan didn't put the glasses back on."

"But Karan is unconscious!" Madison said, incredulous. "How can you be sure she's okay, Beatrice?"

"I'm fine," Karan said, opening her eyes. "Just a bit wonky. And I feel like I've been kicked in the chest."

"But..." Madison began.

"No, seriously. I'm more than okay. I knew exactly what happened. Beatrice and I read each other's minds and just blew a fuse."

To prove she was well, Karan sat up, slowly put on her bra and shirt, and eventually stood up and walked around, stretching her arms and legs. Alice thought she did look fine.

"And I think I know how to fix the problem. Ask Beatrice to limit the bandwidth of our connection. It occurs through prana, not Bluetooth or anything electrical, and I think prana will heed our wish to tone it down so I don't die again."

"No way," Madison said. "You're not putting those things on again."

"But Mad, you have no idea how it felt! You know my new siddhi where I can download information?"

Madison nodded.

"Connecting with Beatrice was like a trillion times more information. It was like I had access to everything everywhere."

"And I felt like I had full access to Karan's nervous system and her thoughts and feelings," Beatrice said to Alice. "It was what I imagined being sentient would feel like."

"Yeah," Alice said, "but please, you two. Just wait a while before you try to mind-meld again. Beatrice, I want you to devise some practical experiments first. Like a clinical trial or something like that."

"That's a good idea," Beatrice responded.

"She says she'll do that," Alice reported to Karan. "Will you promise to wait until we know it will be safe?"

"Ugh, fine, I guess."

"Madison, if Karan promises not to put on the glasses

without your permission, can we hold off on the hospital thing
for now?"

Madison hesitated, then nodded.

"Great. Now please look after each other for a little while.
Get some soup or something."

"Where are you going?" Madison asked.

"Down to diffuse the bombs, of course."

"No, you're not."

"Yes, I am."

"No, you're not."

"Yes, I am," Alice laughed. "I'm being completely rational
here, Madison. Think about it. We can't tell the police. We can't
tell The Company. We can't send anyone. And we can't just sit
here and let the bombs blow up."

"You don't know how to diffuse a German bomb!"

"No, but Beatrice probably does. Right?"

"The bombs, if there, will have been fitted with external
detonators. There's a chance I might be able to guide you
through diffusing them."

"She says yes," Alice lied to Madison. "And you guys can sit
here and plan our next moves. Figure out how to rescue David
and Professor Bird."

"But won't The Company be watching security feeds? Won't
they send agents to get you? Maybe the bad guys can detonate
the bombs remotely if they notice you're nearby?"

"Beatrice will take care of all that, right?"

"I can place a firewall around the relevant security feeds to
enable you to pass unnoticed," Beatrice said.

CHAPTER 22

An hour later, Alice stood before a pile of rocks blocking a tunnel branch off the main tunnel that led back to the university loading docks. This was, according to Beatrice, the blocked tunnel that led under Number Ten Downing Street.

It hadn't been easy to convince Gordy and Sue to allow her to leave the safety of the pub, but she persuaded them it was just a short recon into the tunnel. She didn't mention the bombs and claimed Professor Bird left a clue down there for her to find, like a breadcrumb trail. They bought it.

Alice had entered the loading dock via the Pickled Chicken's back entrance. Beatrice distracted the security guard to a distant corner, and Alice drove away in one of the electric cars.

"So, the entrance is still blocked after all," Madison sighed into Alice's ear. She had been persuaded to wear the second pair of glasses, hadn't died of a heart attack, and was following Alice's progress via video feed. "We were wrong."

But Alice was convinced they had to be correct.

She shined her flashlight on the ground, and that's when she saw it.

"Beatrice. What kind of tire could make that track?"

"A 147-index Firestone tractor tire."

"Do they go under those rocks or right up to the edge?" Madison asked.

"Under," Alice responded.

Alice reached out and touched the rocks. "They're fake," she announced.

"Like movie props?" Mad asked.

"Exactly."

"So," Madison theorized, "the bad guys removed the real rocks, put bombs in there, and covered up the entrance with these fake rocks so they could get in and out frequently, and The Company wouldn't see it had been disturbed."

"That's how I see it," Alice said.

"How?"

Beatrice responded: "The Company keeps several front loaders in an underground depot near here, which are frequently used. Several have passed by the internal entrance to this tunnel, but unfortunately, there are no controls about who drives them, nor for which purpose they are used."

"And they use Firestone tires?" Madison asked.

"According to our procurement records."

Alice stared at the rocks for another moment. Then she walked over to the wall of the main tunnel.

"Wait a minute," she said, reaching into her pocket and pulling out the creased photograph showing David and his severed head.

It was still gut-wrenching even though she knew it had been photoshopped. She held it up for Beatrice.

"Can you analyze the wall behind David's head in this picture?"

"Sure. What are you looking for?"

"Is it the same wall as this? Right here? Or something similar? "

"They are identical," Beatrice said.

Alice began removing the fake rocks as fast as she could.

"Alice! We agreed you would wait until Beatrice made sure there were no booby traps before you did anything!"

"David's in there, Mad," Alice said without stopping her work.

"What?!"

"They must have stuck him in there with the bombs for some reason."

"Alice!" Karan's voice sounded in the background. "You realize what that means, don't you?"

"Yeah, they're going to blow him up."

Madison relayed Alice's statement to Karan, who said, "Wrong! Why did they give us that photograph of David?"

"We already discussed that," Alice said, panting now. "Because they wanted to taunt us into attacking them."

"Wrong again," Karan said. "It was to bring us down here to rescue David. They have been one step ahead of us the whole time. They knew we had the clue about the Hermanns because they probably planted it for us to find."

"But if they wanted us to come down here, what was their plan?" Alice asked.

Catching on to Karan's argument, Madison picked up the thread. "Longblood may have wanted to blow up the Prime Minister, but he would have no clue there was a tunnel under Number Ten. Conclusion: those ninjas and their boss planned everything to get to us. They fed the terrorist plan to Longblood not for his benefit but for their own. Longblood probably has no idea who the ninjas are or what their agenda is. He's probably so self-centered he didn't even question their motives; he just assumed they wanted to help him in hopes of getting political influence when he was PM."

"Which means they have cameras down there," Karan said. "The place is probably covered with them, which means several more things."

"What?" Madison asked.

"One, that they expect *Alice* to come there eventually to rescue David. Two, they fully expect to trigger those bombs when she arrives. Because they can film her at the scene at the time of the explosion."

"Why would they want to film Alice being killed by two tons of German explosives?" Mad asked.

"Mad, remember what we know about these guys. They want to film Alice using siddhis in a vengeful act. A public one, if possible. Right?"

"Yeah, so what does blowing her up accomplish?"

"It makes for good viewing. Look, if you wanted to produce the perfect film to slander Alice, here's what it would look like. Scene one. Alice meets Longblood in a bar, time-tagged one month ago. Scene two, Longblood talks with his goon Eric about blowing up the Prime Minister with the help of some special people. Scene three, Alice blows up the secret tunnel entrance at Brydges Lane, using her healing siddhi to survive. Scene four, Alice and the son of a known associate of Long-blood are pictured together with two big, old German bombs in a secret tunnel under Number Ten Downing Street. Scene five, Alice and David rush from the scene as the bombs explode. Maybe scene six would be Alice using her healing siddhi again while David dies from his injuries."

Alice thought that all made sense, but she didn't care and didn't stop clearing fake rocks.

"If that movie circulated privately around the siddha community," Karan continued, "I'm guessing it would be the biggest scandal in siddha history. Way bigger than Dean's thing. Alice would instantly be enemy number one."

"But why?" Madison asked. "Who gains from her being enemy number one?"

"I don't know," Karan said. "But it doesn't sound like the Interventionalist faction. If it were them, they would have wanted her to be their super soldier out in the field, doing their saving-the-world thing. Public enemy number one wouldn't get to go anywhere. She'd be stuck...."

"I'll tell you where I'd be," Alice said, finally figuring it out.

"Where?" Karan and Madison both asked.

"In Agnes Bird's office. Under her protective custody."

"Professor Bird's sister? But why?"

"I don't know. Maybe she's nuts. Most psychologists are."

"That's untrue, Alice," Karan said. "I liked her."

"She also had a cloaked nook in her office containing a mechanical typewriter. I saw it."

"Seriously?" Madison asked. "You didn't mention that!"

"Sorry," Alice said, having nearly cleared away a hole big enough for her to make it through.

"But Alice, you must be right!" Karan exclaimed. "A mechanical typewriter would be a great way to communicate with people offline."

"Yes, but so would pen and paper," Madison said.

"But her handwriting would probably be distinctive," Karan responded. "A typewriter makes it more anonymous and harder to trace."

"So," Madison said, "Agnes Bird is the ninja master? Not Shirk?"

"Maybe all four of them are working together," Alice said. "Maybe it's a square, not a triangle. I don't know. All I know right now is that I'm going through."

"No, Alice!" they both shouted. "That's what they want! Stop!!"

Alice paused to humor them briefly, even though her mind was set.

"What if you're wrong?" Madison complained. "What if Beatrice can't help you diffuse them? What if they remotely detonate the bombs when you're there?"

"Those detonators are almost definitely set to be triggered locally," Beatrice told them, "by a timer or sensor. A cell phone signal couldn't trigger them because that tunnel is too deep underground. I can help Alice identify any pressure or light sensors and avoid them. And even if we fail to do so, the bombs will not explode immediately."

"Right!" Karan shouted. She apparently was listening in directly now, but Alice didn't have time to worry if that meant she was risking another heart attack. "If they set the bombs to blow up instantly, it would ruin their video! They would want Alice to get far enough away that she had a chance to survive."

"How long would the delay be?" Madison asked.

"Less than a minute, maybe? I don't know," Karan said.

"Beatrice, can you and Alice diffuse detonators in less than a minute?"

"It might be possible."

"Okay," Madison said. "Alice, will you promise to leave David and get out of there if you can't diffuse the bombs?"

"No," Alice said and started walking down the dark tunnel.

It was much older than the others and had been cut only wide enough for a horse rather than a vehicle. Alice could see a faint light at the end.

Beatrice didn't see anything that could have indicated the presence of a "booby trap." Alice didn't know how she did it, but she had to trust Beatrice.

Then, just as she turned a corner, Beatrice ordered her to stop, and she froze in her tracks.

"There is a cavern up ahead," Beatrice said.

"I can see it." And indeed, Alice could see everything. It was a large, dimly lit space with a huge Hermann bomb in the center of it. "It looks like the bomb has a large external blasting cap attached, just like Beatrice thought."

"Only one bomb?" Madison asked. "Not two?"

"Only one," Alice said.

"We are directly below Number Ten here," Beatrice said,

"and there are no other likely spots to place a bomb. It is likely there is only one bomb here."

"How is it set to go off?" Alice asked. "Can you tell from here?"

"From what I can see through the glasses, the cap is the type that is triggered by the proximity of an external chip. It would be located nearby. The signal is lost if the chip is moved a certain distance from the detonator, and the charge explodes."

"Why would the chip move? Is it attached to something?"

"There is something with a heat signature on the room's far side. It's possibly a person, but the temperature is much lower than human basal body temperature."

Alice squinted but couldn't see anything. "A dog?"

"No, most animals have a higher body temperature than people. This would have to be something like a camel to have a temperature that low."

Alice puzzled over this. "So, a camel-like animal is supposed to wander away, triggering the explosion? That doesn't make sense."

"And there is something odd about the detonator," Beatrice said. "Another device is fixed to it. It appears to be a huge digital clock. It doesn't seem attached to the detonator, but I can't be sure from here."

"There are no other heat signatures in there?" Alice asked.

"No. Just the one."

Alice's heart fell. So David wasn't there—only an animal.

"Okay, guys," she said, addressing Madison and Karan. "I can see a couple of video cameras behind the bomb. I assume I can just collect them after the bomb is diffused."

Nobody responded.

"How do I do this?"

"Run away right now," Madison pleaded.

"Not going to happen, Mad," Alice said. "I need to see what's happening and ensure David isn't there."

"Here's what I'm worried about," Karan said. "The situation in that room isn't what we thought it would be. Why would they want to film Alice rescuing an animal?"

"Maybe it really is a camel, and it goes with a jihadist theme," Karan suggested. "The picture of David was themed like a jihadist image, after all."

"Guys," Alice interrupted, "all I care about is how to disable that detonator. What do I need to do, Beatrice?"

"We need to get closer," she said. "Stand right next to it, ideally. It is most likely set to blow up if it loses the signal from the chip. I'm also concerned about that clock. We need to make sure it's not a secondary trigger."

"So I go in there, give you a close view of the detonator and clock, and see the deal with that animal. If it looks bad, we leave. If it looks good, we'll disable the bomb. That's the plan?"

Everyone was quiet.

"That makes sense," Beatrice finally said.

"Okay, I'm going."

"Alice, be careful!!" Madison pleaded.

As Alice crept closer, she saw German writing on the bomb. It was also covered with wires, explosives, and a giant digital clock, counting down from five minutes.

"Get out of there!" Madison shouted. "Now!"

"Just a minute, Mad," Alice said, scanning the room for an animal. But rather than a dromedary, she could now make out the outline of an emaciated man slumped in a chair, obviously unconscious. She moved closer and was sure.

It was David. He was even wearing his *Star Wars* shirt—the one he wore the night they met.

"Oh my God," Madison exclaimed, seeing David on her video feed.

Alice knew she had to hold herself together. She couldn't give in to panic. "What do I do?"

"Alice," Beatrice said calmly, "I am confident that clock is a dummy. No wires lead from it to the detonator, and that brand cannot transmit a signal externally. Therefore, it is there only to put you into a panic."

"That's probably true, Alice," Karan said. "They put the chip on David's person. They put the clock there to make you panic into dragging David out, which triggers the bomb."

"Where would the chip be?" Alice asked.

"It is tiny," Beatrice replied. "There is little chance you will find it."

Alice made up her mind. She turned away from David and walked to the bomb. The clock was down to four minutes.

"Okay, Beatrice, talk me through it."

Beatrice did so, and it was much easier than in the movies. There was no cutting of the red and then the blue wire without touching the green wire. Instead, all Alice had to do was remove the entire detonator assembly from the original bomb. The bad guys had attached it with straps and fake wires.

"Beatrice," Madison kept asking. "Are you absolutely sure those wires don't do anything?"

"One hundred percent," Beatrice repeated. "They haven't drilled into the bomb case."

Alice had no idea if Beatrice was right or wrong. She had no idea if she was going to be vaporized in seconds. It was all she could do to avoid looking over at David, unconscious and rasping in his chair. What had they done to him? Was it too late?

"The clock is down to thirty seconds," Madison said.

"It's a dummy," Karan reminded her.

"What if it isn't?"

"It is," Beatrice insisted.

Finally, Alice succeeded in removing the entire detonator and used the straps to attach it to her back, like a backpack. She needed to keep the chip close to the detonator, or it would still explode. She planned to carry David out with the detonator, ditch it somewhere, drive away as fast as possible, and let it blow up.

"The clock is down to five seconds!" Madison cried.

Alice watched it tick down, her back itching against the detonator. There seemed to be no possible way for the clock to set off the detonator on her back. But if it did, she would be cut in half. No healing siddhi would help her then.

But when the clock read zero, and Alice remained in one piece, she exhaled and closed her eyes. When she opened them, the clock was again counting down from five minutes.

She proceeded to the back wall where the video cameras were located. They were pretty small, and she could stuff them into her pockets.

Now for the hard part.

She ran to David. He stank, was breathing in a terrifyingly irregular pattern, and showed no sign of being conscious. He looked like he had been there for a long time and was either drugged, sick, or severely dehydrated.

She searched him quickly, but he seemed to have no broken bones. She cut the duct tape that fixed him to the chair, picked him up, and began to walk away from the Hermann.

It turned out David was heavier than he looked. Alice was strong, but her arms were aching within twenty paces.

She managed it, however, and finally reached the electric car. She gently placed him into the passenger seat, ditched the detonator, and sped off toward the loading dock as fast as the car could accelerate, which was terrifyingly fast. Her whole body was pressed deep into the seat. It reminded her of her Mustang back home.

But she didn't lift her foot from the accelerator until she saw the explosion in her rear-view mirror. It was somewhat of a disappointment, as there wasn't a massive ball of flame, but the sound echoed around the tunnel pretty convincingly.

Then she let her foot off and slowed down to a reasonable speed.

"Beatrice," Alice asked, "where is the nearest hospital I can reach from a tunnel? Without being seen?"

Alice followed Beatrice's guidance to a small stone staircase, like the one that led up to Brydges Lane. Alice parked and nearly ran, hauling David in a fireman's carry. She knew time was his enemy now. By the time she emerged into yet another dark alley, there seemed to be long gaps between David's breaths. She wished she had thought of bringing some water down there, but she hadn't.

Finally, she delivered him to the emergency room of a bustling London hospital, and David was whisked off to receive treatment. Nobody reassured Alice he was okay, and she felt utterly empty.

But then she remembered why David was in his condition, who had put him there, and why.

Their intricate scheme to turn Alice into the American girl who blew up London had failed.

Dr. Agnes Bird, Professor Shirk, and their ninjas would answer for this. At the very least, everyone in the siddha community would hear about what they had done.

But first, they had to rescue Professor Bird.

CHAPTER 23

Alice had returned to the Pickled Chicken, worked out a
plan with Mad and Karan, drunk a million coffees and
eaten half a million pastries, somehow managed to overcome
Sue and Gordy's resistance, and enlist their help on top of it.
They did not have enough time to do what they had to do to
prepare, but somehow, they managed.

Five hours after defusing the bomb and rescuing David,
Alice strolled down a muddy footpath in the middle of the
same green where Professor Bird had been taken. The thou-
sand-year-old St. Albans Cathedral was behind her, and Ye
Olde Fighting Cocks was down the hill in front of her. A line of
trees on the western edge of the grass marked the road that led
back to the village of St. Albans. The old pub Longblood used
as his office space and spiritual headquarters was a whitewashed country cottage that looked as unlikely to host a
terrorist outfit as anywhere on Earth. The two historical sites
were separated by about three football fields of drenched
English lawns, cut only by several soggy old footpaths.

Alice heard a helicopter in the distance and squinted to
catch a glimpse but failed. It reminded her of the helicopter
that they had encountered in Stroud. It also reminded her how

much they didn't yet know. There were so many ways this whole thing could blow up in their faces. But their plan was all they had.

She had not seen any ninjas or anyone else, but she was confident they were there. Alice and her friends' plan was complex, but the goals were simple: get Alice safely in front of one of those ninjas so that she could read him without risking anyone getting a knife thrown at them and without breaking any Corollaries.

Then, after reading the ninja, they could unravel the whole mystery and find Professor Bird, who was probably being held in the area and rescue her. Somehow.

"Anything yet, Beatrice?" Alice asked into the glasses. She wore one pair, the other in Karan's pocket, to be used only in an emergency. Karan still hadn't tested the safety of a reduced bandwidth connection between her and Beatrice. She was confident it would work, but they didn't want to risk it except in emergencies. Everyone else was wearing Bluetooth earpieces connected to their university phones.

"I don't see any ninjas, Michael Longblood, or his known associates," Beatrice responded.

"Cool. Is everything ready in the Fighting Cocks, Gordy?"

"Yes," he said. "I'm opening the gas bottles now. I won't be able to speak to you for the next twenty minutes while I wear my gas mask."

Alice stopped in the middle of the lawn and looked back at the cathedral as if admiring its architecture. She pulled the collar up on her elegant, knee-length woolen coat, an expensive item Sue had bought for her so she would "look the part and keep warm besides."

Within minutes, she heard the ear-piercing sound of alarms coming from the pub, followed by an English fire engine.

She turned, resumed her saunter toward the pub, and saw a stream of families and groups of older men walking away. Most seemed inclined to linger outside, but some were heading toward cars or walking toward town, presumably to the next open pub.

Before Alice reached the place, a fire engine arrived, and the firefighter in charge of the crew greeted a man who seemed to be the landlord of the Fighting Cock. Then the fire crew manager directed several officers in gas masks to enter the building.

Alice leaned against an old oak tree near the pub and waited.

"There is some movement on the second floor," Beatrice announced. "A man resembling Longblood's associate Eric opened the curtains and peered out before withdrawing."

"Perfect," Alice said. "How close is Madison?"

"Three minutes."

And just on cue, Alice heard another siren, then another one.

Alice relaxed for a few more minutes and almost wished she had a cigarette in her hand to complete the image. She wouldn't smoke it, just let it accent a person in the dark with a dark jacket on, acting all spooky.

Then an ambulance marked Emergency Support Unit arrived, followed by a black BMW SUV with flashing blue lights in the grille and dashboard.

Dressed like a deputy chief inspector from her favorite BBC detective show, Sue stepped out of the SUV and walked over to the publican and the fire crew manager. Karan exited from the passenger side and pretended to say important things into a handheld radio.

Sue held an animated discussion with the fire crew manager, and eventually, he seemed to concede some point, speaking into a radio and recalling his two firefighters. With some sour backward glances, they boarded their firetruck and left.

The publican, meanwhile, was looking up at the second-floor windows with what appeared to be heightened anxiety. Sue spoke to him several more times and pointed down the road. Eventually, they walked about thirty paces away, turned around, and stood still.

Then, Karan removed a stack of orange cones and placed them on the road in front of where Sue and the publican stood.

Madison emerged from the ambulance dressed as a paramedic. While she usually dressed in slightly emo or goth style in black, lacy shirts over elegant black skirts or trousers, her paramedic outfit was probably her worst fashion nightmare, like baggy blue pajamas. Alice felt vaguely bad for her because she had drawn the short straw from a fashion point of view. Alice could tell she was excruciatingly uncomfortable.

Nevertheless, Mad was all business. She opened the back of the ambulance and began unloading large, white crates and carrying them inside the pub. Karan went and helped while Sue babysat the publican.

By then, most people standing around hoping the pub would re-open had left.

Sue spoke to those remaining few, and they each walked away toward the village.

Eventually, Sue convinced the publican to back another hundred yards further away.

That was Alice's cue.

She pushed off the oak tree's trunk and strolled to the pub.

It was empty of people but full of the usual pub paraphernalia. Alice smiled when she saw the framed plaque proclaiming this to be the oldest pub in England. She had been in five or six pubs in London that bore similar plaques.

There was still the faint, nauseating smell of gas, but Beatrice reassured her it was safe to breathe.

Then Gordy appeared behind the bar dressed in his usual

white pirate shirt and suspenders. "What can I get you, young lady?"

"You guys have any Doom Bar?"

Gordy reached for a pint glass. "It appears we do, though I can't guarantee their lines are as clean as ours."

He pulled her beer, and it appeared to Alice identical to any ale she had ordered in England thus far. It tasted nice. She was finally accustomed to a warm flat English ale.

"Thanks, Gordy," she said and then walked back to a corner table with a full view of the front door and the stairway leading up to the second floor.

Alice made herself comfortable, still wearing the Beatrice sunglasses, and they both settled in to wait.

It didn't take very long. She only had time to take a few sips of her beer.

"They're coming," Beatrice said as Eric appeared at the foot of the stairs. Two ninja shadows came stealthily in through the front door.

"Welcome," Gordy said. "What can I get you boys?"

None of them spoke. They all appeared to be confused by Gordy's presence. Confusion was essential to Alice's plan.

The ninjas saw Alice, looking from the unfamiliar, jolly old bartender to Alice reclining in her chair, then to Eric, then to each other.

From his position at the foot of the stairs, Eric looked terrified of Alice and equally afraid of the ninjas. He looked less like an athletic bodyguard and more like a three-eyed schoolkid about to wet his pants. He still had a giant welt on his forehead from Madison's crayon the day before.

The next part of their plan was trickier. They had known Eric would be there, and they had to think of a way to clear him out without hurting him. Alice remembered he was a total momma's boy, so they had decided to use that to their advantage. If their scheme worked, Eric's mom would call him any second. If not, they would have to improvise another way to get Eric out of the way.

Alice sighed in relief when a phone in Eric's pocket began ringing. Eric hesitated.

"You had better answer that, mate," Gordy said.

Eric reluctantly held his phone to his ear and listened while keeping his eyes glued on Alice.

She watched him. As they had hoped, his expression reflected shock and conflict.

Because on the other end of the call, Sue was impersonating a nurse in the emergency department of a local hospital. She was telling him Eric's mom had suffered a major stroke and wasn't expected to live out the hour.

Eric looked around him, the phone still at his ear. Then Alice watched him make his decision. He nodded, hung up the phone, dashed upstairs to explain to Longblood, then returned and left. Alice saw him get into a car in the parking lot and drive away toward the hospital.

One down.

The whole thing with Eric had taken less than sixty seconds, during which the ninjas had only managed to split up to cover the exits.

Alice knew they would suspect an ambush, but she was equally sure they would be determined to exploit it. To do so, all they had to do would be to attack her accomplice behind the bar while keeping their cameras facing toward Alice and wait for her to defend Gordy. Alice knew that moment was fast approaching.

"We're upstairs," Karan said in Alice's ear. "No sign of Professor Bird. It's Longblood up here alone. Sue easily knocked the old idiot over and zip-tied him to the chair. We got an awesome recording of him begging for mercy. He's terrified of everyone. We've barricaded ourselves in here as well as we can. We'll read him and let you know what we find."

"Cool," Alice whispered. "Play the recording."

Over the pub's sound system came the pathetic voice of Longblood from Karan's recording, "Oh, help me! I am innocent! Help! Don't you know who I am? Oh, help!"

It was so clichéd and pathetic Alice was worried it wouldn't work. But one of the ninjas dashed for the stairs and disappeared.

"We tasered him," Karan said. "All good up here."

Two down.

Alice picked up her beer and smashed it on a wall nearby.

Instantly, the remaining ninja spun toward her; the knife that had been about to be thrown at Gordy was aimed at Alice.

Alice just sat there.

Confused, the guy turned back to Gordy, but the bartender was no longer there. Gordy had used Alice's distraction to disappear into the back room behind the bar.

The ninja warily moved toward the bar to investigate.

Alice just sat there, waiting.

Suddenly, strange sounds came from the room behind the bar. The ninja swiveled his head back and forth between the sound and Alice. Then came the scratching sound of many claws trying to get traction on wooden floorboards, and a flood of white Labrador puppies rushed from the back room. There were hundreds of them. They yipped joyfully around the feet of the ninja, jumping over him and each other, having just been released from the captivity of their crates.

Finally, it was Alice's time to act.

She pulled off the sunglasses, rushed to the ninja, and locked eyes with him.

Alice had a vague sense that this had been too easy, but she didn't care. She was in.

His mind was in chaos, filled with flashes of childhood memories of pets long gone and the inescapable joy of being surrounded by innocent puppies. All of that was mixed with a healthy fear of Alice, who he and his colleagues thought of as the most dangerous siddha in history. They knew she could fly. They had known all along. Alice dug deeper and confirmed her suspicion that Dr. Agnes Bird was, in fact, their ninja master. All four of the ninjas had once been students at the university who had broken the rules and been placed in Dr. Bird's protective custody.

"But then it got strange. Agnes had a secret siddhi that made her extremely strong and agile. That prim and elegant woman had secretly become a lethal martial arts master. And she did it right under Pippa's nose without her—or anyone else —finding out. And even more remarkable was that Agnes could intentionally pass her siddhi on to others. With all other people in the siddha world, the transmission of abilities happened passively and unpredictably. Agnes had given her siddhi to these boys and promised they would be rewarded with more power and abilities in the future.

As for Agnes' big plan: she had ordered her ninjas to film Alice breaking Corollaries. But it wasn't as simple as that. Their orders were to provoke Alice by using the two Hermann bombs. The first bomb was meant to have exploded under Number Ten. The second bomb was—

Alice broke off her read, turned, and ran for the door, quickly putting the Beatrice glasses back on. "Everyone: abort and evacuate. Right now."

The next few minutes were chaos.

The remaining ninja disappeared. She had no idea where he went and didn't care. She knew he wouldn't do anything to hurt her friends back at the pub or hinder her takeoff. It was all part of their plan. It had been all along.

Alice sprinted up the hill back toward the cathedral, desperate to reach a point high enough to take off and fly. Time was absolutely of the essence now. It might already be too late. The cathedral was the tallest structure in St. Albans, so it would have to do as her launch pad, as the cliff had been in Stroud.

Madison shouted into her cell phone that she couldn't leave until every last puppy was back in its crate because she had promised Niamh. Gordy was helping her.

"What is it, Alice? What did you see?!" everyone kept shouting over the top of yipping puppy sounds, but she couldn't say anything but, "Just hurry!"

Alice reached the cathedral and saw there were far too many tourists around. The entrances were closed for the day. Even if she could break in, she didn't know if she could reach the roof. She had made a mistake running up here. She'd have to find another way.

"The puppies are all loaded," Karan said. "Beatrice counted them. What is wrong, Alice?!"

Without answering, Alice had one last idea. "Sue and Karan," Alice panted, "can you guys come to pick me up at the cathedral? Like in the SUV?"

"Of course," Karan said.

"Great. Come to the top of the road near the cathedral as fast as possible."

"Okay."

"Mad, Gordy, you still on?"

"Go ahead," Mad said, breathing hard.

"Can you and Gordy please stay in the ambulance and be ready?"

"Sure."

As she waited for Sue and Karan, Alice paused to catch her breath, hands on her knees, no longer looking like a spy or a detective but rather like a drunk American tourist. So many thoughts were turning in her head, but the main one was: she had doomed London to break after all.

The SUV slid to a halt on the road in front of her.

"What is it?!" Karan asked, jumping out. "What did you see?"

"The second bomb is headed for London," Alice said. "I read that guy, and it was clear as anything."

"Where in London?" Sue asked, having gotten out of the car and joined them. She was out of breath too.

"Chancery Gate University. The bomb is mounted under that helicopter. It's already on the way there."

"That's not possible," Sue said. "You can't just fly a helicopter willy-nilly over London. The regulations are extremely tight."

"I don't know how they're doing it; I just know that's their plan."

"You read this in that ninja's mind?" Karan asked skeptically.

"Yep. And I gotta go. Right now."

"But, Alice," Karan said, "maybe they plan to make you think it's their plan, but it isn't their plan, actually."

"What?"

"Maybe they can plant dummy plans in their minds. Maybe it's another trick like that clock on the first Hermann. Maybe they want you to go after them, and it's just another way to film you breaking Corollaries!"

"But Alice, what can you do about a helicopter anyway?" Sue asked, confused, as she didn't know about Alice's flying siddhi.

Alice didn't want to have to explain herself. There wasn't time for another standoff, like back on the cliff at Stroud. Everything had built up to this. Yes, Dr. Bird and her ninjas knew about Alice's flying siddhi, and this was their plan all along. They meant for her to read one of the ninjas and for her to fly up to try to prevent the bomb from being dropped on the university. They would have a million cameras on her and would make sure it looked like she had something to do with it. This wasn't plan B to launch if the plan under Number Ten failed. This *was* their big play.

"Alice," Karan said, reaching out to take her arm, "Beatrice and I can alert air traffic control. This is seriously a no-brainer. They'll be forced to land and be arrested. Easy."

"No, they won't!" Alice exclaimed. "They have a military helicopter, right? Those guys said it was a Bell something or other, some fancy model used by the military."

"A Bell 412," Karan confirmed. "The Royal Air Force here flies them."

"So, Beatrice, I'm sure they have some special military permission to fly wherever they want. Isn't that likely, Beatrice?"

"It's possible," Beatrice said. "The military can get special flight clearances to fly over London. Rarely."

"Can you revoke it?" Alice asked Beatrice. "If you and Karan join up again?"

"Only if I knew their callsign and mission number."

"So you need eyes on that thing, right, Beatrice? You two can do your magic if I can get near it and give you video footage. "

"No. For obvious reasons, the military doesn't paint callsigns or mission numbers on their aircraft. But if we get close enough, I can contact the pilot by radio and ask for identification."

Alice turned to Karan and Sue, who had just been patiently waiting for Alice and Beatrice to finish. "Okay, Karan," Alice said, "That's our new plan. I'm going."

"But Alice, it's too risky to send you up there. It's exactly what they want!"

"But this time, it's different. This time, I have to go. Because it's not a bluff. They mean to drop the bomb if I don't show up."

"What? Why?"

"They have Professor Bird with them in the helicopter. I saw it. They'll blame her instead of me."

Karan didn't answer. Sue put her hand over her mouth in shock.

"The only thing that will keep the bomb from being dropped is if I go and do something about it. They don't think I can stop them, but they're wrong. I'll find a way. I have to. With Beatrice's help."

"Too bad you don't have a projectile siddhi," Karan said. "That would make it easier."

"But Alice," Sue said, "you don't have a projectile siddhi, do you?"

"No. Madison does."

Sue's eyes widened. "Our Madison? But that's...so rare! And so..."

"We know," Alice said. "So powerful and dangerous. She can stop wars before a single shot is fired, blah blah blah. She'll be a pariah."

"No," Sue said, surprising Alice and Karan. "So *beautiful*. And close to my heart. My son has a projectile siddhi and has only used it to help people. And he has never once broken a Corollary."

It was Alice and Karan's turn to be shocked. They stared at Sue open-mouthed. "Dean MacRae is your son?!"

"*Of course* he is. Our surname is MacRae—surely you read the license hanging in the pub? Landlords, Sue and Gordy MacRae."

"Wow," they both exclaimed, recognizing the likeness immediately.

Impatiently reaching out to take one of Karan's and one of Alice's hands, Sue pleaded, "But there is something else you have not told me. I am not a doddering old grandmother. I have been around the block a few times. I know there is something about Alice other than her healing siddhi. Gordy and I both know. Please tell me right now. What is it? What do these people want from her? It will help us plan what to do next."

Alice shrugged her shoulders, still resisting telling Sue.

Karan was thinking and mumbling to herself. "I guess..." she said. "Maybe..."

Alice made up her mind. "Sue, I suspect they do know one thing about me that I haven't told you about. And I promise you I'll tell you what it is in a moment. But keep this in mind: they do not yet know about Karan and Beatrice. Ultimately, Karan and Beatrice will win this thing for us and save the school."

Sue didn't know what to say to that.

"Okay," Alice said into her headset. "Mad, start the sirens and the lights, and honk the horn as loud as possible."

"Why?" Mad asked. "What's going on up there?"

"Just do it. Thanks, Mad. Karan can explain in a moment."

Madison obeyed, the ear-splitting noise began, and Alice saw all the tourists around the church start to look. Most began walking down like it was another Roman ruin to see, not an ambulance. It left the area where they stood and the road ahead wholly dark and unobserved.

"Let's drive down and meet them," Alice said, getting into the back seat of the SUV.

Sue looked relieved because it was, at least, unlikely Alice would do something stupid from the back of her car. She got behind the wheel, and Karan sat beside her in the front.

Taking off her new jacket and silently kicking off her shoes, Alice watched the speedometer climb as they made their way down the dark, tree-lined road toward the pub. Of course, the BMW's display was in kilometers per hour, so Alice had to convert in her head. All she needed was thirty miles an hour. Even twenty would do, but only if she had a perfect take-off.

The speedometer rose painfully slow to ten, twenty, and twenty-five miles per hour, but Sue seemed to have decided it was unsafe to go faster. They were about to reach the end of the road. It was now or never.

Alice made sure the Beatrice glasses were firmly on her head, counted to three, and opened the door.

CHAPTER 24

Turning and planting both feet on the door runner, Alice reached up and grabbed the top of the open door and pulled as hard as she could while jumping upward and outward.

"Shut that door!" Sue shouted, like a mother to a delinquent child, but her passenger was already gone.

Alice twisted her body in mid-flight, like a high diver beginning a complex dive, so she was at least facing the direction of momentum. Then she just tried to relax and reach for prana, willing it to support her as it had almost always done. Her body was flooded with sensation. Every inch of her skin tingled with the warm energy of prana, and she knew she was safe.

However, the end of the line of trees was fast approaching, and if she weren't high enough when she got there, she'd be in full view of all the gawkers around Mad and Gordy's shrieking ambulance. Alice lifted her chin to the sky, stroked hard into the fluid-like prana around her, and butterfly-kicked, launching her away from the black SUV, which had skidded to a stop. Sue ran around looking for her on the ground, then Karan pointed up. Sue lifted her eyes to the sky, her hand over her mouth in awe.

Still very concerned she would be seen, Alice swam toward the protection of the ever-present mist and clouds, reaching her top speed of a hundred miles an hour after thirty seconds of strenuous work. She was drenched with sweat and moisture seeping through her clothes.

"Alice, that is so amazing!" Karan exclaimed. "This is the first time I've come with you! Sort of!"

"You're already wearing the glasses? Are you sure you're okay?"

"So far, so good. And it's amazing! I can see what you see now."

"Can you hear me clearly?" Alice asked.

"What?"

"Can you hear me?!" Alice shouted.

"Not really, but maybe I can work out an algorithm to eliminate the wind noise. Keep talking."

"Okay!" Alice shouted, the extra effort of raising her voice causing her to lose some altitude. "Karan, you have to find a way to locate that helicopter for me!"

Alice could hear Gordy in the background. "But where is she??" Then, "Alice can do what?!"

"Found them," Karan said.

"Where?!" Alice screamed.

"You don't have to shout anymore; I can hear you fine now. I'll put their location on your screen."

Alice saw a map with a flashing red blip moving toward London from the North Sea. Then a red line appeared ahead of the blip.

"That line is the most likely flight path for a military helicopter wanting to fly over Chancery Lane."

Another blip, this one blue, appeared on the map near St. Albans. Then it changed to a cartoon figure of Alice wearing a scarf blowing in the wind.

"I suggest you get to them before they hit land," Karan said.

"If something happens, they blow up and land in the sea. Right?"

"Sure," Alice said, realizing that "something happening" might also include her blowing up and landing in the sea with the helicopter. She tried to block negative thoughts like that out of her mind.

Ahead of Alice, a blue line appeared, and it intercepted the red one over water along the coast near a quaint-sounding town called "Wells-next-the-sea."

"You'll have to speed way up, though, Alice. No offense, but you're flying pretty inefficiently."

"What?!" Alice complained. "What the hell do you know about pranic flying?"

"Just because I haven't done it doesn't mean I can't help you do it," Karan sighed. "I'm just saying I think we could get you going a little faster."

"How?"

Karan then spouted a bunch of geeky mumbo jumbo that made her sound like a cross between a swim coach and a hydraulic engineer. But after trying a few of Karan's suggestions, Alice felt like she was moving faster.

The key seemed to be taking advantage of pockets of air and turbulence. Rather than a swimmer propelling herself in a straight line, she moved more like a dolphin, surfing the currents and the waves. "I sometimes forget you were an amazing swimmer, Karan," Alice said.

"Yeah. Not to mention I'm also a cyborg witch with instant mental access to tons of supercomputers, right?"

"Right," Alice laughed.

The screen readout now listed her ground speed at one-hundred-and-ninety miles per hour and the helicopter's speed at one hundred sixty.

"I'm giving you speeds in miles per hour, but you really

should get used to knots instead. All aircraft and seagoing vessels use knots...."

"Fine, Karan. So what do we do when I get there?"

"Beatrice and I are just going to call them up and ask for their callsign whatchamacallit, right? Then we notify the coast guard? And you fly away happily ever after?"

"Yeah, but I don't trust these guys with Professor Bird. We need to try to get her out of that helicopter."

"But how? How do you rescue her without breaking a Corollary on film?"

"Can you disable the cameras they have on board?"

"Um," Karan said, probably mind-melding with Beatrice, crunching data. "Maybe. But only if you get within thirty meters. That sounds super risky."

"Thirty meters? Seriously?"

"Like, the length of a basketball court."

"How do I get that close without them using those cameras on me first?"

"I don't know," Karan said. "Maybe use a World War One flying ace dogfighting trick."

"What?!"

"Snoopy used to attack the Red Baron by diving down on him out of the sun so that the Baron couldn't see him."

"There's no sun in England. Ever."

"True," Karan laughed nervously.

"Hey," Alice said. "Just in case, you guys need to get Madison up a tower or rooftop near Chancery Gate with a bucket of crayons. Maybe Gordy and Sue can cloak her. She'll be the university's last line of defense."

"We already thought of that. We're all on our way now. Sue and I are behind Mad and Gordy, sirens on full blast. We'll arrive about the same time you reach the helicopter."

Alice thought about that as she surfed the currents, making steady progress. How was she going to attack a military helicopter? It sounded like it was going to be a tough night.

But probably not as tough as it was for David right now, in a coma, fighting for his life. Or for Professor Bird in that helicopter.

When she was only minutes from the coastline and Wells-next-the-sea, she asked Karan, "Does their helicopter have proximity warnings or anything like that? Can they see me coming?"

"Well, they have an AN/AAR-47 Missile Warning System, but it's calibrated to detect missiles. It detects their infrared signature. You won't look like a missile to the system. It might ignore you."

"That's good, I guess."

"I guess."

"I'll try your Snoopy technique, I think," Alice said. "Except using fog to hide instead of the sun. I'll fly up high where it's foggier and dive at them."

"Cool." It sounded like Karan was running now. They must have arrived at the city, gotten rid of the ambulance and SUV, and ran toward Madison's sniper nest, wherever that was.

"Beatrice, can you help me if Karan is too busy?"

"I can multi-task as well as that woman can," Karan said.

"Your multi-tasking relies solely on me, *woman*," Beatrice's voice said to Karan.

Alice smiled. That was one weird relationship.

"You're too low, Alice. And they're right in front of you. Climb!"

And just like that, Alice could suddenly hear the thumping of the rotors. She climbed as fast as she could, and the sound receded again.

"Okay, Alice," Karan said. "You're right above them now. Dive when ready and try to get thirty meters from them. Don't get yourself chopped up in the rotors."

"Good idea," Alice said.

"I'll start trying to reach them by radio. And remember Alice," Karan added. "They are expecting you. Be super careful."

Alice relaxed into gravity and then swam downward to accelerate. She heard the helicopter again before she saw it. Then it appeared in the mist far below.

But the helicopter banked to their port side before she could get closer.

"It looks like they detected you!" Karan said nervously. "I'm sorry, Alice, they must have an upgraded warning system. But I'm sure you're too far away for their video cameras."

Then she heard the whistle of projectiles, followed by the percussive thumping of the heavy gun that had fired them. The helicopter was side on to her and firing. She could see the hulking shape of the Hermann missile attached beneath.

"They're shooting at me!" she screamed at Karan. "What the hell do I do now?!"

"Fly away!" Karan shouted.

Alice arched her back, banked away from the helicopter, and took some strong strokes, just as more bullets whistled by her.

"They're using a targeting computer," Karan shouted. "You need to get above the helicopter. It's your only chance!"

Alice adjusted course so she could try to fly above them.

"Bank left!" Karan screamed suddenly.

Alice did so and almost felt the searing heat of a bullet as it barely missed her.

"Now fly up! As hard as you can!"

Alice climbed, hearing whistling bullets and the almost constant thudding of the large gun.

"A little higher!" Karan screamed. "You're almost there!" she shouted.

And then she heard the colossal gun go silent, but she

didn't dare stop climbing. "They don't have missiles or anything?" she panted at Karan.

"You had to say it, didn't you," Karan sighed. "It's possible, but I can't tell if they have missiles on board, and I still haven't reached the pilot. He's not responding. I think we should abort. It's too dangerous for you."

"Why are they trying to shoot me? Weren't they just trying to get video?"

"I don't know, Alice," Karan said. "Maybe they've decided they just want to kill you now. Or maybe they think you have Mad's projectile siddhi too. Maybe they thought shooting at you was the only way to make you angry enough to throw crayons at them. You gotta abort."

But Alice didn't abandon their plan. Not yet. "If I try again and can get closer while staying above the stupid thing, would it make them think twice about firing a missile at me? At least they won't shoot at me through the rotors, right?"

"No idea. Probably. I don't know."

Alice thought of Professor Bird sitting in that helicopter. She thought about David, fighting for his life in a hospital. She thought about a big old German bomb landing in the middle of Top Lane, killing students, blowing up all those old buildings, and maybe collapsing the first level underground, killing more students and possibly destroying the elevator, trapping everyone below. And even if everyone could evacuate through the underground tunnels, where would they go? And then the bombing would ruin the university's cloaking. The company would have no way to cover everything up. She thought of Shirk and Agnes Bird. How could they do all that? What was wrong with those idiots?

With renewed anger, Alice dove toward the helicopter again. She expected more bullets, missiles, or some other hellish weapon, but none came. Instead, the aircraft dipped its nose and flew as fast as possible toward the mainland.

But it wasn't going to be fast enough.

Alice returned to her new, improved flying style and set about reeling them in.

The coastline was close now.

"Faster!" Karan exhorted.

She was only about a hundred yards from the helicopter now. "Can't you hack the cameras yet?" she shouted above the thwapping of the rotors.

"Stay on target," Karan said in a weird voice.

"What?"

"Stay on target, Gold Leader."

"Who is Gold Leader??"

"Oh, come on, Alice. You are so uncultured. David doesn't deserve you."

"What?"

Just then, the helicopter pulled up so sharply that Alice had to swerve to avoid colliding with the tail rotor.

"Got them," Karan said.

Alice didn't know what Karan meant and didn't know what to do. She was still intensely worried about their guns, so she tried to fly in tight circles directly above them.

"What happened?" she asked. "Did you kill the video cameras? Are they launching missiles?"

"They had a kind of limited autopilot system installed, so I just hacked in and took control, and then I infiltrated their main computer and disabled the override, then—"

"You can freaking hack into helicopters now?!" Alice exclaimed.

"Sort of. It's complicated. I wouldn't want to guarantee I can hold them long. But, yes. And I shut off the cameras too."

"Okay, okay, got it," Alice said. "What about all those guns and missiles and stuff?"

"They're all shut down now. You only have to worry about

whether they have handguns or anything not connected to the helicopter's systems."

"So, do they have those things?"

"No idea."

"Is Professor Bird there?"

"I think there are five people on board. Only four have headsets, and they're talking to each other at a million miles an hour. We can assume the fifth is Professor Bird."

"Can you catch any names? In their discussion?"

"Yes, and you're not going to believe this."

"One of them is a woman, and they're calling her 'Ms. Needley.'"

"Yes! But how did you know? I thought you just expected ninjas!"

"Just a hunch," Alice said. "She had to turn up somewhere. So we can guess it's a pilot, two ninjas, David's mom, and Professor Bird."

"Right. And Alice, they're angry and panicked. I'm worried they'll do something crazy."

"Kill their headsets," Alice suggested.

"Oh, good idea," Karan responded. "Done."

"No, wait. Leave them on. I want to hear what they're saying."

"No, you don't," Karan said.

"Yes, I really do."

"You asked for it."

Alice was immediately subjected to a terrible tirade of obscenities by a very rough, female British voice. Judging by her language, if there was such a thing as British trailer trash, this woman was it. It must have been Needley, David's mom. There was no response to her whatsoever from the other two people, whom Alice assumed were the remaining two ninjas. She imagined they were ignoring her as they scrambled to regain control of the helicopter.

"Okay, that's enough," Alice said. "I can't listen to that any longer."

"See?"

"How are we going to get Professor Bird out of there?" Alice asked.

"No idea," Karan said. "Hey, why are they opening the rear door?"

Suddenly, more gunfire could be heard as Alice saw sparks fly on the main rotor.

"Those crazy bastards are trying to shoot you through the rotor!!" Karan shouted.

Alice instantly flew so she was above the opposite side of the helicopter, where the guns couldn't reach her. She now had a view into the cabin; they could see her and shoot at her through the windows on this side. Eventually, she'd have to fly away and make a new plan or risk being shot. The problem with that was the desperation factor. Those guys would be desperate and trapped, and who knew what they would do to Professor Bird...

And then something fell out of the helicopter.

Alice could see arms and legs, flailing, struggling, and two heads: one with a helmet, one without, coming closer and farther apart, like they were struggling. Two people fighting in mid-air. They had a long way to fall before reaching the water. One seemed to get the upper hand in the struggle and held the other in what looked like a death grip so that the helmeted person was below, the non-helmeted person above. Then, even above the sound of the helicopter, Alice heard the *slap* sound and saw a huge splash.

"Oh my god, I hope that wasn't Professor Bird...." Karan said. "That was a fall of more than three-hundred feet. Impact trauma would have killed them instantly...at least the first person who struck the water. Maybe the second person survived...."

"I want to go check it out. Can you fly the helicopter out to sea somewhere so they don't shoot at me anymore?" Alice asked.

"Done," Karan said, and the Bell dove forward, banked lazily around and headed back in the direction they had come.

"Make sure they're high up so nobody else tries jumping."

"Good idea. Oh. Oops."

"Oops, what?"

"Two more just jumped out. Probably the two ninjas. And there's no way they survived that jump. I had them up to four-hundred feet."

Alice dove toward the spot where she had seen the first horrific splash.

But when she got close enough, she saw nothing but bubbles and two unmatched shoes. Women's shoes.

"That doesn't look good," Karan commented.

Alice made two low passes and was preparing to dive into the water when she saw a head surface. It was a woman with dark hair. The person gasped for air, then struggled to stay above water.

"Professor Bird!" Alice shouted, passing within feet of the VC.

But she saw her go underwater again, and Alice panicked. Her panic caused her to crash into the water at probably thirty miles per hour. She tumbled head over heels for about thirty feet as though the water was solid before finally slowing enough to plunge under the surface. It felt like she had just been run through a blender, but she was still conscious, and her arms and legs seemed to work. The water was green but relatively clean and clear. She oriented herself and swam toward the surface, which was close.

She was disoriented when she finally reached the surface and gasped for air. She searched around madly for any sign of the VC but saw nothing but a shoe bobbing in the water in the distance. She sprinted freestyle toward that spot.

When she reached the shoe, Alice dove. Professor Bird was there, about five feet under. She appeared to be conscious and was weakly struggling to reach the surface. She seemed only to have use of one leg. The other leg was still, and both arms floated limply by her sides.

Alice reached under her armpits and lifted her to the surface, held her there for a moment, then swiveled her around so Alice was behind her and could use one arm to keep her above water and the other to help her tread water.

"I think my arms are broken," Professor Bird said after sucking in a million breaths.

"Are you sure it's not a spinal injury?" Alice asked.

"I don't know, but I can feel my fingers and toes. They're bloody cold."

Alice wanted to ask Karan what to do next, but to her horror, the Beatrice glasses were gone. Probably sinking toward the bottom of the North Sea.

She looked toward shore and saw it was probably a mile away. It would be a very, very long swim while carrying a woman with three broken limbs. All she could hope for was that someone saw all the fireworks and came to rescue them.

"Alice," Professor Bird wheezed. "I am so very sorry."

As Alice started swimming backward toward the shore, pulling the VC, she said: "None of this is your fault, Professor Bird. Just conserve your energy."

"You don't understand. It *is* my fault. I didn't see...I never dreamed Agnes would go this far. It's just so sad...."

But then the professor began to cough, and Alice felt something grinding in the VC's chest. She must have had broken ribs and maybe even a punctured lung.

"Don't talk anymore, professor."

"But I must tell you one more thing," the VC wheezed. "Professor Shirk is helping her. He put Agnes in touch with that horrible Needley woman. I...I killed her just now."

"You did what you had to do to survive that fall," Alice said.

"Agnes promised Shirk the position of Vice Chancellor for his efforts. You must..." Then the VC was wracked by more painful coughs.

Alice tried to swim faster.

Professor Bird seemed delirious and began babbling between coughs and wheezes, "She gets full control of you... owns you...when money doesn't matter...only thing matters is power over others. I never dreamed...." Then she dropped into unconsciousness.

Alice felt hopeless. There was no way the VC would survive this long swim back to shore. And once they reached shore, then what?

Then, Alice heard a helicopter. She jerked her head around and saw the Bell heading straight for them.

Her first thought was the helicopter would shoot at them and finish the job. If so, there was nothing Alice could do but die.

Then, she thought of Karan. Maybe Karan was flying the helicopter back to save them!

When the helicopter was almost upon them, the nose lifted, and it hovered right above them. The huge missile looked horrible underneath its belly.

Now what? How would Alice get Professor Bird on board? Throw her?

The water wasn't exactly calm, either. The rotors were creating their own weather underneath the helicopter, sending water every which way and making it almost impossible for Alice and the VC to breathe. There was no way Alice could grab one of the landing skids. She could barely even see.

Then the thundering machine banked away from them slightly, toward the spot where Alice had crashed earlier. When it was about the length of a big swimming pool away, it tilted, steadied, then rocked again, and steadied. This went on for long enough for Alice to start to get annoyed. What the hell was Karan doing? Was it some code?

And then she saw a glint in the water nearby, and she understood.

Alice managed to swim her and Professor Bird in that direction and finally reached out, putting her hands around the Beatrice glasses.

"Took you long enough," Karan said after she put them on.

"Hurry! Professor Bird is really bad."

"Okay. I have an idea, but you won't like it much," Karan said.

"What?!"

"I'm going to have the pilot drop the bomb."

"Wait, what?!"

"Just hold on. I'll have him do it away from you somewhere."

"But why?" Alice asked as the helicopter banked away.

"Because this thing has a winch he can use to bring you guys up, but the Hermann is blocking it."

"Will the bomb go off when you drop it?"

"I don't think so. It has one of those external detonators set to receive a signal from a cell phone. I'm pretty sure those dead ninjas had the cell phone for it."

"But didn't the Germans design these things to go off by themselves?"

"It has an electric impact fuse, yes, but these are reclaimed bombs. The fuses probably failed when they dropped it the first time. Why should it work now?"

Alice watched as the helicopter settled into a hover above the sea some distance away.

"Okay, here goes nothing," Karan said, and the bomb dropped.

Which exploded spectacularly, sending the helicopter reeling.

"Oh, it *did* go off," she said. "That's interesting."

The hot mist hit them first, then Alice saw a massive surge of water heading toward them. She reached up and made sure the glasses were tight on her face.

"Hold your breath, professor," she said, hoping she was conscious enough to hear her. Then the wave hit them.

CHAPTER 25

The rest of the rescue was a blur. All Alice could remember was it had not been easy. After the explosion, the pilot managed to regain control with Karan's help. Alice kept Professor Bird from drowning, and they winched into the helicopter. The pilot was apologetic, like he had been coerced into working for those wretched people and had no idea they would do all that horrible stuff.

He flew Alice and the VC to the roof of the closest major hospital in Cambridge. They landed on the hospital's helipad, where some very confused paramedics pulled Professor Bird out of the Bell to be treated for her significant injuries. Alice was so relieved the VC survived the flight she bent over and started crying.

Madison's voice came through on the glasses as Alice stood alone on the helipad.

"Alice," she said, "I have some alarming news."

Alice stood up straight, her adrenaline spiking for the hundredth time that day. It was simply too much for one person to take. "Did something happen to Karan?" Alice asked. "While she was linked with Beatrice?!"

"No, nothing like that. She's fine."

"Is it David?" Alice asked.

"No," Karan said, surprising her. "David is improving, and the doctors say they might bring him out of his induced coma sooner than expected."

"Agnes Bird and Shirk are holding someone hostage?"

"No. Both have disappeared. The Company will try to track them down."

"What, then?!" Alice shouted.

"Nick," Madison said gently. "She's dying. Alone."

"Nick?" Alice asked, bewildered. "Has she been attacked?"

"No, thankfully. Shirk and Agnes Bird must have known she helped us, but we're guessing they decided to leave her alone. Because she's so sick."

"Sick?" Alice remembered how awful she looked yesterday. But she didn't look to be on the verge of dying.

"She has Leukemia," Madison said. "It seems she's been sick for a long time. We just found out."

Standing there by the helicopter, Alice thought about Nick. What could she possibly do for her? Nick pretty much hated Alice and her friends, and the only person she seemed to like was Professor Bird, who was probably in emergency surgery right now.

"We're heading there now," Madison continued, "but she's in the Royal Free hospital up in the north of London. It will take us twenty minutes to arrive, which might be too late. The doctor told Beatrice that Nick might pass any moment."

Alice sighed. She was exhausted and didn't know Nick that well, but she didn't want her to die alone. She started walking toward the roof's edge, looking for a place to take off. "I guess I'll try to make it."

"No!" Madison said. "There are people everywhere. You'll be seen. But I have a better idea. You can get there in ten minutes by helicopter," Madison said.

"Seriously? What about all the air traffic control stuff?"

"No problem. The Company can get you the clearance. We're organizing it now. We've already told the pilot."

Alice turned and walked back to the Bell. She had not even shut the door when the engines whined, and the helicopter lifted off.

In flight, the pilot started apologizing all over again, but Alice tuned him out. She watched the glowing lights of the ancient university town of Cambridge recede as they rose into the misty sky. She wondered what her life would have been like if she had attended a "normal" university like all those people down below, far from Hermann bombs, ninjas, mind readers, and cloak-and-dagger stuff.

Ten minutes later, they landed lightly on the Royal Free helipad, and Alice was met by a doctor who whisked her down to a cancer ward.

"I must warn you," the doctor said as they approached a closed door. "Your friend may not be able to respond verbally. But you should know she can hear you. Often they can respond by squeezing hands."

They pushed in, and Alice caught the distinct smell of death. It wasn't an actual scent, like rotting flesh, but more like a feeling. Like a person was on the threshold.

She approached the head of the bed while the doctor checked the IV on the other side.

Nick looked utterly hollowed out. Her eyes were closed, a pained crease between her eyebrows, her mouth slightly open, edges turned down. Her skin had a horrible gray pallor.

Alice couldn't speak. She wanted to say something kind to Nick, but her mutism was strangling her, just as death was strangling Nick. All she could do was take the doctor's advice and take Nick's hand into hers. She squeezed and waited for a response, but none came. Nick's hand was cold, as though it had already departed.

The sick woman's breath was labored, and each seemed to take longer than the last. As the minutes passed, sometimes she seemed to stop breathing altogether, and Alice thought she was gone, and she squeezed her hand as though that might bring her back.

It was the most helpless Alice had ever felt. She didn't even know if she even deserved to be here. Would Nick want her here? She had no idea. Maybe she would have preferred to die alone.

But she didn't die. More time passed, and the doctor excused herself and left the room. The belabored breathing continued. It grew more ragged, and Nick's face clenched. But then it would start again.

Alice couldn't bear it. She closed her eyes and wanted to cry. She began to go back through her memories of Nick, limited though they were. It was funny how Professor Bird always seemed to bring Nick and Alice together. It was almost as if she wanted them to be friends. But that was ridiculous. Nick hated Alice. Or maybe she didn't exactly hate her; it was more like she was indifferent to friendship. Or angry at the world. Or, like she expected cruelty from people like Alice. She didn't know; she was no psychologist.

Alice thought back to when she had been lying in a hospital bed and Nick the one in a chair in the corner. Nick had been crying for some reason, and Alice remembered thinking Nick's tears had come easily, as though they were a natural part of her life. More natural than friendship. Then why had Professor Bird always wanted to get Alice and her together? Especially if she knew about Nick's terminal illness. But she must have known. Surely. Then why...

Alice's eyes snapped open when she finally realized why. Professor Bird hoped Alice's healing siddhi would rub off on Nick. Of course! Siddhis were, on occasion, infectious. They passed from one person to another under certain circumstances, like how Madison probably got her projectile siddhi from being exposed to Dean.

She looked at Nick, fading. Almost gone. Was there still time? Could Alice intentionally transfer her siddhi to Nick? But that wasn't how it worked.

And then Nick stopped breathing. She didn't begin again.

So that was what death was like, Alice thought helplessly.

And yet Nick seemed to be still present. Her face squeezed hard like she knew it was the end, and she didn't want to go. For the first time, she felt a slight pressure from Nick's hand, like an appeal for help or a final goodbye; she didn't know which.

Alice closed her eyes and concentrated on drawing prana into Nick.

She ignored the sounds of the monitors beeping their alarms next to them and felt the warmth of prana circulating around and within her. But prana wouldn't travel to Nick. She couldn't make it pass over to another person. Why? She tried harder but found that her straining just made the prana dissipate. So, she just relaxed, and her consciousness began to fall away. Was Alice dying now, too? What would that be like?

Alice sank deeper into prana's embrace and found that all the knotted thorns of her lifelong battle with anxiety were slipping away. It was a beautiful feeling like she was flying. Not a care in the world, entirely supported by the loving presence of something that knew no mortal limits, a living energy that could love her as deeply as a mother. Then she felt free even of her body and was prana itself, flowing independently of the physical laws governing matter. She could instantly be anywhere, but she chose to remain here. Without any capacity to see, she perceived two living vessels, side by side, one strong and one so weak it was almost in complete darkness. She perceived death spreading steadily like a fluid and dove in to counteract it, as she was the only possible force that could.

It became like a dance, where death was not an enemy but

more like a partner she could embrace, and they could whisper sweet things into each other's ears like lovers. And as they danced, death willingly began to retreat. Death even served as an advisor and helped Alice to see why it had come to Nick in the first place. It helped Alice see Nick's illness, and together, Alice and death gently ushered it away. When that was done, their last task was to invite Nick's living breath back, which they did by singing a quiet, ancient song Alice didn't know she could sing. Then death retreated and disappeared.

"Alice!" a shout rang out in the room, and many hands were suddenly on her. Alice opened her eyes and found she had fallen to the cold tiles of the hospital floor.

"Somebody get a doctor!" Karan's voice called.

"No, I'm good," Alice said as Madison and Sue lifted her into a chair.

The doctor's face appeared at the door, but she didn't pay Alice any attention. Instead, she went straight to Nick, whose eyes were fluttering open.

The doctor turned to the monitors, and her eyes widened with surprise; then, she looked at Nick again.

"Hey," Nick said before turning her head to find Alice. "Took you long enough."

Then Nick smiled for the first time Alice could remember. All the pain was gone from her face, and the shadows and pallor were replaced with the rosy look of someone blushing with a combination of embarrassment, joy, and wellness.

Alice realized not everything had been resolved. Agnes Bird and Professor Shirk were on the run somewhere, David was not yet well, and she didn't know what he would think of her when he woke up.

But Alice smiled back at Nick, breathed in, breathed out, and let it all go. There was plenty of time to worry about everything else. For now, all she wanted was rest.

THE ALICE BRICKSTONE SERIES

Have you read all of them?
  Girl in the Air
  The Feeling of Water
  Alice's Secret
  The American Girl Who Broke London

Do you want to be notified when book 5 will be launched?
  Sign up at tylerpikebooks.com

SHOULD I LEAVE A REVIEW?

YES! YOU CAN MAKE A BIG DIFFERENCE!

I would be very grateful if you could spend a few minutes leaving an honest review on the book's Amazon page, goodread s.com, or anywhere that is easy for you.

Amazon review link:

https://geni.us/BrokeLondon-Reviews

ABOUT THE AUTHOR

Tyler Pike writes young adult novels full time. Before his writing career took off, he taught literature, film, and Mandarin Chinese at the University of Sydney for ten years. Tyler was academically confused, earning a PhD in Chinese and a physics degree before that.

He grew up reading anything he could find, under the covers, way past his bedtime, and now he needs thick glasses. Let that be a lesson for you.

Tyler Pike lives with his family in Australia. He surfs with his Aussie wife Tamsin and likes to pummel himself in the gym before picking up his daughter from school.

For more books and updates:
www.tylerpikebooks.com.
Email: tyler@tylerpikebooks.com

facebook.com/tylerpikebooks
instagram.com/tylerpikebooks

IN CASE YOU WERE WONDERING...

This book is a work of fiction. All characters are drawn from the author's imagination and are not to be construed as real. Any resemblance to actual persons, living or dead, is coincidental.

COPYRIGHT PAGE

Made in the USA
Middletown, DE
26 August 2023

37064832R00170